DON'T BLAME THE SNAKE

DON'T BLAME THE SNAKE

by Tony Fennelly

Top Publications, Ltd. Co.
Dallas, Texas

Don't Blame the Snake

First Edition

Top Publications, Ltd. Co.
12221 Merit Drive, Suite 750
Dallas, Texas 75251

Printed in the United States of America

Prelude

"Hardly a natural death."

"Seems like the most natural death in the world to me, Lieutenant." Officer Duffy waved an arm. "I mean this here was a pretty small man and that in there was a mighty big snake."

Lieutenant Frank Washington took a step back out of the narrow space between the emperor-sized beds.

"But unnatural at least in the sense that Eastern Diamondback Rattlers aren't indigenous to New Orleans, much less to French Quarter hotels."

Officer Duffy glanced around the penthouse suite, decorated in Italian Provincial with its oil paintings executed in the styles of some minor renaissance artists. "Why would a guy who can afford all this let an eight-foot rattlesnake in his room, anyhow?"

Ridley P. Schuyler should not have. The slightly built victim lay spread-eagled with one foot under each bed, his head propped on the shelf of the phone table and his swollen lips still frozen in an "Oh" of dumb shock.

Washington took in as much he needed to, then averted his eyes. "What do we know so far?"

"Forty-five minutes ago, at eight P.M., the hotel maid, Mrs. Watson, came in to turn down the bed and found him like this," Duffy pointed. "Then she looked into the bathroom and there was the snake, on the toilet."

The lieutenant's mustache bowed into a frown.

"It was using the *toilet*?"

"Not *that* way. Like for a nap, just curled up on the lid.

The seat is heated, you know?"

"And even in July, these air-conditioned hotel rooms are like freezers." Washington shivered, not faking it. "Smart snake."

"Yeah. Seems the maid had the presence of mind to shut the bathroom door before she punched 911. She's braver'n me." Duffy rolled his eyes. "I'da just run out screamin'."

The Medical Examiner, Nat Lawson, had already made his notations on a printed silhouette of the male anatomy but now bent in close for a final look at the body.

"Say, Lieutenant? Want to see something here?"

"Not much, no."

He stepped over anyway and squatted between the subject's splayed feet.

"What we've got here is a clear two-point puncture wound on the victim's left wrist. You see the necrosis there, where it's all black?"

The lieutenant folded his arms. "Mm hmm."

"That means the snake venom has already digested this late gentleman's flesh. It's a tremendously powerful protein poison. You'd be surprised."

"*He* was."

"So it was injected right into the artery and charged straight up to the heart. Bingo."

"Bingo."

"He probably helped it along by hollering and flailing his arms, making it travel faster. Natural thing to do." Lawson pulled a form out of his black bag and uncapped his pen. "He's a Mr. Schuyler?"

"Ridley P. Schuyler, it says on the register."

"Ridley P.?" Duffy raised his head. "Where'd I hear that name?"

"He used to be a famous novelist," Washington straightened up with a grunt and turned away from the body. "Top of the best-seller list some ten years ago."

"Yeah?" Duffy changed places with him to stand over the corpse and wrinkled his nose. "Well, this guy doesn't look any smarter than me. How does someone get to be a best-selling writer, anyway?"

"That particular one had a gimmick," Washington said. "He'd begun his career as a second-story man."

"He was a crook?"

"Nothing but. Schuyler enjoyed an extensive record of arrests and convictions beginning at the age of fifteen. During the next twenty years, he was checked into and out of a dozen state and county institutions. And, as usual in those cases, each stretch served as a training program to help him become a bigger and better crook."

"I've heard that story before," the M.E. called out. "A good boy turned bad by the system?"

"Never a good boy," Washington countered. "The guy was a real skel, from babyhood probably. He never wanted to be anything but a career criminal and never earned an honest dollar in his life."

"We got a million like that."

"Fortunately, for our side, Schuyler wasn't too good at his job. He knew all the tricks about disabling a burglar alarm in an expensive house, but was too dense to realize he couldn't move among his betters without being conspicuous. So he'd only manage to pull a few jobs before he'd arouse somebody's curiosity, be caught in the act and go back inside. He spent his thirty-fifth birthday exactly where he belonged, in the Ossining Correctional Facility."

"Affectionately known as 'Sing-Sing'," the M.E. sing-songed.

"And he should have grown old in there, but then Schuyler got the single big break of his life. He hooked up with one of those 'Behind Bars' creative writing programs."

"Creative writing in prison?"

"The class was immensely popular, too." The mustache twitched. "You'd think literary expression was every hard-timer's dearest wish."

Duffy said, "Hell, they'll volunteer for anything to get out of the laundry room for a few hours."

"So Schuyler's heartfelt sincerity earned him the guidance of some good-hearted young liberal arts graduate and after a few months' tutelage, she realized he had the makings of one good book in him. Some major New York publisher agreed with her and it came out as '*Deep Lock*'."

The M.E. looked up from checking boxes on his form. "*Deep Lock*? I remember that one."

"You should. It was the literary event of the early eighties. It got a three-column rave in the New York Times, for its 'gritty realism' and all the ways they can say that."

Duffy was still standing over the deceased. "I recall that this cutie looked different when he was talking to Jane Pauley on the Today Show. More hair maybe."

"*Deep Lock* won several prestigious awards and sold to Hollywood for six figures." the lieutenant continued. "Nick Nolte, or somebody like him, played Schuyler in the movie."

"How do you know so much?" Duffy wondered "You must be a genuine fan of the guy."

Washington snorted. "I'm nothing of the kind. I took special note of Schuyler's career at the time because it made me a bit angry."

"Angry?"

"All his fawning publicity fostered the impression that criminals have a lot more on the ball than we good guys." He lifted his broad shoulders and blew out a sigh. "You know that little punk was lionized in the east coast literary circles. A bevy of effete intellectuals lobbied to get him an early parole and had enough ink and prestige among them to put him back on the street."

Dr. Lawson shook his head. "Those yankee liberals never did have any sense."

"Never did. So the scumbag was given the cover of New York Magazine, and the best table at Elaine's. He got invited everywhere and interviewed by everyone. One of those Park Avenue society hostesses even threw her young daughter at him and he married the girl."

Duffy whistled low. "Fame and fortune, the hand of the princess and half the kingdom to boot. He sure came a long way from Cell block D."

"A long way up and then a short trip back down." Washington smiled at his metaphor. "The main problem was that Schuyler had told everything he ever knew in the first book and after he'd spilled his guts in that one, there was nothing more to write about."

The M.E. was still bent over, completing his form, but the pen paused and he laughed.

"Easy come; easy go."

"The ride wasn't over quite yet, though. Schuyler already had the reputation and momentum so he got more book contracts anyway. There was no quality whatsoever left in his writing but somehow, he kept the public's interest by changing his style. He started a series of gruesome thrillers, the "Dick Duel Adventures"."

"Dick Duel?" Lawson frowned. "That was some crude, low-rent imitation of Mike Hammer, right?"

"Right. They made him the first prestigious writer to present graphic descriptions of mutilation murders."

"Gross-out." Duffy made a face as though he had just swallowed bile. "We have to read that trash in police reports but who the hell would *want* to?"

"Some sick people I guess. And there must have been enough of them to keep Ridley Schuyler in suits for a few more years."

"I knew I hadn't heard the name in a while," the M.E. allowed.

"No one has. By the late eighties there were a dozen new authors who could dream up descriptions that were even grosser and more disgusting than Schuyler's and could write them with more style. So every book climbed a little lower on the best-seller list, and suffered more returns from book stores and made less money."

Washington pulled a pair of disposable plastic gloves out of his pocket and slipped them on. "His last book was the bomb it deserved to be. It nearly broke the publishing house and they had to down-size across the board. By the early nineties, Schuyler had slid from literary figure to has-been. His young debutante wife packed up and divorced him while he still had some money left to divide."

He took the victim's wallet off the dresser and flipped it open. "His publisher told him his latest manuscript was garbage and asked for the advance back. Schuyler said he'd already spent it. His debts exceeded his assets. His yacht was repossessed. He went bankrupt. The society hostesses suddenly got it that their golden man of letters was nothing more than an ill-mannered punk."

The M.E. zipped up the body bag in a final gesture. "So this man's fifteen minutes on top stretched out awhile."

"Nearly six years. Then it was all over. He became the subject of the season again in 'How The Mighty Have Fallen' articles." Washington showed the wallet. "A five, three singles, and a Discover card. – And I got to take some comfort in just being a one of the 'good guys'."

Duffy snickered."So we have to figure that since Schuyler came down in the world, he got to be lonely and bought himself a pet, a cuddly little pit viper? I wonder what he was doing down here in 'The City that Forgot to Care' anyhow."

"That one I can answer. He was scheduled to appear at a crime writers conference on the cruise ship, Santa Luisa."

"Say, lieutenant," a freckled young patrolman called from the doorway. "I just talked to the desk and found the bellman who showed the victim to his room. Nobody saw any snake."

"It could have been carried in a large pullman case." Duffy offered. "Like that one by the T.V."

"Yes," the lieutenant conceded. "He might have been

able to cram it in there. Snakes are flexible."

"Sure they are." Duffy bobbed his head. "As I reconstruct the scene, poor Mr. Schuyler was just sitting there on the bed playing with his scaly pal when there was some kind of misunderstanding between them. Could be something he said that the snake took exception to, right? Then chomp! Death by misadventure."

"You make it an accident then."

"More'n likely."

"But, hold on." Washington stepped over to the closet in two strides and opened the door with a plastic-covered thumb and forefinger."Here we have two suits.. three sport coats..two pairs of trousers.. " He looked down and pointed. "Brown shoes, black dress shoes, athletic shoes." He turned to the dresser and pulled out its three drawers. "Jeans, sweat shirt, t-shirts, briefs, socks, shaving kit.." He turned. "All this gear would have pretty much filled that one suitcase. Don't you think?"

Duffy scratched behind his ear. "Yeah, I guess so."

"And, if you'll notice.." Washington swept his hand around. "There aren't any other pieces of luggage in the room, not even a brief case."

"Uh. Well, yeah."

"Then tell me, Duffy, how did Mr. Schuyler carry that snake upstairs? In his loving arms?"

"Ah.."

"Hey, Loo!" The freckled officer by the door chortled. "What're you gonna do? Hold the rattler for questioning?"

"I'd prefer not to hold it at all." Washington said. "Where's the guy from the zoo?"

"Right behind you, chief!" A stocky man, uniformed in khaki, emerged from the bathroom dragging a canvas bag that had been secured with a leather belt. The bag was writhing with rope-like bulges. "Did you get a load of this fella? – 'Course it might be a lady snake. I didn't take the time to sex the critter."

"'Get a load of'?" Washington returned. "If you mean did I open that bathroom door and have a visit with the rattler before you showed up, the answer is no."

"Some people claim to love snakes but then they don't respect them enough," the zookeeper advised. "A man may see that a rattler is several feet away and think there's safety in distance. What he doesn't realize is that one of these can strike the entire length of his body."

"Do tell."

"I guess you don't really want me to open this bag and show you."

"That guess is accurate."

"But you should come down to the reptile house to see him behind glass. I will say this is the finest specimen of crotalus adamanteus I ever laid eyes on. A real beauty."

The M.E. closed his bag with a snap. "At this time, Mr. Schuyler wouldn't share your enthusiasm."

The zoo-keeper moved his head from side to side. "Listen, you guys, this big boy was probably just slithering through the woodland minding his own business when some sociopathic poacher dropped a loop over his head, stuffed him in a bag, carried him up here and got him riled." He stooped and patted the bag. "Don't blame the snake."

CHAPTER ONE

First there came the intrusive "Knock-Knock-Knock" on my bedroom door. Then followed the annoyingly wheedling, "Oh, Margo? Dear Margo?"

"I'm *naked*."

"Yuck!"

The door stayed shut. Julian isn't the want-to-see-me-naked kind of husband. He's gay.

"Rise and shine! Come on, Margo! It's two o'clock on Saturday afternoon, for pity's sake."

"Leave me alone!"

Saturday was named for Saturn, the ruler of the first hour after sunrise. Saturn is that mean old skinflint of a god who demands self-denial, discipline and hard work.

"Saturday's Child works hard for a living."

So, a few thousand years ago, the smart Hebrews declared this the Sabbath so they could sleep an hour later and make it a Jupiter day. Jupiter being the jolly, generous god who tolerates exceeding laziness and self-indulgence just so long as one at least drops in on a religious service some time before lunch.

Julian knocked again.

"Margo?"

"Go away! I can't be reached."

Here it was, a July afternoon in New Orleans and too hot and humid to do anything but lie splayed out under my ceiling fan covered only in a wet towel.

"Put something on in the way of clothes'" He persisted through the door. "It's time to get up."

"No sale. There's nothing worth getting up for."

It was the weekend, after all, so the O.J. trial wouldn't be on TV. The Oklahoma City bomber was still in custody and the Unabomber still wasn't. The U.S. shuttle Atlantis had already docked into the Russian space station, Mir. The astronauts and cosmonauts had partied then parted, leaving the Russians to clean up the mess in their quarters.

("Phew! I thought they'd *never* leave. Sure glad they took that American wonk, Thagard, with them. What a pain in the neck *he* was. Da.")

I held up my towel to let some cool water drip on my chest then let it fall back with a wet slapping sound.

This Summer of '95 is said to be the hottest in recent memory, with record-breaking heat waving all over the mid-west. Up in Chicago, so many elderly people, trapped in their stifling small rooms in hundred-plus temperatures, had died of heat prostration that the city morgue didn't have enough bins for them all and they were being stacked along the corridors like cordwood.

A woman in Tennessee left her two babies locked in her car in the blazing heat of a motel parking lot while she sashayed into one of the units and loved and laughed for nine hours. By the time anyone noticed, the children had already suffocated to death. The nonplussed mother was arrested for negligence or carelessness or something.

Right here in New Orleans, a bulldog named Winston was shut up in the small compartment of an S.P.C.A. van for two hours and died from the intense heat and lack of oxygen. An S.P.C.A. supervisor lost his job over the tragedy.

Channel 6 News gave more air time to poor Winston than to the cordwood seniors or the suffocating babies.

Which is only natural as the dog at least was pedigreed. Which reminded me. I made the supreme effort of lifting my head.

"Hey, Julian? Where's Catherine?"

"She's burrowed into the cool dirt under the porch."

"That sounds pretty good. You think there might be room down there for both of us?"

"I can offer even better accommodations." Julian tapped the door panel again. "How about joining me for seven days of sun and fun at the Riverside Crime Writer's Conference."

"A writers' conference?" I put my head back down where it belonged. "Go blow. I don't want to meet a bunch of nerdy writers."

"Nerdy writers, yes, Margo." He put on his cajoling voice. "But just think about this. They'll also be cool, comfortable *air conditioned* writers."

"Air conditioned?" Now, I was feeling all of a sudden literary. "Where's that?"

"On the cruise ship, Santa Luisa. The company reserved a cabin for me with twin beds. That means *two*. One for me and one for you."

"The Santa Luisa?" I addressed my humming fan. "I should think that boat would be a little too upscale for your rinky-dink establishment."

Julian is the first vice-president of Vieux Carré Publishing, a four-man outfit that specializes in regional interest. Their best-sellers are Cajun cookbooks.

"Our trip will be a tax write-off under 'Promotion'. Free to you and me."

"Free? That's almost within our budget."

"And, may I repeat, *air conditioned*."

"Okay, I'm in." I hoisted my shop-worn body upright and over the side of the bed. "Bon voyage to us." I wrapped myself in the top sheet, in lieu of garment, opened the door and, brushing past my pesky husband, gracefully lurched down the hallway to the bathroom.

After a five-minute shower, I had gathered strength and flexibility enough to towel off, dress up as far as a slip, and drag out my make-up bag. As I faced the comely, though slightly ravaged image of the Margo in the medicine chest mirror, Julian flounced into the bathroom and took a seat on the edge of the tub.

"I called our good neighbor Ken and he's agreed to babysit Catherine."

"Aren't we imposing on the poor man?"

"Maybe, but someone has to take care of her. It was either Ken or that guy who feeds her cookies over the fence so she won't bark when he comes back at night to rob us."

"Ken is better. – I wish we could afford a full-time house sitter."

"Maybe we should invite Kato to stay in our back room. I hear he's looking for a place."

"Good idea." I pulled my hair back to clear the field for make-up. "You know, I think Kato gets a bad rap. He's just an unemployed actor who accepted an offer of free lodging as would any young bachelor."

"I agree. If he'd only landed a feature role in the next Quenton Tarentino film or got cast in "Friends", the guy would be a hero. But since he's still waiting for his first break, they call him a bum."

I ran a brush through my lovely russet hair which would be long enough to cover my bosoms if they didn't sag at all.

Julian eyed the exercise somewhat critically. "I thought there was a rule somewhere that women within spitting distance of fifty are supposed to cut their hair short and devote the remainder of their lives to good works."

"My hair is too gorgeous to cut and I don't *know* any good works." I leaned toward the mirror. "See this? Teri Case made it red with blond highlights and brown roots. Isn't that brilliant?"

"Why is that so brilliant?"

"It looks like my hair is growing out *brown* not *gray*. Get it?"

"Oh, now I see. You might just be taken for a young

woman trying to look glamorous rather than a post-menopausal crone simulating fecundity in a pathetic last bid for masculine attention."

"Yeah."

"I like it."

"Thank you. Trouble is, that magic was wrought nearly two weeks ago and now I've got about an eighth-inch of real root showing."

"So, no problem; you'll get to show off your hat collection. You'll be glad you decided to come to the conference. Honestly, it will be fun."

"I'm counting on cool, Julian. I won't even *hope* for fun."

"But really. There will be two dozen lectures of interest to crime writers. They've lined up a pathologist from Houston and a toxicologist from Miami with all the latest research on poisons."

"Scientists? Bore, bore, snore." I glowered at the tell-tale glimmer of gray under the brown and wondered how some people can call it "silver" as if it were in any way pretty or valuable.

"Not all the experts will be dweebs, my dear. Your friend Frank Washington has been engaged to speak on crime scene procedures."

"Good old Frank? Well, that's something." I curled a piece of my forelock (tinted an almost-believable auburn) over the treacherous gray. "At least I'll have one interesting person to talk to."

"If you like interesting, I heard that the most prolific spewer of slice and dice novels, Duncan Steel, will be on hand to receive his blood-thirsty public."

"Steel? That old pervert is so gruesome, it isn't even cute."

"I'll have to agree on that. The inside of Steel's mind must be putrefied and crawling with maggots. But now I'll give you the deal-closer. This could turn out to be an historic occasion as the star speaker of our program will be none other than the prize-winning author, Ridley P. Schuyler."

I reached into my make-up bag. "Schuyler's going to be speaking? Well, that would be historic all right. He's dead."

"No, he isn't!"

"Dead as good manners. Norman Robinson said so last night on the ten o'clock news. Norman wouldn't lie about something like that."

"But what happened?" Julian rose to confront me in the mirror. "How did he die?"

I shook up my bottle of Clinique Ivory. "Bitten by a snake in his penthouse hotel suite, on Bourbon Street."

"A snake?" He shook his head as though something were clanking around inside it. "How did he get hold of a snake? Was it one of those from the conference?"

"What's that?" Now at long last he'd piqued my interest. "You're saying there will be snakes at your silly conference?"

"Well, yes. The poison expert is actually a herpetologist. Snakes will be part of his demonstration."

"That's neat!" I stuck my middle finger in the bottle of make-up and smeared it over my cheeks. "I love snakes."

"Never mind the snakes you love. Tell me what the news report said about *Schuyler's* snake?"

"It was a humongous diamondback rattler, eight feet long; that's all it said."

"Where did the thing come from?"

"No one could tell where. Maybe it just slithered out of the toilet bowl."

"That's an engaging picture, but not possible. An eight-foot rattler would be too big around to squiggle up to the top floor through all those yards of plumbing." Julian assessed my efforts at beautification in the mirror. "If you really want that foundation to look natural, you should set the base with a wet sponge."

"I hate sponges. They remind me of cleaning."

I reached for my eyelash cream and, on the way back, knocked over a tube of Wildroot hair oil. I fumbled for it but missed and it toppled into the grubby sink and bounced twice. I rescued the bottle and found a place for it on the toilet tank.

"You know what, Julian? It just occurred to me that this bathroom is an unholy mess."

"Not until now?"

"Trouble is, no magic elf is going to come in here and clean it all up."

My suave but lazy better half resumed his perch on the edge of the tub and raised his hand. "I nominate Margo the elf. Do you disdain honest labor?"

"Not at all. I've just found that being a slob leaves me a lot of free time to do important stuff. Anyhow.." I frowned at his reflection. "What about Julian the elf? You're the one who's been shaving over this sink. Look at all those disgusting little whiskers. Why can't you clean up after yourself?"

He squared his shoulders. "Don't you think I'm too effeminate already without further sissifying my image by flapping some soapy rag?"

"You can do it in some real butch way, wearing a leather jacket, tattoos.."

"Nose ring.. 'male itch'.."

I smeared some lipstick on my cheeks, blending it in with the foundation to make a cheap and easy matching blusher.

"Tell me, Neg, why are you hauling your cookbooks to a crimewriters' conference anyway?"

"We're not flogging gumbo recipes this time, dear. Vieux Carré Publishing is about to launch our new 'Storyville Classics' series."

"Which is?"

"A line of hardcover mystery fiction."

"That sounds rather ambitious for your meager little operation. How many sailors did you have to put out for to raise the capital?"

"I was able to do the sailors for free, because there wasn't much capital to raise beyond plant costs."

"Why not?"

His reflection smiled brightly. "We don't have to pay the authors."

"How economical."

"Because all the copyrights have expired. Our whole list is nothing but reprints of depression-era mysteries some once-popular authors, for reasons of their own, decided to set in Fictional New Orleans."

"Fascinating." I struck a pose for the mirror. "I adore the city of Fictional New Orleans where everyone speaks with a Georgia accent."

"Except for the Cajuns," Julian reminded. "Who have never been out of South Louisiana, so naturally they speak with a *Parisian* accent."

"Mon dieu, Monsieur."

"The first of the series comes out next month. *Mask Of The Delta*."

"A mask? Hold on! Let me guess the plot." I paused a moment to draw a burgundy line around my lips. "Someone gets killed during Mardi Gras."

"Naturally," Julian agreed. "Every day is Mardi Gras in Fictional New Orleans."

"And now my uncanny psychic ability tells me.." Fingers to my brow. "The killer was wearing a *costume*, right?"

"Of course. And you can bet your rhinestone harlequin mask that everyone else in the story was wearing a costume too. No one in Fictional New Orleans ever wears normal clothes out at night. So the victim was a beautiful showgirl named..?"

I filled in the burgundy line with Max Factor's Fantasy Rose.

"Colette La Mont!"

"That would be the girl, of course. Everyone in the city has a French name. So who was the last to see her alive? It was that person seen going into Madame La Mont's suite dressed as.."

I stabbed the air with my lip brush.

"Jean LaFitte!"

"Yes, it would have to be Jean LaFitte. But who was dressed up as LaFitte that night?"

"Why it was none other than *Pierre*," I declaimed. "My late sister's only son."

"Ah," Julian exclaimed. "The prodigal Pierre."

I held up my amber mascara. "But I know the murderer can't be Pierre because he swore to me that he didn't do it and he has cute freckles. So who else rented a Jean LaFitte costume yesterday?"

"Golly, I have no idea."

"Then it's off to the costume shop." I pitched my voice higher to play the ingenue. "Here we are in the costume shop, but where is the proprietor? Yoo Hoo, Mr. Chepetti!"

"Hark?" Julian flung an arm ceilingward. "Is that a foot sticking out from behind the counter? Why look, it's poor old Mr. Chepetti! The culprit must have killed him so he couldn't reveal the name of the man who rented the second Jean LaFitte costume."

I brushed on the mascara in short, upward strokes.

"Why, that big meanie. Now, we'll never be able to prove Pierre innocent and he won't be able to marry his sweetheart,.. uh.. Fifi."

"'But wait!'" Julian leapt to his feet. "Now, I remember! The Jean Lafitte who went into Madame La Mont's room wore his watch on his right wrist, so he had to be left-handed." He snatched up a roll of toilet paper and accused it. "It was *you*, Antoine du Bois, the master chef! When you took me on a tour of your kitchen, earlier, I noticed that your sauce pans all had their handles pointing to the left'."

"Let's write this stuff down," I twirled my mascara. "We've got an HBO Original feature for sure."

"Waste of time, Margo. Our story would never play on cable. There are no vampires in it, no car chase, and no part for Eric Roberts."

"You don't think..?"

"Sorry, this treatment doesn't suit their needs. Best of luck in placing it elsewhere."

"How's this? – Ooh!" I leaned away from the mirror and clapped my hands to my cheeks "I can't believe it! Are.. Are, you *kidding*?   All these TV cameras! I mean.. this is so exciting! I never won anything before!"

Julian slapped my rump. "What on earth are you doing?"

"I'm practicing my reaction for August 8th."

"What's supposed to happen August 8th?"

"That's when the American Family Publishers' truck will come here to the house with my gigantic check for ten million dollars." I addressed the mirror again, throwing my arms out. "I never *dreamed*..! Oh, Mr. McMahon, I'm so glad I sent in my entry!"

"Margo, you have a better chance of ascending to the papacy. Why don't you rehearse for *that*?"

"What a drip. Well, if you're going to be so negative about my windfall, I won't share the new RV and simulated pearls with you."

CHAPTER TWO

The muddy Mississippi flows by only three blocks from the sauna-like environment of our house on Piety Street. But thanks to the breezes coming off the river it was blessedly cooler out on the Julia Street Wharf.

Our vessel, the Santa Luisa, awaited us dockside in all her seven decks of majesty.

Julian shaded his eyes and gazed up at the teak railings and brass fittings. "That ship looks very comfortable."

"A lot more comfortable than out here on the dock in the heat of the bleeping day." I swung my hatbox. "I can't wait to get inside our cabin and paste myself against the air-conditioning vent."

The only obstacle to that ambition was a podium at the top of the gangway, blocking the entrance. It was ours to convince the ship's officer behind it that we were entitled to climb aboard.

We assumed our places at the end of the long line and nearly twenty minutes of shuffling earned us the right to be greeted by a standard-issue social director, clipboard in hand. He had a white uniform and a face like a Cabbage Patch doll which perhaps couldn't render any expression but bright eyes and a closed-mouth smile. Julian pulled out our boarding passes and the sight of them impacted on him like flipping a switch. "Good afternoon." He dropped the passes in a box behind him and ran his finger down his passenger list.

"Welcome to the luxury liner Santa Luisa, Mr. and Mrs. Fortier. I'm Ed Richter, your cruise director. I see that you're with the Riverside Crimewriters group."

We admitted it.

"The schedule of regular shipboard activities will be placed in your cabin every night. If there are any events you would like to know more about, feel free to contact my office at any time."

"We certainly will," Julian assured for both of us.

"You already have your shipboard I.D. cards which are used to charge extras to your cabin. You're one deck up on A, Stateroom 29. The elevator is to your right as you go in." He handed us two little plastic plaques with holes in them. "Here are your keys. Would you like help with your luggage?"

"No need," Julian said and picked up our bags as Richter waved over our heads to greet the next passengers in line. "Let's find that elevator."

But we didn't get ten feet down the corridor before being waylaid by a hair-sprayed matron wearing a sailor dress and a pasteboard "Hello, I'm.." badge.

"Hi, there." She waved a tote bag bearing the ship's logo. "Welcome aboard the Santa Luisa. I'm Patsy Pickering!"

I hate people with cute names like that but have too much class to say so. "Good afternoon, Patsy," I managed. "Umm.. Nice boat."

"It sure is," she patted her blond bubble coiffure and handed me a printed schedule. "I overheard Mr. Richter mention that you're two of our 'criminals' on board for the Riverside Crimewriters' Conference."

"Close enough." Julian put our garment bags down and took her proffered hand. "I'm Julian Fortier, with Vieux Carré Publishing. And this is my wife, Margo."

The greeter-girl wrinkled her up-turned nose. "Vieux Carré? I thought you people did cookbooks."

"Not exclusively." Julian switched on his pre-programmed public relations pitch. "We're introducing our exciting new mystery imprint, the Storyville series. We plan to bring out six gripping classic novels in the next year."

"How fascinating," Patsy twittered as she rummaged in her tote bag and came out with a manilla envelope labeled "Conference Materials: Mr. And Mrs. Fortier".

"Can I look forward to meeting some of your Storyville authors here on the cruise."

"They're not expected, I'm afraid. They happen to be dead."

"Dead?" She drew back. "How *awful* for them."

"Not so awful, really. Those particular books were all written back during the twenties and thirties. It would be rather more awful to still be alive after all those years, don't you think?"

"Oh. I see what you mean." She recovered her natural state of perkiness. "Well, we do have some famous *living* authors on board whom you'll enjoy meeting. Though most of our attendees are fans and um.. 'pre-published' writers."

I nudged Julian. "'Pre-published' writers?"

"It's a wistful term," he explained. "'Pre' in the sense that I'm a 'pre-prosperous' millionaire."

"We're chock full of activities this week." Patsy Pickering clasped her hands together. "We're honored to have Sara Luke who has just made the bestseller list again with her cozy series. We've got a whole slate of crime-detection experts who will be speaking on their specialties." She stopped and notched her mood downward. "Of course, Ridley Schuyler was going to be our biggest attraction. His untimely death was a great loss to us."

"He must have hated it too."

That remark sailed right past her.

"We've almost made up for it though with an eleventh-hour addition to our program! " She lowered her voice as if fearing that its normal volume would break the spell. "We have the privilege of welcoming the greatest literary star of the post-war generation. Holden Webb, himself!"

"Holden Webb?" Julian showed a rare reaction, actually opening his eyes wide. "But that man is an obsessive hermit, the biggest recluse in the publishing world. Why did he agree to come on this cruise?"

Patsy bit her lip a moment before admitting, "I can't imagine why and I wouldn't have dared to ask him either. I can only tell you that three days ago, out of the blue, Mr. Webb contacted me by e-mail, offering to participate in the conference. Though he stipulated that he didn't want to have a scheduled assignment or give a speech."

I cocked my head. "What good is he then?"

"At least he's promised to say a few words at the closing ceremony. But I'm so thrilled just to have him on the same boat, aren't you?"

"Astonished is the word."

"He's so shy, he made me send his boarding credentials to a mail drop in New Orleans. He didn't want to have to identify himself to the stewards."

"He had to anyway, to get on board."

"No, he could have just shown the pass with the stateroom number."

"Have you seen the great man yet?"

"Not that I know of." She looked annoyed with herself. "Come to think of it, Mr. Webb could have walked in with the 'Silver Fox Travel And Social Club' and I wouldn't even have noticed."

I heard a staccato grunting sound behind us and turned to observe two tired, gray women trudging up the gang plank, each wheeling a battered suitcase a tug at a time.

Julian looked at his watch. "We're almost ready to sail. They must be last-minute passengers."

As the weary and disheveled women stopped to identify themselves to Mr. Richter, our welcome waggin' turned away from them as though the sight depressed her. "Oh.. They're just Alice Heckman and Fanny Stumpff."

"Room maids?"

"No. Mid-list writers." Patsy Pickering made a face. "We let them come to fill out the roster since they don't really cost us anything. I had the porter clear out an inner cabin for them next to the boiler room."

"That should be comfy.– Thank you, Ms. Pickering." Julian checked the cabin number on his I.D. card, picked up our garment bags and led the way to the elevator as I followed on his heels with my hat box.

I pushed the square "Up" button and it lit. "What did she mean by 'mid-list' writers?"

"They're not 'top of the list' best-selling authors," Julian explained. "So their advances are very low; their publishers only run off a few thousand copies of their books and don't waste any money promoting them. They basically just sell to libraries and a few dedicated genre fans."

"If the mid-list authors have to sleep next to the boiler room, where do they put the *low*-list authors?"

"There's nothing lower than mid-list."

The elevator doors slid open and we took it up to A Deck and made for our stateroom which was about the length of a city block down the corridor. When we at last reached the door marked 29, Julian put down the bags and shoved one of the little plaques with holes in it (the new-fangled key) into a slit which responded with a green light to signal admittance.

"Neat," I said. "This kind of lock can't be opened with a skeleton key or a credit card."

"Don't count on it. Security technologists invent new locks every year and make things more complicated," Julian cautioned. "They're pretty good at keeping the amateurs out. But the professional thieves are only half a step behind them."

"I don't see how, with this mechanism."

"Consider that the housekeeping staff must have master keys. Just one crook among them breeches any security."

He pushed open the door and I followed him into Stateroom 29. Our home for the next six days would be a cheery cabin the size of a decent hotel room, decorated in colonial style. There were two closets on my right, across from the bathroom. Then came the dresser, across from the couch, holding a TV. And, as promised, there were two twin-size beds. Dropping my hat box on the dresser, I walked between them and pulled aside the curtains of the porthole, a window-sized squared circle, to look out at the poor saps who had to stay ashore, outside in the heat. "These are pretty nice accommodations for a boat." I appropriated the right bunk which was closer to the television, and pulled back the bedspread.

"Oh no, Julian! Look at these sheets! They have horizontal stripes."

He had hung my Ultravalet up in the wardrobe and was unzipping it for me to open like a closet.

"So what?"

"So I'll look fat while I'm sleeping."

"Forget it. You're not exactly a sylph when you're awake."

I flopped on the bed, pulled off my shoes and socks and rubbed my bare feet over the cool sheets as I paged though Perky Patsy's program. "I'm looking for a picture of Holden Webb. But the program must have been printed before his last minute inclusion."

"You're not likely to find a photo of him anywhere. According to Esquire Magazine, Webb hasn't allowed anyone to take his picture since the late fifties."

"I don't understand that attitude. Me, I *live* to get my picture taken."

"Webb has other things to live for. For example, his third book, *Life Under The City* became an overnight classic and was translated into every written language. It was required reading back when I was in high school."

"For me too. I couldn't help identifying with the character."

"The beatnik or the giraffe?"

"The Good Humor man.– I wonder why they never made a movie out of that book."

"The big studios wanted to, all right. Webb turned down

a fortune in film offers, saying he wouldn't trust his vision to the Hollywood treatment. Anyway, he made enough money from the print editions to buy himself a tract of woods in some small town in Maine and be left blessedly alone. Since then, he's written the occasional short story for the New Yorker and has been an acerbic reviewer in a few prestige publications." Julian dug into his bag. "Webb hasn't been seen in public in over thirty years. That's why it's strange that he would make his debut on a cruise ship of all places."

"And at a small-time crime writers' conference at that."

He unpacked his shaving kit. "It's doubly strange that Webb would agree to set foot on the same ship as Ridley Schuyler. They hated each other."

"Did they? How did a New York criminal and a New England hermit ever meet in the first place?"

"No-how, but Webb had been one of the eastern literati who raved endlessly about "Deep Lock", touting Schuyler as one of the great new voices."

"Then how did he feel about Schuyler's subsequent works, the disgusting 'Dick Duel' series?"

"As if he'd been slapped in the face with a cesspool mop. By the fourth abomination, some five years ago, Webb had become angry enough to write a critique of Schuyler's oeuvre for the New York Times Book Review. A brutally honest one, as I recall. He said he didn't understand how the brilliant mind that had conceived *Deep Lock* had degenerated to the point of spewing verbal sewerage about mayhem and sadism. After that, Schuyler blamed Webb's column and not his own execrable writing for the collapse of his career."

I left the bed to unpin my wide-brimmed afternoon hat and rummaged in my hatbox for a soft one. "Before we assail the conference, will there be anything worth wearing heels and a girdle for?"

"Probably not." Julian unfolded his copy of Patsy's schedule and held it under the light of the porthole. "According to the program, the only event going on this afternoon is in the assembly room on the Promenade Deck. Pete Jarvis's poison lecture."

"Poison? Oh, is he that guy with the snakes?" I pulled on a cotton hat in egg shell with a cluster of pink roses and smeared on my matching pink lipstick, just in case someone would be taking pictures and give me a chance to jump in front of the camera. "Great, let's go."

"Ladies and gentlemen!" We heard from some kind of loud-speaker out in the hall. "Welcome aboard the cruise ship Santa Luisa. Now we ask for your cooperation in our mandatory lifeboat drill. Please put on your life jackets which have been stored in your closets. The alarm horn will sound six long tones and one short, then you are to proceed in an orderly fashion to your lifeboat station, the number of which will be found on the card inside your door. This is a requirement of the maritime safety code. Thank you. To repeat..."

As the announcement was read again, Julian opened the closet door, pulled down two bulky, garish life jackets, and held one out to me."

"No!" I waved my arms at him. "I can't wear that."

"Why not?" He slipped his own over his head and drew tight the strings at the waist.

"They're *orange*."

"Of course they are, for optimum visibility when you're bobbing around in the dark water."

"But I'm a *summer*. I look *terrible* in orange."

"If the boat actually sinks, I won't make you wear this and then you'll drown and turn a becoming shade of blue which will go with everything you have on. But just for the drill, we have to be cooperative." He stood over me and slipped the hideous traffic-cone colored contraption over my head and pulled the strings to secure it. Grudgingly, I tugged my shoes and socks back on and followed Julian out to the corridor where we folded in with the other sheep being guided by painted red arrows, climbed the indicated stairs and made our way out to the appropriate station.

There we joined the throng of passengers who didn't look any better in orange than I did and were addressed by the top of a white hat wagging over the heads of the grumbling crowd.

"Good afternoon, ladies and gentlemen. I will call out the numbers of your staterooms. And when you hear your numbers, please identify yourselves."

"In the unlikely event of a real emergency.." A hand pointed up. "The lifeboats now suspended over your heads will be lowered into the water, and a crew member will assist you into your assigned boat."

I tapped Julian on the jacket. "I hope you remember our number."

"Twenty-ninc."

After the tedious, boring, drill, in which presumably every passenger on the whole boat swore to being present and accounted for, I pulled off the tasteless life-jacket and followed Julian back to our cabin.

"I was hoping to get a glimpse of the famous Holden Webb."

"How would you know him if you saw him?"

"He would look really literary and reclusive."

Even with Julian's fantastic sense of direction, it took us nearly ten minutes to stow our life-vests, then negotiate the elevators and corridors to the promenade deck where the poison lecture was being held. The speaker, Pete Jarvis, was a home-spun type, a tall, sandy-haired drink of water. By the time we slipped into the assembly room, he had already begun his talk in front of a slide screen which now displayed an exceedingly fat spotted fish.

He welcomed us with a wave as we tip-toed toward the back and found ourselves two empty seats, but didn't pause in his lecture.

"We have here the 'arothron meleagris', the species of white-spotted puffer fish found in the tropical Pacific. This is named for its ability to blow itself up to a globular shape when threatened. The poison, tetraodontoxin, is formed in the internal organs of the pufferfish or, as they call it in Japan, the fugu." He pointed to the picture with the red beam of his laser pointer.   "This tetraodontoxin has a toxicity rate of 6, the highest on the scale, and is not destroyed by cooking. Ingestion of the improperly cleaned pufferfish results in convulsions and respiratory paralysis. The death rate among affected humans is sixty percent and there's no known antidote." The red beam turned off.

"In Asia, unfortunately, fugu is considered an ambrosial morsel due to the slight tingling and numbing sensation caused by trace amounts of that very poison. Some precautions are taken. For example, it may be prepared only by specially-licensed chefs who have been trained to remove the poison sack surgically without breaking it. But every year, hundreds of Japanese gourmets die for daring to partake of this deadly dish."

There was a general murmur as each member of the audience asked himself or someone else why anybody would risk his life for a fish filet. Jarvis waited for the noise to subside then announced, "That's it for the poisonous fish." He smiled. "Now we move on to venomous snakes."

"Yippie!" I bounced in my chair. "Snakes!"

Julian gave me a subtle elbow.

The slide switched then and Jarvis turned and pointed his laser beam at the red, yellow and black ringed snake on the screen behind him. "The coral snake is of the Elapidae family, so it's related to the fearsome Cobra. The coral is found in the southern United States and is one of the deadliest in this hemisphere. Its venom has a toxicity rate of five. Very fatal."

"Beautiful though," someone said.

Jarvis grinned. "I'm glad you appreciate it as I brought one example of the species with me. Some of you may have seen him in the terrarium in the next room. He will remain secure behind safety glass all week. That's a vital precaution because I let him keep his venom sacks. You see not only does a snake's venom help him kill and digest his food, but it also has valuable medical uses."

At this moment, the curtain behind him stirred as a colorful ringed serpent emerged from beneath it and came slithering down the platform. This appearance precipitated a great commotion among the assemblage. Some women shrieked and men were kicking their chairs over in their mad scramble for the exit. I popped up too, but in my case to move *toward* the unexpected visitor.

"Hi, Snakie!" I sprinted to the platform, scooped up the writhing intruder and kissed at its forked tongue as the rest of the company watched in a paralysis of horror. All, that is, except for the lecturer himself. Jarvis just shook his sandy head and chuckled.

"I see the red-haired lady is on to us. Okay, joke's over, folks." He walked over to me and put his hand on the snake's head. "Say hello to Pedro, my Mexican milk snake, which I just had a steward release behind the curtain. Unlike the similarly-marked coral, this one is absolutely harmless."

A chorus of "Ohs" echoed around the room and from out in the corridor to which the fleeter of foot had quickly repaired.

Patsy Pickering had sought safety behind a folding chair and now raised her head just high enough to peer through the back of it. "Now Mr. Jarvis.. you're saying that k-kind isn't p-poisonous?"

"No, he isn't. But the fact that he *resembles* a poisonous snake is Pedro's protective coloring. Predators are afraid to molest him."

Patsy pulled herself to her feet. "But, Mrs. Fortier, how did you know the difference?"

I kissed the snake again and wrapped him around my neck like a pretty scarf. "I just remembered the old rhyme about the order of the rings. 'Red meets black,'" I touched Pedro's colored rings to demonstrate. "'Friend to Jack. – Red meets yellow..'" I pointed to the picture of the real coral snake up on the screen. "'Kill a fellow.'"

"That's not a hundred percent accurate," the lecturer cautioned. "But basically it serves as a guideline. That rhyme is repeated to keep farmers from destroying helpful snakes due to mistaken identity."

Throughout all the tumult, Julian had moved only to cross his legs. "My wife likes snakes," he muttered. "I hate to think what that says about her."

Pete Jarvis was nice enough to let me hold Pedro for the rest of the demonstration.

CHAPTER THREE

Walking up the grand staircase and through the atrium lobby, I took Julian's arm. "You know this ship is just like one of those luxury hotels downtown, with potted trees, and a concourse of upscale shops. You wouldn't even know we were at sea."

"Yes, it's much more lavish than the 'Love Boat' in that old TV series."

My eyes skidded to a halt at the window of the "Bella Luisa Boutique". The display featured a variety of t-shirts and sarongs draped around models of sailing ships. I pulled Julian's sleeve and steered him. "Hey, let's try this one."

He hung back. "What exactly are we supposed to do in here?"

"Browse. Maybe we'll find something neat."

"You think so? What can you find in a ship's gift shop that you can't buy for half the price on dry land?"

"Ash trays with an etching of the riverboat." I stepped inside and yanked him in after me.

"We don't even smoke."

"The idea is to find a souvenir that looks presentable so we don't have to be ashamed of it." I stopped and picked up a strand of pink pukka beads and held it under my chin. "Would I wear this?"

"Not in *my* company, you wouldn't."

"Well, I'll bet you'd like a bow tie with little semaphore flags on it."

"Guess again."

"Then I'll look for something practical." While rummaging through a display of sun visors, I noticed a merry-looking young man in a blue sweater standing at the full length mirror, trying on sailor's caps and laughing at his reflection. "Look over there, Julian! I'm sure I've seen that guy before."

"Really? Where?"

"I'm trying to recall where. This is embarrassing."

"Why? He probably wouldn't know you, either."

Then the blue sweater spoke to the clerk, "Excuse me, Miss. Does this captain's hat come in black?" and it hit me.

"Why now I remember!" I clutched Julian's shoulder. "That's Father Kevin Dawes from St. James The Less Church in Gentilly. We've got to go say hello, and.. – Ugh!"

That last remark was in response to Julian's having abruptly grabbed my arm with which he yanked me around behind a shelf of sea-green windbreakers.

"What're you..?!"

"Shh!" He put his finger up to his lips then leaned down and hissed into my ear.

"When you see a priest away from his parish, wearing civilian clothes, you *don't* recognize him!"

"Don't..? But that would be *rude*, I.."

I poked my head around a postcard display and snuck another glance over at Father Dawes. Then I saw that a younger, taller man in a red sweater had just joined him.

"Hey, Kev, I'm getting this bow tie with little semaphore flags. See?"

"How utterly tacky!"

The two then hugged and laughed together.

My jaw dropped. "Why he must be..?"

Julian took my elbow and turned me toward the door. "As which of us is not?"

"But.. But..," I sputtered. "That's against the rules. Priests are supposed to be *celibate*."

"To most of them, celibacy just means not doing it with a woman. Let's duck on out of here." He propelled me out to the lobby and back toward the grand stair case.

"But it's not right."

"You're very proprietary about the Church."

"Why not? I'm a loyal Catholic."

"You haven't been to Mass since they were saying it in Latin."

"Well, I don't exactly have time to practice now, but I'm counting on the church to be there when I need it."

"Which will be when?"

"When I get too old to sin. – How do you think the secretly light-footed Father Dawes got himself invited on a cruise devoted to crime fiction?"

"I surmise that it was his companion who was invited. The red sweater is Ward Newcomb, the up-and-coming freelance illustrator. He's done some book covers for us."

"Handsome guy. Is he any good?"

"He is if you want all your men to look like Fabio."

"That wouldn't be so bad. Whom does he make his women look like?"

"His mother."

"Why did I ask?"

The staircase brought us up to the Observation Deck. The outside door to it was opened by a handle instead of a knob. Julian let us out into the stifling fresh air. The sun was still out and leaving the ship's air-conditioned climate was like stepping into a steam bath.

I ran my hand along the brass rail. I was more conscious now of the roil of the waves and bent my knees in rhythm with it.

"Look down there at the end of the deck." I used my elbow, subtly, I hoped. "I recognize none other than that master of slice and dice thrillers, Duncan Steel."

"What do you know!" Julian squinted against the reflection of the Sun off the water. "The old soak looks even worse than his dust jacket photos."

"Much worse." I got the impression that Duncan Steel

still had a big set of teeth left over from his youth, but through the decades, his face had aged and shrunken around it, leaving only the grin.

"It looks as though half his total mass is mouth."

"Right." Julian murmured. "He reminds me of that species of african ant, the head of which still keeps biting even after its body has been pinched off. You know the kind I mean?"

"Yes. Tribal physicians use them as sutures."

There was a striking blond on Steel's arm, slender, soigneé, all dressed in black spandex despite the heat, and tall enough to eat dinner off the top of his head.

"Who do you think she is?"

"Maybe his trophy wife."

"I always wanted to be a trophy wife."

"Well, Margo, *you* would be analogous to a third place *bowling* trophy in some small-town seniors' league."

"That's not nice."

"In Bunkie, maybe."

The blond had looked young and beautiful from the other end of the deck. But as the two drew closer, I could make out the lines around her eyes and lips and the tell-tale tight lids of an eye-lift. Not so great after all, I thought nastily.

The unlikely couple moved past us, looking neither right nor left, he taking small, precarious steps and she with a tight grip on his left arm, as if she were holding him upright.

"Julian," I said. "My hat is wilting. Let's get back into the cool."

Once indoors again, I intended to shamble right down to our cabin but Patsy Pickering was crouching in wait behind the next potted bromilliad.

"If it isn't the Fortiers! Hey, you two, the fun is just starting."

"Really?" Julian asked. "Have you talked to Holden Webb yet?"

"No, I went by Cabin 84 and knocked but there was no

answer. So he must be roaming around the ship." She looked slightly irked for two beats. "But next on the conference program is our 'Welcome Aboard' cocktail party. I hope you both will join us."

"Thank you," I said. "But I already heard the snake lecture, so I'm going back to my air-conditioner."

"If that's where your interest lies.." She blinked like "I Dream Of Genie". "Then you'll definitely want to come. Mr. Jarvis said he would have all his snakes on display in terrariums during the reception."

"Neat!" I tugged Julian's sleeve. "I want to go visit them."

"You *observe* snakes, Margo. You don't *visit* them."

Patsy aimed her little nose at my blank breast pocket. "But of course you both would have to wear your badges."

She smiled as though her face were making a curtsey and went on her way.

"Badges?" I nearly spat. "We don't need no stinking..!"

"Don't fret, dear. I've got ours all ready." Julian pulled the fool things out of his shirt pocket and handed me one. It was a white rectangle with a blue border and "Riverside Crimewriters Conference" in gothic typeface over a cartoon that looked like John. J. Fadoozle with a magnifying glass, studying my name for clues.

"The very concept of the name tag is stupid. Like I don't have the communicative skills to tell someone my own name if I want to meet them. Besides it doesn't go with my dress."

"It doesn't go with anyone's dress but wear it just the same." Julian unfastened the pin and stuck it on my pocket. "It's a security measure. They're not supposed to let you into conference events without it."

"Who would try to crash a dumb-ass writers' convention?"

"A starving Haitian stowaway, perhaps?"

"He'd be the life of the party."

Sure enough, there was an officious-looking, if dowdy, label checker posted at the door who took her commission with dead seriousness. She squinted at my "Hi, I'm Margo" badge and nodded curtly.

We had arrived much too early for our "Welcome Aboard", seeing as the crowd wasn't one. There were about two dozen uncomfortable-looking people milling around, probably publishing-world hustlers scrambling for someone who could do them some good. Julian must have spotted a suitable target of his own. He let go of my arm. "If you'll excuse me, dear, I see a book seller I'd better play patty-cake with."

That was agreeable to me because I had spotted one familiar face in a room teeming with dippy strangers. Good old Frank Washington had just walked in, looking as uncomfortable as anyone else. I skittered up to him. "Hi, Frank. I'm glad to see you joined the festivities."

"Hello, Margo. That makes one of us." As a waiter swept through waving a tray of appetizers, he picked up a saucer of shrimp and turned it to offer me one. "Actually, this is the last place I want to be. I have a red-ball case on my desk back at the office, just shrieking for my attention, but I'd already committed to this silly conference." He clicked his tongue. "My wife says we need the lecture fee for a new hot-water heater."

"Red ball? Hey!" I clapped my hands. "Would you be the primary on the case of Ridley P. Schuyler versus the snake?"

"Who else would be? Is there anyone in Homicide unluckier than I am? And did I originally sign up for this cruise in the hope of getting away from it all?" He looked heavenward. "Irony of ironies, there are more authors on board here and more snakes too than I had to deal with back at the crime scene."

"Fantastic!" I grabbed his hand, which still held the plate of shrimp and pulled him into a corner away from the increasing traffic as other duly-labeled conferees wandered in. "Tell me about it. At least whatever's on the record."

We passed a side table on the way and Frank took the opportunity to abandon the plate. (No resident of New Orleans will ever be impressed with catered dishes.)

"At first glance, it read like an accident. Schuyler brought his pet snake up to the hotel room with him and they had a falling out."

"It happens."

"The only problem with that scenario is, no one ever knew Schuyler to have a pet snake."

"And that would sort of stick in someone's mind."

"Aside from which, there was no way he could have conveyed an eight-foot rattler up to his room without attracting somebody's attention."

"So what's an alternative theory? Some other guest accidentally left his snake in the room?"

"Nope." Frank shook his head. "The hotel maids clean very carefully after each guest. They empty the waste baskets, scour the sink and bathtub, throw out any snakes."

"So someone else had to have brought the little love to the room."

"No one admits to it though."

"Of course not. Who would admit that his careless snake-handling resulted in a lethal bite? That's good for 'reckless disregard', at least. Maybe even manslaughter two."

"Assuming that the bite was unintentional."

"Assuming? You think the rattler might have been carried up there secretly, intended as a murder weapon?"

"Why not?" Frank returned. "A snake is not as messy as a knife. It's quieter than a gun and doesn't have any serial number. Impossible to trace. Did you ever try to get fingerprints off a pit viper?"

"Add mystery to the death of a famous crime fiction writer and you get a big shock to the publishing world."

"Famous, right. To me, though, he was a thief. Period."

"But Schuyler supposedly retired from stealing in '85."

"That was the story he gave out."

"You don't believe it?"

"That skel was a hobby of mine for a few years. During the summer of '88, someone using his M.O. broke into the

Mountain Lakes mansion of the Chemical Magnate, Frederick Ihde, and eloped with a prize Fabergé Egg."

"What else?"

"Nothing else; just that. He stole light."

"He went to all that risk for only one item?"

"Don't worry, it was a very good haul all by itself. I read about that artifact. It was gold mesh covered with precious stones, one of Fabergé's most intrinsically costly pieces. Czar Nicholas II presented it to his wife in 1902 to commemorate the birth of their youngest daughter, the Grand-Duchess Anastasia."

"The real one, not the imposter."

"Who?"

"'Anna Anderson, who tried to pass herself off as the Grand Duchess Anastasia."

"You mean, the one Ingrid Bergman played in the movie?"

"But in the movie the character actually *was* Anastasia. In real life, she was a Polish farmer's daughter named Franziska Shanzkowska.

Now I recall that back in the thirties, 'Anna Anderson' had all of café society convinced. She acquired more celebrity as a phony Romanov than any of the real ones ever did."

She wouldn't have convinced me," I declared. "I always thought she had some nerve impersonating a woman whose native tongue she didn't even speak."

"Anyhow," Frank continued. "The burglary was committed in broad daylight, around three in the afternoon. According to the Jersey police, the caper was so slippery smooth that it matched Ridley Schuyler's old style exactly. The whole family happened to be out at a Legion of Mary function. The maid was grocery shopping. The alarm system was disabled by an expert and the locks picked."

I waved my hand. "But in a suburban neighborhood on a summer's day, there must have been a lot of people milling around, barbecuing steaks, mowing the lawn in plaid Bermuda shorts."

"Not really. Heat of the day in July, most sane people are indoors, behind noisy air conditioners."

"There wasn't one convenient snoop peeping through her venetian blinds?"

"Maybe one. Ihde's neighbor two doors down saw a man fitting Schuyler's general description on the block but she didn't get close enough to see his face. She noticed that he was also driving a diesel Peugeot like Schuyler's. Naturally she was curious about the stranger but not curious enough to take down the license number."

"Could Schuyler himself be placed in the area?"

"Actually, our man was in Manhattan. That's a world away, culturally, but In terms of time and space it was only about a thirty-minute drive down Route 3. And he didn't have every minute of the evening accounted for either. But who would? He was divorced and he lived alone. In New York City, most people don't notice the comings and goings of their neighbors. And the law can't demand that a person prove that he *wasn't* in a certain place. Still, if Schuyler hadn't been rich and famous at that point, the police would have picked him up and sweated him. But there were no witnesses inside the Ihde's house watching the theft of course, and no prints or other physical evidence to give sufficient cause.

"They followed up on the mysterious stranger?"

"Sure, the local cops went from house to house and questioned everyone young enough to see and old enough to talk. But no resident of the neighborhood admitted to having a visitor of that description."

"Was Schuyler the only suspect?"

"Pretty much. The New York police picked up another former thief of roughly the same description and M.O. and leaned on him for 36 hours but that guy finally came up with an alibi and they had to kick him loose. He wasn't their first choice anyway."

I shook my head. "None of that makes any sense. In '88

Ridley Schuyler was already a millionaire and still making the best-seller list. Why would he have risked everything he had by committing grand larceny?"

"There's another factor. The perp might well have been someone who didn't need the money. See, the egg was never offered for ransom and has never turned up in anyone's collection either. So it's not likely that the crime was done for profit. That's why the motive remains a mystery to this day."

"Maybe it doesn't exist any more. Suppose the thief simply dug out all those precious stones and melted down the gold?"

"I can't believe that. The egg is worth exponentially more as a work of art than the sum of its components."

"Bet it was insured."

"Under-insured, actually. Poor Fred Ihde bought a policy when he purchased the egg in 1962, but then he never increased the amount to reflect its escalating value over the years. He's down more than four million."

"So say the wandering stranger was a lucky coincidence. Maybe he was peddling Fuller brushes. And this Ihde character steals his own Fabergé egg, sells it secretly to some Arab oil prince for his private collection, slurps up the insurance pay-off and lives happily ever after."

"I'll admit that was a widely-held theory at the time." Frank said. "The buzz was that Ihde had arranged to burgle himself. Trouble is, the man's reputation had been spotless up to that point, but he's been under a cloud ever since. The poor guy has spent most of his fortune on private detectives trying to get a line on the real thief, locate his treasure, and clear his name."

"Oh, Lieutenant Washington." Patsy Pickering had appeared from behind him and applied a Vulcan sleeper grip to his shoulder. "The conference director has been dying to meet you. Excuse us, Mrs. Fortier."

"Certainly."

As she coaxed Frank across the room, I turned my

attention to the real attraction of the event, a flank of terrariums with nice snakes inside. I peered in at a little four-foot python named (of course) "Monty" and tapped the glass to attract his attention, but he preferred his own coiled company to mine and took no notice. Beside me was a bearded man with glasses peering into a terrarium holding a young coral snake. He held something square in a brown paper bag under one arm while, with the other, he fed himself a roast beef sandwich. I nodded politely, then stepped around him to check out the other snakes but they all seemed to be curled up and bedded down for the night and obviously didn't want any truck with me so I cast around for other diversion.

There were at least two women in the room who didn't look exactly like idiots. The downtrodden mid-list writers, Alice Heckman and Fanny Stumpff, had a table to themselves in the corner under the porthole. I sashayed over to introduce myself, leaned across their table, grunted like an ape and thumped my "Hi, I'm Margo" sign.

The taller woman grunted similarly in reply and slapped her "Hi, I'm Alice" sign. Her companion, mouth agape, grunted, shook her "Hi, I'm Fanny" sign and waved at an empty chair which I sank into gratefully.

"I don't know quite what to do with myself here. I guess you two are right at home at a writers' conference."

"Wrong," Fanny said. "I'd rather be at my real home any time."

"We only come to these deals because we're desperate for some kind of recognition." Alice explained.

Fanny bobbed her head. "Trying to acquaint people with our books." She asked her colleague. "How many readers do you figure we pick up per conference?"

"Maybe three in a good year."

"Sounds like a losing fight," I ventured.

"How true," Fanny said. "But in July this is the only game in town for writers who can't fly to Spain for Paco Taibo's Semana Negra. What's *your* excuse?" She read my name tag again. "Margo?"

"My husband Julian is the vice-president of Vieux Carré Publishing. Right now he's rooting around begging booksellers to stock their new line of fiction reprints."

"The humiliation game," Alice stirred her drink. "That's what we're all here to play. – Say, glom that man with the beard and glasses." She nodded toward the terrariums. "The one eating a sandwich by the snakes."

"Yes."

"College professor."

"You know him?"

"Never clapped eyes on him."

Fanny nodded agreement. Liberal arts. Has to be."

I sneaked another look at the subject. "How did you deduce that?"

"I see that his beard isn't trimmed neatly enough for someone for whom appearance is important. So that rules out that he's a lawyer or an executive with a big company. But then again it's not as shaggy as that of a professional recluse like a writer."

"And he's too tall to be a rabbi." Alice put in.

"Okay, Fanny. I copy all that. But how do you get liberal arts?"

"He doesn't have any stains on his clothing, so I don't make him as an absent-minded scientist."

Alice tapped my shoulder. "He's just finished his sandwich. Let's go see if we're right."

"Who's 'lets'?"

"You, Margo." She got out of her seat and pulled my arm. "Go over and ask him who he is."

"Why me? I don't care if that jamoke is the King of Spain."

"Just on the off-chance that he *is* somebody important," Alice persisted. "Come on, I don't want to go by myself and look like a groupie."

"Also, if he isn't anybody, he'll be more impressed with

you than with either of us," Fanny added emphatically. "Nobody is impressed with *us*."

That was indisputable so I let them urge me out of my chair.

Alice placed her hands on my shoulders and pushed me ahead of her through the chattering revelers until we were directly in front of the bearded man, then addressed him from behind my left ear. "Hello there." She stuck her hand out. "I'm Alice Heckman and this is Margo Fortier. Her husband is Vieux Carré Publishing."

"Part of," I amended.

Fanny had been right. The poor man actually looked impressed. "Really? A publishing house?"

"A teensy part."

"I'm Gordon Magnuson." His blue eyes smiled behind thick lenses.

"Hello, Gordon. I guess you're a mystery fan."

"You *know* it. I did the Bouchercon in Seattle last October, Malice Domestic in Baltimore in April, and Edgar's Week in New York in May. And I'm leaving this boat in Cancun to attend another crime seminar in Mexico."

"That sounds interesting. Have you been enjoying this conference so far?"

"As much as possible, I guess. I'm terribly disturbed about what happened to Ridley Schuyler."

"Oh, did you know Schuyler?"

"Not yet. I hadn't had the privilege." He shifted the brown paper package so that he was holding it like a baby. "You see, I came to the conference just to meet him. I've been making an intensive study of his novels for the past three years."

"A three year study on *him*?" I fear that I may have appeared tactless with my eyes bugged out like that.

So he hastened to explain. "More specifically on the reaction the public had to his prose. His popular appeal. I wrote several articles for scholarly journals delineating the shift of his novelistic style from the literary to the popular genre. Last year, Schuyler got word of my articles and sent a note thanking me for taking an interest in his work." Gordon smiled in remembrance of his claim on history. "Then I had the opportunity to speak with him several times on the phone. But this cruise was to be the occasion of our first face-to-face meeting."

"Then it turns out that you're a writer, yourself!" I gave Alice a "Nyah nyah" look.

"Somewhat. In fact, I ..um.. Well, I haven't had any novels published yet. Right now I teach College English in Virginia." Alice winked an "I told you so." back at me. "This will be the first one."

"What will?"

"*This* will!" And then, like a bank robber unleashing his weapon, Magnuson snatched the brown paper bag off his parcel to reveal what looked like a bale of scrap paper in an imitation leather binder. The thing was the size of the Greater New Orleans Telephone Directory and had to be close to a thousand pages. He opened the mess up to the title page and presented it proudly. Alice and I exchanged a look of sheer panic. I just gave it a glance, then automatically took a step back, half afraid that he would try to hand me his proud bundle. Alice managed to slip around behind me again and I accidentally stepped on her foot which must have hurt but she didn't want to call attention to herself by yelling "Ouch."

So she just bit her lip and grunted.

"The Second Awakening." I breathed, as though marveling at its creativity.

"I realize the title is very cryptic, " Magnuson said. "That's part of the suspense." The "pre-published" wonder held the bag under one arm and fanned the manuscript open. "But the significance is clarified here on page eight-hundred and forty-nine. You see, the 'first awakening' is birth itself. And then, during the denouement, the 'second awakening' is finally revealed to be the onset of maturity."

"Oh, my goodness." I folded my arms with the hands safely inside. "Amazing."

"The material part of the story is set in Wauwatosa, Wisconsin in the summer of 'seventy-two." Magnuson ran his finger down a page as though quickly re-reading it and delighting in every word. "Mrs. Schneller, in my writers' group, said this conveyed an uncanny sense of place."

"And.." Alice sounded ingenuous. "Who would know better than Mrs. Schneller?"

"Exactly." He nodded, closed the manuscript and tapped it with manly affection. "That's what *I* say. You'll find that the plot is profound on several levels. The framework is a story about an idealistic young PhD. candidate who's trying to get his driver's license renewed but he runs into a wall of bureaucratic fascism just because he has moved recently and doesn't have any proof of his local address."

"Gracious!" I felt behind me and groped for Alice's hand but she was doing some kind of moonwalk to get away without looking as though she were leaving. I tried to achieve the same effect with a dainty shuffle. "What an exciting theme."

Magnuson was oblivious. "And at the same time he's going through an identity crisis precipitated by unjust criticism from a sociopathic faculty advisor." He looked from me to Alice and back again. "There is a stream-of-consciousness internal monologue that I know you ladies would find fascinating."

By now we both had backed well out of reach of the manuscript. Alice pressed herself against the buffet and I was in danger of falling into the crab dip. "Well, gee!" I jabbered extemporaneously. "Too bad I don't have my glasses with me. On board. But you can bet I'll be first in line to get your book at the library once it's published."

He looked thoughtful. "That will probably be next year."

"Sure it will, yeah."

"Once a discerning editor sees this..."

"What a lucky guy *he'll* be. – See you later." I reeled around and tore off so fast that I bumped into Alice who was still tactfully walking backwards along the wall. She grabbed my arm and we jerked around and skittered back to our table where Fanny still waited.

"Save me from those," she breathed, collapsing into her chair.

"Those what?"

"Wannabee authors. At least twice a week I get letters from people purporting to be fans. But they're actually just amateurs trying to con me into reading their lousy manuscripts."

"They want you to criticize their work?"

"To *not* criticize it. There are Gordon Magnusons all over the world and everyone of them thinks he's written a best-seller."

Fanny nodded sadly. "We writers all go through it, Margo. Our line is supposed to be.." She put both hands up to her cheeks like Macauley Caulkin in "Home Alone". "My stars! This is the most spell-binding work of great literature I've ever had the honor to read! I just sent it on to my editor who has offered three million for hard-soft. Ron Howard is dying to film it with Kevin Costner and Geena Davis!"

Alice shook her head, "More likely Penny Marshall with Hanks and Roberts."

Fanny shrugged. "Scorcese, De Niro, Streep."

I chimed in. "Houston, Bogart, Monroe."

A waiter stopped by and asked if we needed anything at this table. I said, "A Coke, desperately. No ice."

Fanny and Alice ordered daiquiris desperately.

Five minutes later, Julian apparently ran out of marks and found his way around to our table. "I think I'm getting hoarse from all this schmoozing. I was never cut out for saleswork."

"Then sit down with us. – Fanny and Alice, this is my husband, Julian."

He took an empty chair. "I just got some scuttlebutt. It seems Ridley Schuyler had arranged his appearance at the conference to promote his new book."

"A new book?!" I was sipping my Coke and almost did a spit take. "But I thought his work had degenerated to the point where he couldn't even get published anymore."

"Just barely. He had to resort to dealing with Meechum & Gould."

"Meechum & Gould?" Fanny echoed. "That bad, huh?"

"Yes, it shows you how far he'd come down in the world."

"They're not good publishers?" I asked.

"They're not good *payers*." Fanny advised. "I did my first book with them. The advance was pathetic." Her eyes rolled. "Harvey Gould assured me that it didn't matter because I would get it all later in the form of royalties. But I'm still looking for a royalty check."

"They have the reputation they deserve," Alice said. "Their contract reads like a feudal serf mandate. They grab all the control over the work and fifty percent of all rights forever."

"That's not industry standard," Julian remarked.

"To put it mildly." Fanny shrugged. "But it looked reasonable to me fifteen years ago. I was a small town school teacher with no publishing credits but the church newsletter."

Alice patted her shoulder. "Of course she didn't have an agent."

"I'd never even *met* an agent. And I was desperate for a book contract to validate my existence."

"When you've been in this business a while, you get clued in about Meechum and Gould." Alice laughed mirthlessly. "They brought out my first series book."

"That's good, isn't it?"

"Not the way *they* do it. They're notorious on Publisher's Row for their creative accounting. Every time I get a royalty statement from them, it seems my book has sold fewer copies."

"I guess those were supposed to represent returns from the book stores," Julian offered.

"After nine years?"

"Um. No."

Alice finished off her daiquiri with a slurp of her straw before continuing. "I met those scam artists back in the mid-eighties when Sara Paretsky and Sue Grafton had just come into their own, so books about tough female P.I.'s were suddenly all the rage. Harvey importuned me to write one of that sub-genre for his winter list and offered the highest advance I'd ever got, half on signing and half on acceptance. So I wrote it."

"It was great too," Fanny put in. "She sent me the manuscript."

"But by then every other house had come up with the same idea and was busy recruiting its own Grafton clone. In the five months it took me to finish the thing, the market had become saturated with female P.I.'s of every size, shape and color and the trend had peaked. Now the theme was cold. So Meechum and Gould claimed my manuscript was unacceptable and demanded back the part of the advance they had paid."

"She had to sic the Authors' Guild legal department on them." Fanny said.

Alice sighed gratefully. "They wrote an amicus curiae letter and convinced the judge that according to industry custom and practice, 'acceptable' didn't depend on the whim of the editor or the market place. It meant 'professionally written and fit for publication'. The court read the manuscript and upheld the contract."

"It's their usual M.O.. to give a desperate but promising young writer a token advance then do a small print run and don't invest anything in promotion. If the reviews are good, they get just enough sales from libraries to make a decent return on their investment. Then they let the book go out of print and sit on it."

"Sit on it?" I tapped the table. "Hold on. What good does that do them?"

"They've got the rights to the property forever, see? Then if and when said promising young writer gets a *major* publisher and cracks the best-seller list, Meechum & Gould simply reprint the earlier work for nothing but the cost of paper and ink. By keeping expenses for each book to a bare minimum, they can divide their capital eggs among a whole slough of baskets."

Alice leaned across the table.

"It's like this, Margo. Imagine that *you* controlled all the rights to an early and obscure John Grisham novel. And you didn't even have to pay him an advance."

Now I got it. "That would be like winning a Sweepstakes."

"Better. Film rights alone could bring you more than the state lottery jack-pot."

I nodded shrewdly. "Then it's all a matter of their being *'atavistic.'*"

Julian elbowed me. "You don't even know what that means."

"Yes, I do."

"Use it in a sentence."

"Um.. I know the meaning of the word atavistic."

"Sorry, I guess I was wrong."

"Yes." I looked past him to the buffet. "Hey, what a beautiful girl!"

Alice swiveled her head around, "Girl? My, but I don't see any little children around here. That person you seem to be indicating is a young *woman*."

"From Margo's perspective, anyone who still menstruates is a girl." Julian explained. "Of course I haven't seen that particular specimen before, but she *is* beautiful."

"That *young woman* is Stefani Wyeth," Alice said sternly. "She edits the literary journal at Columbia. The Riverside Crimewriters managed to lure her here as their creative writing teacher. Tomorrow, she'll be giving a day-long workshop for the pre-published writers."

Ms. Wyeth was tall and lean and looked like a Vogue cover girl or an Ethiopian princess. And smart too? Nature's gifts are not evenly bestowed.

Fanny rummaged in her tote bag and came up with the cruiseline program.

"Tonight in the main room, they're presenting a funny magician," she read. "Then Tuesday night, we'll get to see a funny juggler, and the next night, a funny impressionist. Our last night aboard, we'll see a world famous dog-trainer who is also.."

"Stop," I interrupted. "Let me guess."

"..funny."

"I knew it."

"All the headline performers on the ship are comics and coincidentally, they all seem to be men."

"There aren't too many female comics, in the whole world," Alice said. "And only about five of them are any good."

"It's true that women simply aren't as funny as men," I had to admit. "Why is that, do you think?"

"I hypothesize that men have to develop a sense of humor because they can't get laid," Julian informed us all. "Women don't have that problem."

"Tomorrow night, there will be a name act. The famous recording artist Vinnie Moretti will be appearing with his band in the grand auditorium."

"Vinnie Moretti?" I repeated. "There's a name out of the past."

He had three hit records back in the sixties. They still play them on oldies stations."

"I remember him singing on Hullabaloo. Lada Edmund, Junior was up there in the cage, go-go dancing in white boots."

Fanny turned the page. "There's also an act on upstairs in the Lorelei Lounge running nightly. 'Schmelvis'."

"'Schmelvis'?"

"The resident Elvis impersonator. This says he sings 'Love Me Tender' in Yiddish. That must be very romantic."

"Sounds like it," I said.

"According to his bio, he won a medal at the International Elvis Convention with his stirring rendition of 'Du Bist Gornicht Nor A Prosteh Hunt.'"

"What does that mean?"

"Referring to my high school German, something about a hound dog," Julian supplied. "By the way, Fanny, where are you from?"

"I live in western Montana."

"Oh, really?" I said. "How ..um.. fascinating. That's 'Big Sky Country'. Yeah, uh. mountains and stuff."

"High mountains," Julian added, raising his arm over his head in illustration. "Tall."

"Some of them. Yes."

"Wowee."

I formed a mental picture of her vast blue and gray sky with nothing in it but cloud formations. No cityscapes. And below it, mountains with nothing on them but trees. No buildings. No people. Desolate.

"The life of an author in the mid-west must be .. uh.. exciting," I pretended to suppose.

"Neither of us actually lives the life of an author," Alice offered. "I'm a housewife in a small town outside of Boise and Fanny is a high school teacher."

Then I spotted what looked like an instant bookstore in the rear of the salon. Tables were neatly stacked with books presided over by a young woman in shorts, t-shirt, and belly pack. The sign over her head said, "Mary Maggie Mason's Rare Books."

(Another cute name. All that alliteration. Yeesh!)

"Say, Julian. Let's run over there and buy some books by Fanny and Alice."

"But the sign says "rare books"."

"Don't worry," Fanny said. "*Our* books are rare." She got up and walked over with us.

We found two books by each of our new friends and

brought them back to the table to be formally autographed.

I said, "Those aren't so rare. Right in front, she had titles by Parnell Hall, Alan Russell, Michael Connelly, and Harlen Coben."

"That's true, Fanny said. "And you can bet her name is in every one of those books. I swear Maggie would sell *Mein Kampf* if Hitler had Tuckerized her in it."

"What does that mean? 'Tuckerized'?"

"The word comes from a Science Fiction writer named Wilson Tucker who likes to put his friends in all his books. Mentions their names.. Gives them parts.."

"So Ms. Mason's name is in all the books in those stacks?"

"As one of the characters, yes."

"Ladies and gentlemen!" A loudspeaker blared right behind us, jolting the whole table. The intrusion was the fault of none other than Patsy Pickering who had climbed up on a little stage which I hadn't heretofore even noticed. She tapped her microphone with her finger to make sure it was on. "It's wonderful to see you all here. Welcome to the Riverside Crimewriters' Conference!" She paused to allow for a spontaneous ovation then had to continue without one. "This is the first time it is being held here on the cruise ship Santa Luisa. And we sincerely hope it won't be the last!"

Half the audience applauded politely at this optimistic projection.

"Thank you so much. We are thrilled to have every one of you here at our 1995 Conference, and hope you'll all have an enjoyable time reacquainting yourselves with old friends and making new ones." She punctuated that thought with a winning smile.

Some people applauded around me so I took the cue and clapped my hands together a polite four times.

Then Patsy switched from the smile to a look of pious concern. "But this is also a very sad occasion. For we mourn the tragic loss of our friend and colleague, Ridley P.Schuyler."

At the dead silence generated by this pronouncement, someone automatically started to clap, then realized it inappropriate and managed to stop at one.

"We pray that the heartless criminal who took Mr. Schuyler away from us will be discovered and brought to justice very quickly." She waved her slender fist in the air vigorously enough to elicit a few cries of "Yeah..yeah!" from the company.

"So we'll begin this conference with a moment of silence." She folded her little hands under her tummy and looked down at her shoes for what might have been a minute but seemed longer. Fanny and I shrugged at each other.

Then Patsy looked up again as though coming awake.

"At this time, you, Ridley's fellow writers and fans, are invited to share your memories of him and his work here in an informal memorial service.

A middle-aged kewpie doll of a woman just behind us raised her chubby hand. "Excuse me? I have something to say."

"Yes, Letty. You knew him, didn't you."

With no more encouragement than that, Letty made her way to the platform and climbed up.

"Ridley Schuyler was such a giving person," she said into Patsy's microphone. "He went out of his way to help us pre-published writers. I'm proud that he was my friend!" She nodded emphatically at this claim and the brief applause it garnered then climbed back down while Patsy called on someone else.

As Letty passed us, returning to her table, Alice caught her hand and whispered, "I was touched by your words. I hadn't known Schuyler ever helped anyone."

"Oh, but yes! He was really nice to me." Letty's eyes sparkled. "One time Ridley actually introduced me to an editor. How many famous writers would take the trouble to do that?"

Fanny looked dubious. "His *own* editor?"

"Well, no," Letty said confidentially. "Actually, it was a

young man who worked for another publisher."

"I see." Alice put in. "And did he set up a special meeting for this generous career-making introduction?"

"Not exactly." The kewpie doll looked at the ceiling to reconstitute the glorious memory. "It happened at a 'Meet The Editors' reception given by my writers' workshop in New York."

"So your great benefactor, Schuyler, basically just dragged you across the room and introduced you to some junior editor who was maybe standing over the buffet trying to supplement his meager income by making a meal of withered canapés."

"Well, I didn't think of it that way. I was just grateful."

"And tell me, what came out of this momentous introduction?"

"Actually.. mmm.. nothing."

"You're grateful for nothing."

The kewpie doll flounced off, somewhat peeved at the besmirchment of the most significant relationship of her life.

"You soured the memory of her encounter with a star." I chided.

Fanny made a wry face. "That's an old dodge. The goodhearted writer who offers to be your mentor. You're so grateful for his kindness that you buy all his books in hardcover, run around to all the writers' conferences yodeling his praises, writing effusive reviews of his works, acting like an unpaid publicist. And in return he'll be oh-so helpful."

Alice took up the lecture. "He'll introduce you to an editor but it won't be his own. No. It will be some low-rung assistant who can't even greenlight a project. Then with great fanfare, he'll introduce you to an agent but it won't be his own. He never takes you to Elaine's and you never get to meet his 'A' list."

During this exchange, three or four mumbling fans had taken their places center stage to bear witness to Schuyler's lifetime of selfless good works, then Patsy took the microphone again.

"And now we'll have a few words from the person who was closest to Ridley. His friend and publisher, Harvey Gould!"

Fanny coughed into her drink and swiveled around.

"He's here? That creep? I wouldn't have come if I had known."

"Me neither," Alice said. "But we had no warning. They only listed authors and speakers in the conference materials. That louse wasn't mentioned."

Some people thought applause was called for and others didn't as Harvey Gould, a stocky man sporting a gray pompadour, stepped up on the platform with a salesman's swagger. He paused to accept what acknowledgement was accorded, waiting a little longer than necessary, then held his hands out and began his speech.

"I'm grateful to be able to say a few words about Ridley Schuyler, as I knew him like a brother during the last year of his life."

That seemed news to everyone in the room. Mumbling stopped. Heads were raised. "Ridley's forthcoming book, which sadly will be his last, will reveal startling information about his activities since he was released from prison. This will be a fitting testament to this gifted man's skill and cunning."

"'Skill and cunning' sound like good attributes for a thief," Fanny whispered. "Not a writer."

Gould went on. "..And I expect that what this book has to reveal will provide many vital clues toward the solving of the terrible mystery of this enormous tragedy."

I tugged Fanny's sleeve. "He's talking as though he knows who killed Schuyler."

"How could he know unless he did it himself?"

"It's all hype," Alice scoffed. "Gould would claim to be sleeping with the Unabomber if it would sell books."

When the show was at last over, and we could speak at a normal level, Julian said, "Ironically, our would-be guest of honor got himself murdered just as his career was making a big turn-around. The buzz in this room is that Meechum and

Gould were about to put Schuyler back on top. They were gearing up to make his book a best-seller.

I laughed to show that I got it but he was looking serious. "That's a joke. Right, Julian? I mean you can't *make* something a best-seller."

"Sure, you can."

"What if the public doesn't happen to want it?"

"You *make* the public want it."

I looked around the table then said, "I'll bite. How do you manage that?"

He sat back and folded his arms. "You start by making the bookstores want it. Tell them you're doing a print run of five hundred thousand copies and backing it up with a million-dollar promotional campaign, full-page ads in the New York Times and its counterparts all over the country, tour the author through all the major markets."

"That's a lot of hype."

"Right. So now they know there's going to be a demand for it. Then you give the book such a deep discount that it pays them to push it over a dozen others just like it."

Fanny tapped his arm. "Tell her about the chains."

"Yes." Julian went on. "It's most important to get the chain retailers. They may have thousands of individual outlets, a store in every mall in the land. But only one guy does the buying for all of them. Get it? So what you have to do is bribe that one guy."

I pondered that. "But isn't it against some kind of rule to give a bribe?"

"Not when they call it a 'display fee'. That's what they require just to place your books on a shelf in the stores. If you want them positioned face-out, or as end-caps, that will cost you more." He rubbed his fingers together. "If I were a publisher with thirty-five thousand to spend, I could get Fanny's next book displayed in three major book chains as a featured best-seller for a solid month."

"It's as easy as that? So why doesn't Fanny's publisher

do it for her?"

"Why should he do it for Fanny? He's going to do it for Mary Higgins Clark."

"But that's really a waste of money," I charged. "Because Mrs. Clark's next book would sell no matter what."

"Not if her readers don't know it's available and can't find it in the stores."

"Then how are *Fanny's* readers supposed to find *her* books?"

At this moment, Fanny herself had her eyes toward the ceiling and was humming softly as Julian explained. "They can watch for reviews in Library Journal and Publishers weekly."

"Who reads *those*?"

"Booksellers and librarians. As it plays out, most of Fanny's books have to be hand-sold by dedicated store clerks, recommended by librarians and passed among ardent mystery fans."

"That sounds like some kind of furtive underground action."

"It's not a hopeless cause, though. If her work is consistent and excellent year after year, over time, she'll build up a profitable readership."

"That seems like a long, hard road just make a living wage." I opined. "I wouldn't be happy about it if it were me."

"Me neither." He turned. "But you're happy, aren't you Fanny?"

"Of course I'm happy. Can't you see by my smile?!"

"Look, Julian. She's not smiling at all."

"No, she's not."

"But we may yet catch a break," Alice intervened. "Say Fanny's next mystery gets a starred review in PW, or a rave in the New York Times or wins an Edgar, someone will take notice. And if Tom Cruise decides to play my protagonist in a film, I'll never be hungry again."

Julian nodded. "So getting back to someone like Schuyler, you can see that if the publisher really gets behind his book, it could be positioned as a best-seller before it's even printed and bound. Meanwhile, the public relations department would have been working over-time, to place related articles and personality pieces in the media and escorting the author on a thirty-city tour, appearing on talk shows from Bangor to San Diego.

Fanny said, "Naturally, critics have to react to all the hoopla so they review the book. Favorably or unfavorably, it's all ink. Everyone wants to know what the big fuss is about. By that time, the man on the street is afraid he'll be missing something of consequence if he *doesn't* get hold of a copy.

"Anyhow," Alice said. "Schuyler's death is fun to talk about because of the murder angle, but it's hardly a great tragedy for the literary community."

"I'll admit that I was impressed by Schuyler's first book, *Deep Lock*. I sat down to read it for just a few minutes then it kept me up half the night. The imagery was gut-wrenching. But.." Julian sat back and heaved a long sigh. "The man must have put every original thought he had into the one masterpiece. After that, he completely ran out of ideas and wrote his first Dick Duel thriller."

"I was warned off that book," Alice said. "What was it about?"

"It featured a crazy nut who murdered a series of beautiful young women in a grotesque, ritualistic manner for no reason other than that he was a crazy nut."

"Sounds disgusting. What was the second one about?"

"A crazy nut kills a series of beautiful young women.."

"The third?"

"A crazy nut kills.."

"I'm beginning to detect a pattern there. Sounds like bottom of the rack, paperback original material."

"It should have been. Yet, with a major publisher's promotional machine behind him, Schuyler still managed to stay on the best-seller list just reworking that plot. But after three or four repetitions, the reading public finally caught on that they were getting the same stories, characters, scenes, dialogue."

Fanny said, "The genre books were a waste of pulp, but he was finished with 'Dick Duel'. I had a look at his next book, *In Deeper* and it's the best thing he's ever done. Better even than *Deep Lock*. It was a true-life chronicle of the rise and fall of a criminal cum novelist. He would have regained respect among the literary circles. It would have put him back on top."

"You actually read an advance copy?"

"Well, the first ten chapters. That's all anyone got, including the reviewers."

Alice nodded then turned her head toward the far end of the room. "Hey, there is at least one genuine best-selling writer among us."

I looked where she was looking. "Who?"

She pointed subtly with her right shoulder. "That heavy, purple woman near the door is Sara Luke."

My eyes pulled over to follow the shoulder. Sara Luke was haystack-fat and covered in purple from the turban on top of her head to her patent leather shoes. She looked like "Moby Grape".

"She seems very nice." I allowed. "I just adore enormously fat people."

"Why?" Alice asked. "Because they're so jolly and have expansive personalities?"

"Because I look so thin standing next to them."

"Well," Fanny said. "Ms. Luke's bank account is even bigger than she is. Her last three novels hit the sacred list."

"'Sacred list'?"

"Of the best-sellers in The New York Times Book Review."

"I don't subscribe. What kind of thing does she write?"

"Formula whodunits. Sara has a very popular cozy series about these husband and wife sleuths, Gino and Maria Cucci." Alice grimaced. "I can't abide it."

"Why not?"

"Gino and Maria are supposed to be married. Right?" She leaned forward on her elbows. "They've been together, and sharing a home, including a *bathroom*, mind you, at least ten years."

I glanced at Julian. "That's not so unusual."

"But these saps still behave like *honeymooners.* They're forever slobbering all over each other." She held her arms around air and made kissing noises.

I harkened back to my own marital bathroom and shook the image away.

"I'd say she promulgates an unrealistic picture of married life."

"More like nauseating. Maria is always nuzzling Gino's this while Gino is nibbling Maria's that. And they just can't wait to solve this mystery so they can dive back into their conjugal feather bed and climb all over each other again."

Fanny hmmphed. "It'd rot your teeth out of your head."

"You two would enjoy a series about the Fortiers," I volunteered. "Julian hasn't kissed *me* since the Saints made the play-offs."

He nodded. "1991. That *was* an occasion. — So I'd surmise that Sara Luke has never herself experienced marriage in all its unpleasant realism."

"You're right," Alice said. "She's a spinster lady. I wonder if she's constructed an idealized world for herself just because she's lonely."

"But if that's true about her sales, a million other people must be buying into the same dream."

At this point, Patsy Pickering sashayed our way.

"Hi, may I join you people?"

"Oh, sure." I shifted my chair to the side and Patsy pulled over one from another table, settled in and arranged her skirts.

"I'm so glad you Fortiers are here because I just love books about New Orleans. What do you think of the novels of

Harold Gibbs?"

Julian and I looked at each other. He nominated me spokesman with a raised eyebrow, so I had to say it. "We have negative feelings toward his guts."

"Ooh, but.." she oohed with eyes shining. "I just love his books for their authentic settings. He must really know your city."

Julian unfolded his cocktail napkin "He could find it on a map. Maybe. But he sure never talked to anyone who lives there. Did you notice that all his characters have French names? Even the cops."

"Of course."

"Now, I don't think I've ever met a cop of French descent. They're mostly black, like our friend Frank Washington, and Italian."

"But," Patsy mewed. "His characters are so colorful."

"Some color. I've noticed that in Gibbs's version of New Orleans, all black women seem to be handkerchief-headed voodooists."

"I've been in the city twenty-five years now," I put in. "And I have yet to see a black woman wearing a handkerchief except on a box of pancake mix."

Julian's glass was empty and he pushed it away.

"Gibbs actually has his characters, who are supposed to be native New Orleanians, mind you, refer to crayfish. I mean *crayfish*."

Patsy looked beatifically blank. "But what's wrong with that?"

"I haven't heard that word since I left New Jersey in 1968." I informed her. "'Crayfish' was what we dissected in high school biology lab."

"Oh, I get it now. *You* people say 'crawfish', right?"

"No kidding," I said.

Julian held up a finger. "But the most egregious error is that Gibbs has all of his characters dropping French phrases into their speech. 'Ooh la la!' 'We have to catch that killer, toute suite.'"

"Oh, yes!" Patsy percolated. "That adds a lot of local flavor, don't you think?"

"Of which *locality*? Native New Orleanians don't grow up speaking French. Not a single one."

Patsy shook her silly head. "But I always see it in the movies. I thought Louisiana had its own dialect."

"There are Cajuns out in the country who still prefer to speak French," Julian allowed. "Mostly older people who never had a chance to go to school."

"And theirs is not the Parisian dialect either," I was pleased to enlighten her. "They speak the language of their ancestors, the provincial French of the 18th century supplemented with modern English words."

Alice grinned. "And I'd bet you wouldn't catch any of them saying 'Ooh la la!' if you live to be a million."

"That's something else that makes me want to shriek." Julian made a fist over his napkin. "When Gibbs tries to reproduce a Cajun speaking English. He comes up with some hodgepodge of redneck dialect, urban black jargon and 'faithful Indian companion'. He has them saying 'I be' and 'You be' like bloody rap records."

Julian is the linguist in the family, so it was my turn to shut up as he pulled his chair back to make eye contact with the whole table.

"You see, a Cajun's bad English corresponds to his good French. For example, it's grammatically correct for him to say, 'Moi, j'aime ça, oui.' But translated word for word, it comes out, 'Me, I like that, yeah.' which is poor English and that's the way an uneducated Cajun speaks."

"Who would know the difference?" Alice asked. "Editors and publishers are all anglophones who live in New York."

Suddenly the pre-published Gordon Magnuson appeared among us, leaning over Patsy's left shoulder.

"Say, Mrs. Pickering, since Ridley Schuyler isn't here, there must be a gap in your program."

"That's true, Professor," she replied. "But I'm afraid it can't be helped."

"So here I am to the rescue," He said grandly. "I volunteer to fill that time."

"Fill that time, how?"

"Why, with a reading from my manuscript."

"Reading from your..?"

"Oh, I wouldn't disappoint you, Mrs. Pickering. I can read for an hour and a half at a time without even stopping for water."

"I'm sure you can, but.."

"Let me tell you, last semester, I read the first twenty-three chapters to my freshman English class and they were absolutely fascinated."

"Fascinated?"

"When I had finished, not one of them could say a word."

CHAPTER FOUR

I stepped out on deck for five minutes of warm breezes to neutralize the chill of the air conditioning, then sufficiently thawed, had turned back toward my stateroom to change when I was accosted by the gray pompadour and salesman's swagger.

"Good evening, I'm Harvey Gould." He craned his bull neck to read my name tag. "Margo. Are you enjoying the conference?"

"It's very nice," I said, paying the highest compliment I could issue and kept walking.

Harvey Gould fell into step alongside me. He smiled which, because his teeth stuck out, must have been easier for him to accomplish than any other expression.

"I don't want you to think I'm making a pass, but I noticed you back there at the reception and just couldn't take my eyes off you."

"Really? Why not?"

"Because." He smiled even harder. "You're absolutely the most beautiful woman on the ship."

"Well, how nice of you to say so." popped out automatically. That's my canned reply to unsolicited compliments from strange men on the make.

"Not at all." He made a hand-to-the-stomach bowing gesture. "I would like the honor of taking you to lunch tomorrow."

"Um.." I stopped short. His momentum carried him two steps farther, then he had to turn back. "But, Mr. Gould, how can you take me to lunch? All the meals on board are included in the price of the cruise."

He gave a short self-conscious laugh in the spirit of, "You caught me." then amended with "Actually, I meant that I would like to *escort* you to lunch."

"That's so very generous," I breezed. "But I'll be taking all my meals with my husband."

"Your husband? He's a lucky man."

"Exceedingly so."

Julian was already in the cabin when he heard me scratching around with my key and opened the door for me.

"Dinner will be served at eight-thirty. I put us down for the second sitting."

I went to my UltraValet, picked out two of my dresses and held them up in front of the mirror. "Should I make my grand entrance in pink or green?"

"There's no point in changing, Margo. The custom is not to dress formally on the first night at sea."

"Why not?"

"Because we haven't had time to unpack our clothes and apply an iron."

"Iron?"

"You know, the hot metal thing you use to get the wrinkles out of your clothes."

"That's called a *dryer*."

Julian held up his white linen suit on its padded hanger and shook it out.

"I'll ask the steward to bring one in for us tomorrow. I'm *not* too proud to iron. Or more likely I'm too proud *not* to."

"If it's informal, I don't have to squeeze into anything slinky."

"You can go as you are. But at least have a try at your hair and make-up. We'll be dining at the captain's table."

"The captain's table?!" My startled face gaped back at me from the mirror. "But I thought that was only for V.I.P.s. How do you rate a place there?"

"Personally, I don't. But my wife happens to be an influential society columnist who just may write some wonderfully flattering items about this cruise line."

"That makes sense. But when they assigned the seats, they couldn't have known I was coming. I didn't agree till the last minute."

His reflection smirked and I got it.

"Well, that's all to the good. You knew you would be able to convince me. – At the captain's table I might meet someone worth meeting."

"Translation: rich."

"Yes. So I'm going to show the goods."

I unfurled a breezy Stella Dottir number in lilac. "This one isn't too dressy and will give me breathing room."

"And eating room."

"You know what?"

"Yes."

"I feel sorry for Fanny and Alice. They must be younger than I am but they already look worn out. They're so gray and drab."

"That's only because they're poor, Margo. Most mid-list writers have to work a full-time job to support themselves and do their writing in the odd spare hour, nights and weekends. They don't have the time or the cash for your Teri Case haircolor illusions and Stella Dottir fashions. There's nothing wrong with either of them that money can't cure."

"Did you notice Sara Luke?"

"The purple mountain? Who wouldn't?" Julian arranged himself on the couch with his ankles crossed and one arm dangling off the side. "She just signed a three-book contract for five million."

I stepped back for a full-length view, reflexively pulling my stomach in. "Would I give up being this beautiful to be that rich? No, I don't think so."

"My dear, such an exchange would never be offered even in Faustian fantasy. One:" I saw his hand go up in the mirror, one finger extended. "You aren't nearly as beautiful as Miss Luke is rich. And, two: There are about twenty beautiful women for every rich one."

I changed into the lilac and adjusted the neckline downward to the point where it couldn't honestly be called a neckline anymore.

(I was meagerly-endowed throughout my youth but now in the full bloom of middle-age, I get to buy low-cut dresses for the first time in my life. Maturity has at last conferred upon me the Playmate-Of-The-Month-sized breasts I'd always dreamed about. That far I look good. Of course, below the midriff line, I could be taken for the Playmate's fat mother. But I don't mind.)

"You know, Julian, I used to be on a perpetual diet because I wanted to look good in the nude, but I've finally reached the point where I don't care any more. No one will ever see me in the nude again."

"Because everyone who ever wanted to already has."

"You've got some nerve implying that I was promiscuous." I batted my fiber-enhanced lashes for the mirror. "You seem to forget about all the men who tried to get me into bed over the years and whom I refused."

"Oh, yes. That was one disappointed old Negro."

"Trouble is," I dug out my make-up base. "I've grown bored with the whole courtship routine. I'm afraid that lovers are a thing of the past for me."

"Don't fret, dear. You can always masturbate."

"I don't have anything to masturbate *about*."

"How much longer are you going to try to fight nature?–I'm getting hungry."

"Well, go on ahead. I can find the dining room for myself."

"Okay, see you upstairs."

On my way through the atrium, I spotted Frank Washington, but he didn't see me. He was concentrating on Harvey Gould whom he had backed against a pillar and was leaning over him, somewhat menacingly, it seemed to me.

"Say, Mr. Gould, I need a word with you." He flipped out his badge.

The publisher's eyes shifted from badge to face and back. "What word? Heh heh. What for?"

(I slowed my pace a little so I could witness the confrontation without actually stopping.)

"For what you said back there at the cocktail party."

"I didn't say.."

"Word for word," Frank persisted. "That Schuyler's last book will reveal clues toward solving the mystery of his death."

"Well, you know me. – Heh heh. – That was just *talk*."

Frank spoke through gritted teeth. "This is *serious*, friend. If you know anything at all about the murder of Ridley Schuyler, you have to reveal it."

"Hey!" Gould seemed to be ducking out of the way. "I don't know a thing, Lieutenant. I mean I *lied* up there on the stage."

"Lied? What on earth for?"

"It's all hype to sell books. Hey, I'm a *business* man."

"This is quite a *dangerous* business, you've got yourself into, Mr. Gould."

In the next moment, I had moved out of earshot and couldn't enjoy any more of the threats. Too bad.

The ship's dining room was fully as elegant as one in any movie, with a grand red-carpeted staircase leading down to the room lit with crystal chandeliers. The tables, covered in white damask and laden with silver and china, were far enough apart to allow private conversation. I could pick out the captain's table in the back, by the dance floor, because there was a fair, imposing man in a white uniform, sitting next to a darker man in a sports jacket and across from them was my ever-lovin' husband.

As I made my sweeping entrance, (stretching my neck and pulling my shoulders back to walk taller and thinner than in real life) Julian spotted me and rose and his table mates followed suit. "Captain Yeates, this is my wife, Margo."

"Good evening, Mrs. Fortier." The Captain was handsome, so I slipped into the chair next to his, trying to look casual about it. The captain then inclined his fine profile toward the third man at the table. "And I was just about to introduce your husband to my other guest. We're very honored to have Lord Reggie Micklewhite of Caldster with us."

My pupils must have dilated at the title but I just smiled demurely and tried not to act impressed.

"That's interesting, Lord Reggie." Julian was doing a better job at not acting impressed as he reached over and shook the nobleman's hand. "Where exactly is Caldster?"

"In the Caithness Highlands of Scotland," his Lordship replied breezily. "Near the Loch of Westor."

"Then you're actually a Highland Laird."   Julian pronounced it "Heeland".

"That's wha' me Land Title Deed says." Lord Reggie didn't seem interested in the subject of himself and quickly picked up the leather-bound menu. "Grite variety 'ere. The beef special looks good."

"It does." Julian turned to me. "Are you going to have the soup to start?"

"Wait. I've got to study on this." I made an inventory of my place setting. "We must be getting the whole Maine lobster tonight. This is my favorite dinner."

We had been furnished with all the tools necessary to properly eat a crustacean: the nutcracker to crack the shells, the thin little forks to hold the meat and the picks to dig into the tight places. When I was a kid, I used to break and clean out every single antenna. But nowadays, I lack the necessary ambition and make do with the easy-to-eat tail, claws and body.

I bent over my menu. "I don't know if I'm gonna like them 'jours' they put in the soup here."

Julian gave me a George Sanders look down his nose. "Margo, that joke wasn't funny the first time."

"I think it's an excellent joke," the captain said.

"Wha' joke?" his lordship said.

"There are still two empty chairs," I remarked."Someone must be late."

"Yes," the captain said, over his menu. "We are still expecting Mrs. Heckman and Miss Stumpff."

Alice and Fanny entered on cue hurrying down the staircase and scrambling all over each other in their excitement. They evidently hadn't been apprised on the 'informal' rule as they wore what to them were elegant gowns, shiny polyester with sashes.

Lord Reggie rose to pull out Fanny's chair and the captain himself obliged with Alice's

"This is an unexpected honor, Captain Yeates." Alice giggled. "We didn't dream we'd be invited to sit at your table."

"My job isn't all a matter of duty, Mrs. Heckman. Happily, I'm allowed to choose my own dining companions." The captain smiled warmly. "My wife is an inveterate mystery reader and a huge fan of you both. She insisted that I meet you."

Fanny glanced around. "But Duncan Steel isn't at this table and he's more famous than we are."

The Captain issued a patrician version of a snort. "My wife seems to think Mr. Steel is some kind of pervert. She didn't want him anywhere near me. Or other.." He made quotation marks in the air. "Decent people."

Fanny asked, "Have you read any of Steel's fiction?"

"I've tried a few, but I had to put them down after one chapter. His novels were so self-revealing, it was embarrassing. I don't want to know a writer is into bondage. Do you?"

"Certainly not, Captain." I jumped in. "Especially not if it's a dried-up old sinner like Duncan Steel." I held up my copy of the conference program turned to the author's photo.

"Be fair." Fanny said. "Maybe it's just the lead character in his series who is so fascinated with bondage.

"No, Fanny. He discusses the subject too much in every single book and in too lip-smacking a detail."

Julian looked at the photo and wrinkled his nose. "Just because Steel discusses something doesn't mean he approves of it."

"But he doesn't just discuss it, Julian. He belabors it as the underlying theme of all his stories. You might as well claim that Tony Hillerman doesn't approve of Indians."

"He's writing what he knows," Alice said. "I can clue you in, small-town people. Duncan is famous as a sexual pervert."

"Famous where?"

"Among his peering peers and peeresess. The world of crime fiction writers is very small. We all know one another."

Alice lowered her voice. "Did you get a load of that gal traveling with Duncan?"

"She's very attractive," I said charitably.

"Attractive in a hard brittle way," Julian opined. "I'll bet she could crack nuts with it."

"Do you think she's his wife?"

"I don't know, but she didn't look like anyone's wife to me."

"Well, when they first came aboard, I assumed they were engaged or she was at least his mistress," Fanny said. "But I sat across from them at the four o'clock buffet. And she was just sitting there and never looked at him the whole time. Just making small talk with everyone else at the table, you know? While he just gummed his fajitas. So naturally, I asked her what she did for a living."

"Naturally?" I let my jaw drop. "But, Fanny, I would *never* ask someone what they did."

"Why not?"

"It's tantamount to asking how much money they make. Not to mention that it's nosy."

"Yeah, right." Fanny turned her back on me and addressed Julian. "So she told me she's a 'psychodramatist'. That sounds pretty impressive."

Julian issued a supercilious smile. "It is or it isn't, depending upon which psycho she's dramatizing."

"How do you mean?"

"Considering the way she looks and what she's accompanying, I'd surmise that Steel is paying her by the hour to indulge him in erotic role-playing."

Now the captain was curious. "What kind of role-playing?"

"I can't say for sure but maybe she dresses up in black leather, barks Nazi commands, and snaps a velvet whip. Whatever the game, I'd bet my next meal Steel's little friend is a dominatrix."

Alice looked scandalized. "She may be a lady of easy virtue, but why do you think she would be into that perverted stuff?"

"Did you get a good look at the poor hag? She's what? Past forty, anyway."

"Past forty?!" I took umbrage and a roll. "What's wrong with that?"

"Don't get upset, Margo," Julian assured. "It's a perfectly fine age for women who are happy to *give* it away. But it's too far along to be in demand as a straight prostitute. So she has to do specialty. Wigs, costumes, props."

"You think Steel needs all that to get his kicks?"

"He looks too shriveled and played-out to perform normal healthy intercourse, wouldn't you say?"

"I can see why he wouldn't fit in here." I turned to the Captain. "Sara Luke is a *cozy* writer. Mrs. Yeates must approve of *her* books."

"Certainly. But Miss Luke has asked to be seated at the corner table with the entertainers."

"The entertainers?"

"Yes. One of them claims to be her biggest fan. All the dancers made quite a fuss over her and she was flattered. — And Holden Webb was invited to sit at this table, of course, but he sent word that he wouldn't be eating in the dining room at all."

Fanny picked up her menu. That's in keeping with his reputation as a recluse."

The captain nodded. "If he sits back here with me, everyone would figure out who he is. But if he settles for the buffet out on deck instead, he can do so anonymously. And if he can't stand the sight of people at all, he has the option of ordering dinner delivered to his cabin."

During the appetizer, the men were occupied discussing the merits of grilled versus broiled and I leaned across the table to the writers. "On my way to get dressed, I was accosted by your erstwhile publisher, Harvey Gould. He offered to take me to lunch tomorrow."

"How can he take you to lunch?" Alice cut an oyster Rockefeller in half. "All meals are included in the price of the cruise."

"That occurred to me too."

"I'll bet cheap men love cruises," she opined around a mouthful of creamed shredded broccoli. "Once aboard, they don't have to buy a woman more than a couple of drinks."

"I wouldn't say so." Fanny interposed. "There's a very nice gift shop on the Promenade Deck."

"I scoped that out already," I said. "But it's not open late at night when you're trying to negotiate a quid pro quo."

A musical quartet had just set up on the landing of the staircase and begun playing "This is a lovely way to spend an evening." There apparently was no 'informal' night for them. They all wore tuxedos.

Fanny leaned across to the captain. "This is a vessel of U.S.-Bahamian registry, right? Where do your employees come from?"

"Most are U.S. citizens." he replied. "Some of the stewards are college kids between terms. But we've got several from various countries in Latin America. Why do you ask?"

"I was just surprised to see a Greek national working up

on deck."

"You mean Aleko." The Captain shrugged. "He's my wife's cousin from Piraeus. The boy is willing enough to work, but he doesn't speak English and I know barely enough Greek to tell him what to do. Sometimes I have to act things out like Marcel Marceau."

"He doesn't have to talk at all. He does a lot for the decor as is."

"Say, Margo?" Alice spoke in a low tone, barely moving her lips. "At three o'clock. It looks as though your admirer, Creep-O Gould, has already transferred his attentions."

I turned in my chair, with elaborate casualness, ostensibly to look at the view, and swept the room.

At a small table near the door, the charmless Harvey Gould was huddled close to our welcome wagon, Patsy Pickering, murmuring intensely into her ear as though he had at long last encountered the grand passion of his life.

I shrugged and swung back around. "That's the normal sequence of events."

"Normal?"

I sat back in my chair as the waiter bent in and lit the candle under my dish of butter. "I'm used to it. For some reason, I'm a magnet for those pussy hounds.

"The reason is that she looks easy," Julian explained gratuitously.

"So," I turned my back on him and addressed Fanny. "When they're out hunting game, they usually start by coming on to me. Then when I blow them off, they set their sights a little lower then get blown off again, delve lower still and down the food chain they go, a notch at a time." I put my fork into the lobster tail which was perfectly moist and tender. "It'll be interesting to see what he ends up with. – Frank Washington rousted him in the atrium. It was a delight to behold."

Captain Yeates swiveled. "Rousted him? Why?"

"Because at the cocktail party, Gould had announced that he had information pointing to Ridley Schuyler's murderer."

"And did he?"

"I heard him tell Frank it was all a lie, hype to sell books."

Alice tackled a claw with her pick. "The only time I believe Harvey Gould is when he says he lies."

Forty-five minutes later, when I had knocked back my mandatory chocolate dessert and there was nothing left of my meal but a bloated memory, Captain Yeates asked. "How was your dinner, ladies?"

"Glorious." Fanny lay her utensils across the top of her plate. "I'd say the fare here is about equivalent to that of a four-star restaurant."

I folded my napkin. "Almost as good as Julian does."

The captain looked interested. "Your husband is a chef?"

"In an amateur way," Julian said modestly. "Cooking is a common preoccupation in New Orleans, especially among the French. We're rather spoiled when it comes to food."

The captain pushed his plate aside.

"About now, I'd like to take advantage of this fine dance music." He smiled at me. "And if you don't mind, Julian, I'd like to take advantage of it with your wife."

"Really?" My gallant husband looked alarmed. "Are you sure you're up to it, Captain? I mean dancing with Margo is like trying to push a hundred and forty-five pound upright vacuum cleaner through a briar patch."

"I stand warned." He stood and held his hand out."Mrs. Fortier?"

I took the hand, mewed, "Charmed, I'm sure." and led the way over to the dance floor.

The captain was tall and broad-shouldered and I enjoyed being in his arms. Most fortunately, he was an excellent dancer, so all I had to do was hold on and let him steer me. I decided it had been too long since I had danced with a man.

CHAPTER FIVE

After dinner, I attempted to shake off some calories with a solitary stroll around the Promenade Deck. This had it all over the cracked and broken sidewalks of my neighborhood which are dangerous after dark in any case. Eventually, I lost count of the laps but, going by the pain in my bad ankle must have covered at least two miles' worth of hardwood planks.

I heard two women's voices up on deck ahead of me. An indigo cloud had just sailed across the moon so I didn't see anything of the speakers but bulky outlines and the lighted ends of their cigarettes.

"Wha'd she expeck? When a young white girl marries a big black buck like that? Woulda been strange if he *didn't* cut her throat, *I* say!"

"And they got more of 'em on the jury," Her companion reminded. "They're gonna turn 'im loose. I bet a week's pay."

"No, Brenda, it's got to be hung. Those white people on the jury won't let the blacks acquit him."

I saw one of the glowing ends move from side to side.

"They can't stop 'em. By Christmas, that murderin' jig will be walkin' around free as a bird, sure's the gospel."

Now the cloud had floated past so that I could look up to the Observation Deck and see none other than Julian leaning over the rail. "Is that you down there, Margo?"

"Hey, 'Neg! What are you doing way up there? Fantasies of Horatio Hornblower?"

"Come on up. We're paying for this view." He waved at

the narrow stairway to my right. "Let's enjoy it."

I hoisted my skirt and climbed the stairway to the Observation Deck then stood beside him to watch the moon shining on the water.

"I'm so glad we got to sit at the captain's table. I'm not used to such distinguished company."

"I suspect you have some romantic illusion about that titled brit."

"I admit it. Though Reggie doesn't talk the way I expect a Lord to. He has a cute Bob Hoskins-type accent."

"It may be cute, but it's hardly appropriate to his self-described station. Who ever heard of a cockney nobleman? Much less an Englishman with a Scottish title."

"You're saying it isn't real?"

His hair was blowing in his face. He turned into the wind.

"I'd surmise that it's real for what it's worth, but don't look for your Lord Caldster in Burke's Peerage. His honorific is probably bought, not earned or inherited."

"How can you buy nobility?"

"In several ways." Julian advised. "You can buy one through a title broker. There are plenty of impoverished blue-bloods eager to sell their birthrights for a mess of pottage. Fifty thousand may get you a fairly decent baronetcy. Or you can pay someone with a title to adopt you into his family. Or resort to Reggie's method."

"What's that?"

"There are tracts of land in the Scottish Highlands that have transferable titles attached. They're good for that and not much else. You can't build on most of them, you can't farm them; they're not near anything. But if I purchased an interest in one of those estates, according to local law and custom, I could call myself 'Laird Julian Fortier of Thistlestick.' or whatever."

"Hey, neat! If you did become Laird Julian, would that make me a lady?"

"Nothing would, I'm afraid. Anyhow, U.S. citizens may not hold foreign titles, so forget it."

"I just thought Reggie was a cute guy."

"But you have to ask yourself why that 'cute guy' would bother to buy and use a meaningless title."

"You think that makes him a phony?"

"No doubt of that. But a phony what?"

"Whee! What a breeze! – Yoo hoo!" This somewhat naive greeting came from Patsy Pickering who appeared around the corner of the deck, clapping. "This is my third voyage on a cruise ship and it's still exciting. I feel just like Tom Sawyer and Huckleberry Finn floating down the Mississippi on their raft."

"It wasn't Tom who went on the raft with Huck," Julian corrected. "It was Jim, the..uh African-American."

"That's what Huck called him, anyway." I offered. "'Ol' African-American Jim.'"

As the wind blew my hair in all directions, I got a good grip on the railing and leaned over. It looked like four stories down to the river. A high dive.

"Hi, gang." Alice Heckman called, climbing up the stairs behind us. She fought her way through the head wind to join us at the rail and gazed down into the water. "It's so brown."

"That's why we call it the Muddy Mississippi," Julian informed her. "It's been carrying dirt, pollutants and factory wastes from as far as Iowa."

"This is the first time I've actually seen this river up close. After all the books I've read about it and all I've imagined, the real thing is a let-down somehow."

"Tourists come here expecting the Mississippi to be blue as the Caribbean and get sorely disillusioned.

Alice leaned over the rail. "It looks fairly calm though. As if you could back-stroke the whole way across."

"Don't try it." Julian stepped over and put a hand on her shoulder. "You're just seeing the top layer of the water. Yes, that's calm. But no more than a foot beneath it, you'd meet an undertow that would suck you down for a bumpy ride along the bottom all the way to the Gulf Of Mexico."

"I lifted the hair off my neck and made the most of the cool breezes. "This is a rare respite from the hanging heat of the city."

"Is it bad in New Orleans?"

"If you step out of an air-conditioned building, it's like walking into a sauna. In my neighborhood, we hang clothes out on the line to get them *wet*."

Alice laughed. "In the mid-west, I'll have to say it's usually lovely this time of year. Seventy-five degrees, average. But not *this* summer. I'm glad to get away for the 'dog days'."

I held my skirt down to keep the wind from lifting it.

"You know these are called the 'Dog Days' because on July 5th, the Sun meets the Dog Star, Sirius, the brightest star in the sky."

Alice swung around and looked in every direction then pointed. "Is that Sirius, the bright star up there?"

"No, that's Venus. You can't see any star or planet when it's that close to the Sun. It's combust."

"What?"

"That means it gets lost in the blaze."

We heard a deep, resonant "Hello up there!" as Frank Washington climbed the narrow stairs to the observation deck.

Alice met him at the top. "I'm glad you're here, lieutenant. How was your interview with Gould?"

"What?"

"About Schuyler's murder?"

"Not fun or profitable." Frank strode over to the railing. He could look in any direction he liked since his "fro" was too short to be blown around.

"Did you at least torture him?" Alice wished out loud.

"That would be rude. But after several minutes of cringing and whining he managed to convince me that he had no information about the case. Then he brushed himself off, regained his bravado and, to my disgust, he initiated a conversation with a tall, fantastically beautiful soul sister."

"There's probably only one of those on board." Alice said. "You mean Stefani Wyeth."

Frank cocked his head. "Stefani Wyeth?   Say, that name rings a bell."

"Does it really?" I asked, slyly. "Someone out of your past?"

"No, Margo. My past wasn't that providential." He stared down at the water as if to call up some recollections. "Now I remember. She was mentioned in a magazine article about Ridley Schuyler. As the story went, Stefani Wyeth met him while working with New York State's 'Behind Bars' college extension program. She was the creative writing instructor who inspired Schuyler to write Deep Lock."

"His first book?"

"His *only* book, if you want to be particular about it."

"That's what they say. I guess he was a better burglar than an author."

"Not much better." Frank smiled grimly. "Schuyler never made the big leagues as a thief. But I just learned that we have a finer example of the breed on board. He calls himself 'Laird Reggie of Caldster'."

"Hey, he had dinner with us at the captain's table! You mean he's a crook?"

"Was. Past tense. Reggie Micklewhite was the most successful cat burglar in London during the late sixties and early seventies. Until technology tripped him up, of course. Even the best of them runs out of luck in time."

"He got caught?"

"En flagranté on videotape. So then he reformed and became an honest citizen." Frank pursed his lips. "As people tend to do when they have no feasible alternative."

CHAPTER SIX

The Lorelei Lounge was the place on the ship where the lovers would go. (Were there any passengers young enough to be lovers.) The lighting was overhead and indirect, augmented by candles in red jars on the tables.

Walking in, we heard the strains of a guitar strumming rocka-billy and I turned and looked over at the stage to see the vocalist, the illustrious 'Schmelvis.'

This impersonator clearly represented the King in his final days, bursting at the seams of his white-rhinestoned jump suit and singing his heart out.

"..Ich vill zien dine klaineh bereleh.."

The tune sounded familiar but I couldn't make out the words. So I cha-cha'd over to what appeared to be the senior citizens' enclave against the wall and addressed a snowy-bearded old man in a yarmulke. His skin looked as delicate as the yellowed paper in an old book that would disintegrate if you tried to turn the pages. I leaned in to get his attention being careful not offend his religious sensibilities by touching him.

"Excuse me, zayde? What is he singing about?"

"He chust vants to be your teddy bear."

"Oh. All right."

The real action was on a long sofa by the wall, where Alice and Fanny had the spurious nobleman trapped between them. There was space enough for me on the end of the couch and I eased into it without interrupting the conversation.

Alice was saying, "Do you enjoy cruising, Lord Reggie?"

"Not me, luv. I'm really scared o' water."

She gave him a fresh cocktail napkin. "Then what inspired you to take part in our conference?"

"Fact is, I only came aboard to 'ave a word with Ridley Schuyler."

Fanny looked surprised. "You were friends with him?"

"'Ardly that. I 'ad a grudge, really. After 'e pinched that bit o' swag in New Jersey."

"The famous Fabergé egg?"

"Yes. Wouldn't you know, the coppers came and put the arm on *me*? Sweated me for thirty-six bloody hours."

"I heard they picked up another former thief," Alice recalled. "So that was you?"

"They knew it was more likely *'is* work but 'e'd become rich and respectable now, 'adn't 'e? So it's me as gets two nights in the 'ot box."

"So you were resentful."

"Can't really say that. I just wanted to 'ave a look at 'im. When I read 'e was comin' here, I wrote the cruise line and offered meself as an expert witness on theft security. By way of singin' fer me supper, you might say."

"You wouldn't have to sing much," I said. "You must have been a very successful thief."

"Not much, no. Truth to tell, I'd been better off in honest work."

"But you were able to buy yourself an estate in Scotland."

"Oh, I paid me life's savings fer that. A landowner was somethin' I always dreamed o' bein'." He laughed softly. "I'd see meself livin' in a big 'ouse out in the country like gentry. Walkin' me big dog in a dewy meadow every mornin'.. Maybe even ridin' one o' those fancy mowers around the lawn." He shook his head. "Always stuck in the city, I was. Fer business reasons.

Fanny nodded. "Considering that cows don't have much

jewelry worth stealing."

"Can't even 'ave a garden for all I'm gone." He sighed over his drink. "Every Englishman should have a garden. So twenty years ago, I bought meself a hundred acres in Caithness . I drove up to the place once, pitched me a tent an' went fishin' in the loch. Got flippin' lonely though, so after three days of it, I packed up and took meself back to London."

"But you're a *lord*."

"Yea, the title came with the Land Deed so I stuck it on." He chuckled. "It don't fool no one as matters. Just meself, I guess."

Fanny said, "Of course that area would be isolated. You shouldn't have gone up there alone."

"'Ad to, I'm a bleedin' bachelor, ain't I?"

That caught Alice's attention. "You don't have anyone?"

"I 'ad plenty o' someones back when I could give a dolly.." He winked. "A bit o' tom. But now I got to be an honest man, those days are gone and the dollies are gone."

I nudged Fanny. "A bit of 'tom'?"

"'Tom Foolery'," she murmured. "Jewelry."

By ten o'clock, Julian had found his way to us, pulled up a chair and ordered a bottle of red wine. It had just been delivered when the herpetologist, Pete Jarvis, entered the lounge moving as fast as a walk-racer and headed for our table. "Good evening, ladies."

"Hi, Pete." I returned. "How is my friend Pedro?"

"He's fine. I just put my snakes to bed."

"How sweet," Fanny said. "Did you tuck them in?"

"I turned off their daytime lights. Say, have any of you seen Dr. Magnuson around?"

"Not since dinner. Do you know him?"

"A long time. I've been running into Gordon at writers conferences for years. But I still haven't been able to catch up with him at this one." Now Jarvis burbled excitedly. "You see, last month, he sent me a note that he was bringing a great big surprise for me. Something that will *thrill* me."

"Thrill you?"

"That's what he said. I can't wait to see what it is."

The next person to come through the door was the afore-mentioned Professor Magnuson, waving hello with his left hand as his right was still clasped around the ubiquitous manuscript, clutching it to his bosom as though it actually had some value. I wondered if he slept with the thing.

"Hi," he greeted. "There was no one I knew down in the Sports Bar, so I thought I'd find the gang up here."

Jarvis rubbed his hands together. "Well Gordon? I think you've kept me in suspense long enough. I'm ready for that surprise you raved about."

"Surprise? – Oh, yes." Magnuson smiled broadly as he whipped off the paper bag with the ease of long practice. "And here it *is*. I've finally finished my manuscript, *The Second Awakening*.."

Jarvis looked down at the messy bale of typescript and his face dropped like a stone.

"A manuscript..? That's .. the wonderful surprise?"

"Of course! I know how long you must have been waiting for it."

"Well.. sure.." Jarvis stammered. "Too bad I don't have my glasses." Then he must have realized that he was wearing them. "I mean I need a new prescription. Can't see anything with these." He swept his hand in front of his face and looked blank as though he couldn't make it out. "But when I do get a new pair, I look forward to reading your manuscript at the earliest opportunity. Really."

"Very well then, Pete." The pre-published pest looked flustered and embarrassed. "Funny. I felt sure you'd want to see my raw copy, before those editors get their hands on it. Who knows what they might want to cut?"

"Yeah, who knows?"

"Hmmpf. Looks like you lose out."

"Yeah. I lose out."

"Well then." Gordon opened the paper bag and carefully

re-sheathed his proud creation. "I guess I'll go track down that New York publisher, Harvey Gould. I'm sure he'd like the opportunity to see this."

"Yes. And he deserves it too."

Once Magnuson had disappeared out the door, Jarvis heaved a long sigh and shook his head. "How about that? You know a guy over fifteen years and then all of a sudden you find out he's an idiot."

"You don't mean..?"

"The professor, yeah." He made a plosive sound with his lips. "Why'd he think I'd be so interested in his stupid manuscript? Did you get a load of the *size* of that thing? I wouldn't read fiction of that length even if it were *good*."

"But it's not exactly fiction." I pretended to enthuse. "It's more like an autobiographical roman à clef about the trials and vicissitudes of a young PhD. candidate."

"Oh, saints above! I'd pay good money *not* to read that crap.– I'm going up to catch the funny bicycle act."

As Jarvis walked out, I looked past him to see Patsy Pickering in the doorway, breathing heavily almost as if she had been trying to outrun something. She glanced around the lounge for a friendly face until she spotted ours then headed our way and stood behind an empty chair.

"Could I join you people?"

"Come right ahead." Alice reached for the wine bottle and handed it to her along with a glass. "I didn't expect to see you on your own tonight, Patsy. I'd thought you and Harvey Gould were getting serious."

"Not on your life." She wrinkled her little nose and looked as though she wanted to spit. "Would you believe that on two hours' acquaintance, he tried to invite himself to my cabin?"

"I sure do," Fanny said.

"And when naturally I told him it was much too soon for me, the creep had the nerve to call me a *tease*."

"He claimed you had been leading him on?"

"Can you imagine?" Self-consciously, she buttoned the top button of her blouse. I mean all I had let him do was *kiss* me. Once! That's only first base, right?"

"Symptom of the times." Julian inspected her stem glass by the light of the candle flame then poured for her. "Men don't think they should have to stop at bases anymore."

"I've noticed that," Fanny swished the wine in her glass. "The bozos must have all convinced themselves they're home-run hitters. Here's to single blessedness."

"You hear that?" Alice sighed. "I was hoping this cruise would prove to be a 'Love Boat' for Fanny. And what does the passenger list have to offer? Harvey Gould!"

"If he were it, I'd jump overboard." Patsy wriggled her shoulders. "But I've already seen better pickings at this conference. Professor Magnuson is an attractive man, don't you think?"

Alice hmmfed. "I suspect you've only seen him from the chest up."

"What do you mean?"

"If you'll look down at his hands, you'll note that he's lugging a ratty old manuscript the size of an unabridged dictionary that he's trying to con us all into reading."

"Is that what that thing is? I'd thought he was carrying his shirts to the ship's laundry."

"He calls it 'The Second Awakening'."

"Creepy. Well, he didn't bother *me* about it."

"He's trying all the writers and editors first, Patsy. He'll get around to you."

Julian shook his head. "I'm a bigger target, for my sins. Magnuson tried to get me to consider his grand opus for our Spring list."

"He doesn't lack faith in himself."

"With excruciating tact, I explained that," Julian held up a finger. "One: I'm not an editor and Two: at Vieux Carré we only do regional literature, focusing on Louisiana, presuming that would end the matter and send him flogging it elsewhere.

So what did the good professor do?"

"What?"

"He offered to change the setting of his book from Wawautosa to Crowley!"

CHAPTER SEVEN

By one A.M., Julian and I were alone at the table. Schmelvis had folded up his sneer and signed off, and there were only a few hangers-on remaining in the Lorelei Lounge. The life of a night person is one of casting around for companionship long after most respectable people have gone to bed.

Julian covered a yawn. "Well, dear? Shall we call it a night?"

"No, I'm not tired yet."

"But all our friends have turned in."

"Hey," I stood up. "That guy in the corner is sitting by himself. Let's talk to him."

"Wait a minute." Julian rose and followed me.

On drawing closer, I saw that the lone drinker was the shopper from the boutique, now sporting a nautical bow tie over his blue sweater.

"Hi," I said. "Oh, it's Father Dawes! I – " Oops, foot in mouth again.

The priest's dark eyes blinked in the light of the candle, perhaps in embarrassment. "I thought I recognized you, Mrs. Fortier. And now you recognize *me*. I don't know what to say."

Julian hastened to intervene. "If you're alluding to your friendship with Mr. Newcomb, don't worry. We of all people are not interested in 'outing' you."

Father Dawes shook his head. "Sit down a minute; will you? I'd like to talk about this to someone." He moved his candle out of the way as Julian and I took the chairs on either side of him.

"You see, I may wind up 'outing' myself."

"That's a pretty drastic move for a priest," Julian averred.

"That's just it. I may leave the priesthood." It couldn't have been alcohol talking in this case. I noted that he was only drinking coffee.

"No!" That came out too loud. The few drinkers left in the lounge turned to see what the commotion was about. I covered my big mouth and fairly whispered. "Why would you do that?"

The priest shook his head. "It's just so wrong to be living this lie."

"It's not wrong at all." Julian put a hand on his. "Listen, sport. Everyone lives *some* kind of lie. I pretend to be straight. Margo pretends to be respectable. It's just manners, really."

I nodded agreement. "Nobody wants to know what anyone else is *really* like."

Father Dawes tapped his cup thoughtfully.

"This cruise will mark a turning point for me. See, I've been in constant emotional turmoil over my sexuality. Since I met Ward, it's been even worse."

"But.." I tried to sound curious, not judgmental. "You must have known you were gay before you took Holy Orders."

"Sure, I did." He emitted a little one-syllable laugh. "But since I was making a lifetime commitment to celibacy anyway, I didn't think it mattered what kind of sex I wasn't having. I asked for special grace and I was able to sublimate those desires. — That is until it just didn't seem worth it anymore. My entire life as a parish priest was beginning to seem a waste of time."

"You don't always see the good you do," I said quietly.

"You know my biggest heartache?" He looked up. "The gay teens."

Julian cocked an ear. "Did you see many of those?"

"Too blessed many. At least once a month, some fourteen-year old boy would wait till the church was empty then creep into the confessional and, in a small, scared voice, tell me he was some kind of pervert. I could just see his shadow through the screen and his shoulders would be hunched as though expecting a blow and then those shoulders would tremble and even shake as he wept that no matter how much he prayed for God's grace, he couldn't be sexually normal." The priest choked up. "And even though he knew how wrong it was, he couldn't help being attracted to other males."

I looked over at Julian and he was nodding slowly.

"What could I tell a kid like him? According to the teachings of the Church he should resign himself to a life of celibacy. But that course isn't for everyone." Father Dawes hugged himself in empathy. "Most people feel the need of the warmth of companionship. And some can't help craving the physical closeness. Some simply can't."

Julian said, "Sounds like they could use a chapter of Dignity."

Now the father's companion, the red sweater, came to the table with a pot of coffee. "Hey, Kev. I had to go all the way down to the buffet for this." He sat down and smiled at Julian and me. " Hi."

"Ward," the priest said, "These are the Fortiers from New Orleans. Margo and Julian."

"Hi, Ward," Julian said. "We were talking about Dignity."

"What's that?"

"A support group for homosexual Catholics."

"That sounds paradoxical to me," Ward objected. "According to the Bible, a 'queer' is condemned as an abomination against God and nature. right? So how can one be a practicing Catholic?"

Julian said, "Some of us believe we have as much right to our faith as anyone else." He turned to Father Dawes "Is there a chapter of Dignity in your area? For those kids?"

"No, of course not."

"Why not?"

"We're a very conservative parish. Who would dare start one?" Then he lifted his head. "Me?"

"Why not you?" Julian put a hand on Father Dawes's shoulder. "I would say that's a ministry as worthy as any other."

"Sounds good." Ward nodded. "Assuring homosexual kids that they're not desecrations of God's law."

"It would be more than a full-time job." Julian affirmed. "There are a lot of us, you know."

CHAPTER EIGHT

In my first morning on board, I pulled myself together while Julian perused the schedule of activities. "The first major event of the day will be the creative writing workshop."

I was sorting through my hats. "We can skip that."

"Don't you want to be a writer?"

"I *am* a writer."

"Oh, indeed you are." He held up an invisible tea cup with his pinky sticking out. "'Bootie Kaufman's debut was the most stunning of the season.. And Mimsie Butterworth just won her first blue ribbon in dressage. Love and kisses, Mimsie'"

"So? You think it doesn't take creative talent to make those dull, rich people sound interesting?"

"Each dull, rich person is interesting only to himself, dear. That's why you have to put all the names in boldface type. So nobody is obliged to plow through the entire column. – Anyhow, the lecturer will be Ridley Schuyler's mentor, Stefani Wyeth."

"In that case, I may drop in on it."

***

After breakfast, I went exploring and my wandering took me along the Promenade Deck, out to the pool.

There was only one corner shady enough for my delicate skin and I would have enjoyed sitting there gloriously alone for ten minutes till Ms. Wyeth's class started. But there was a fortyish man already seated there, tapping away at a lap top. So I had company, like it or not.

"Good morning," I said with no more than the mandatory level of friendliness. "Nice pool."

"Sure is," he agreed. "I may go in later." He stopped tapping and put his hand out.

"I'm Abram Weissman."

I shook the hand and sat down beside him. "I'm Margo Fortier, New Orleans."

(I always add 'New Orleans' after my name as if it were a title or a degree. If people don't find anything impressive about me personally, they'll at least have to admit my city is interesting.)

Weissman was duly telling me my city was interesting when a young steward approached us and handed him a leather-bound folder.

"Mr. Weissman? This is the kosher menu, sir."

"What?"

"As you requested when you booked passage. You understand that we have to have advance notice for the specialty meals."

(It occurred to me that I had never seen such an Aryan-looking Abram Weissman, but it wouldn't be P.C. to mention this.)

"Oh, right." Weissman frowned over the selection for a moment then pointed. "I'll take this one and whatever comes with it."

"Gefilte fish with chrayn." The steward bowed. "Excellent choice, sir." Weissman accepted the compliment with a nod.

"The staff on this ship are very gracious people," I noted. "They want to say *something* nice to us, and they usually have nothing to praise but our choice of entree. – Are you going to the creative writing seminar?"

"No. I'm not here to learn to write."

"What for, then?"

He just shrugged.

Then Ed Richter, the "Cabbage Patch" cruise director, came over and stopped in front of us, clip board in hand. "Mr. Weissman?"

"Yes?"

"Sir, I have come on a discrepancy here that maybe you can help me with."

"Sure. What is it?"

"We have you listed on our passenger manifest as Abram Weissman of Brooklyn, New York."

He half sat up. "Yes, that's right."

"Then there must be a mistake." Richter leaned forward and looked hard. "You can't be more than forty-five."

Abram frowned. "Thirty-eight, actually."

"But I have you signed up for our senior citizens' recreation program, the 'Golden Adventurers.'"

The passenger froze for a second. Then he reanimated and continued smoothly. "Oh, I can explain that, Ed. It was my father who signed up for that program. You see, Dad had originally reserved the cabin, but two weeks ago he slipped in the bathtub and cracked his ribs. It was too late for a refund so he turned the ticket over to me."

Richter tried to stifle a tone of annoyance. "But when you came aboard, you still identified yourself as Abram Weissman."

"And I am." The passenger grinned and pointed to his chest. "Abram Weissman, Junior."

"Very well, then." The round blond head nodded. The explanation made sense to him. But not to me. I displayed a smile that must have looked more like making a face and excused myself. Julian had come to sit on the other side of the pool with his feet in the water. I pulled off my sneakers and socks and joined him.

"I see you lost interest in Mr. Weissman." Julian handed me his orange smoothie. "Somewhat abruptly."

I took a sip and handed it back. "Because the guy's a green-brass phony. 'Junior' my rear-end."

"I overheard the explanation. So he came on the cruise in his father's place. That's plausible."

"No, it isn't." I spread my toes and splashed. "I bet he's

not even Jewish."

"I'll concede that he doesn't look like one, then neither does Goldie Hawn."

"But religious Jews don't name their kids after a living relative, so how can there be an 'Abram Weissman, Junior'?"

"Maybe those Weissmans aren't religious."

"Signed up for the Kosher menu?"

"Things are not always as they seem."

***

I found the creative writing seminar easily, as it was in the same room as Jarvis's previous poison lecture. I poked my head in, spotted Alice at the end of the last row and slipped in next to her.

Stefani Wyeth stood behind the podium and smiled a greeting showing just six or eight of her perfect teeth.

"I'm gratified to see how many mystery fans are brave enough to assail the challenges of the publishing world." She waved long graceful fingers. "I see some manuscripts out there and congratulations are in order for those of you who had the perseverance to follow your dreams. Now why don't we get to know one another and talk a little about our work." She aimed the fingers at the kewpie doll who had taken a seat front-row, center.

"You first. Would you like to tell us about yourself and your story?"

"Yes." The chosen one got to her feet and turned around to address the class. "My name is Letty Buell. I'm a widow. And I live in Tunkhannock, Pennsylvania."

Those in some sort of twelve-step program sang back "Hi, Letty!" without thinking.

"Welcome to the class, Letty." Stefani said. "Now tell us what you're working on."

Letty proudly showed us all her loose-leaf binder which was powder blue with stickers of daffodils and hyacinths in a dainty heart-shaped pattern.

"This is a mystery about a widow who makes the best

Apple Brown Betty in the county and everyone knows it!" Her eyes shifted from one face to another, defying any of us, her fellow students, to claim we didn't know it. "But she never wins the blue ribbon at the baking contest just because she doesn't happen to be the *aunt* of the *deputy sheriff.*" She paused a moment to let this injustice impact on and outrage all present. "I–That is *she* brings her prize dish to the county fair and her rival, this awful woman named Janet Merkle – I mean Mercer. The character's name is Janet *Mercer* – is found dead!" Letty's little lips formed a thin, straight line. "Poisoned! Yes, poisoned with one of her own raspberry compotes that she's so proud of. And she dies *horribly*. All curled up and.."

"Thank you!" Stefani interrupted gently. "That sounds fascinating. And the lady behind you." She smiled over Letty's head at a severely thin brunette. "Would you like to introduce yourself?"

"Yes." The woman arose. "I'm Mavis Ryan. I'm divorced and I have a law firm in Albuquerque. We specialize in corporate liability."

"How interesting," Stefani encouraged. "And what are you writing?"

"This will be a novel about a corporate attorney who works in a city somewhere in the southwest. She gets roped into solving this murder because of her ex-husband." Now she was speaking through clenched teeth. "See, he's a real ass-hole of a mama's boy whom she never should have married in the first place! The best day of her life was when that creep walked out on her, believe you me."

"I see." Now Stefani was casting around for another volunteer.

"And he gets thrown out a ten-story *window.*"

"Wonderful! – You, the young man up here."

An acne-scarred soul in his twenties stood up. "Everybody thinks this guy's a nerd, you know? So he programs the building's computer to squish them all like bugs!"

Alice and I exchanged a "Gotta-get-outta-this-place"

look, made ourselves small and ducked out the rear door.

Out in the corridor, Alice looked amazed. "Did you hear that woman, Mavis? She said she was a corporate attorney. Must be pulling down six figures. Why on earth would she want to be a lowly mystery writer?"

"For the prestige?"

"Ha! What little there is of that goes to authors of 'literature'."

"Isn't that what you are?"

"No indeed, Margo. To write true 'literature' these days, you're supposed to pick your characters up at one random point in their lives and drop them off at another random point without much happening in between. Plots are considered trite. Anything that has a beginning, a middle and an end is considered a trashy genre book. No literature prizes for us. – Hey, I don't want to be late for my panel, 'Modern Cozies'. Fanny is probably there already. You coming?"

"Wouldn't miss it."

The "Modern Cozies" program had a table on a platform which was furnished with microphones, glasses, and a pitcher of ice water. Fanny was already seated along with Patsy Pickering and the purple-swathed Sara Luke. Alice hurried up the aisle to take the vacant fourth chair.

Patsy, impeccable in her pretend Chanel suit, looked at her watch and decided to begin the fun. She turned on her microphone and stood.

"Ladies and gentlemen, thank you for coming, this morning. We are privileged to have Sara Luke with us today. Her Gino and Maria Cucci mysteries are translated into eighteen languages and three of her books remained on the best-seller list over five months and have been made into highly-rated TV movies. We're enormously grateful that she took some of her valuable time to speak to us today. Also we have Alice Heckman and Fanny Stumpff." She paused for applause which was obligingly delivered then continued. "We have a question and answer format for this hour. So our panel will entertain questions from the floor."

One sloppily manicured hand was raised.

"This question is for all the writers."

"Yes?"

"Where do you get your ideas?"

"Oh." Sara frowned then put her lips close to the microphone. "From.. life really."

"Yes," Alice agreed. "From life."

Fanny waved. "Life, me too."

· "Very good answer," Patsy pronounced. "Next question?"

"Say!" From way in back, a man's hand flailed for attention. "Is it hard to get published?"

Sara and Fanny both just stared. Alice opened her mouth, then shut it then opened it again to say, "Well, first you have to write a book."

"I'm going to," the man assured. "My friends all tell me the adventures I've had running my appliance store would make a great book."

"I'm sure they would."

"Say, Ms. Heckman?" The appliance man waved with excitement. "Maybe the two of us could collaborate, huh? I'll tell you about my life and you write it down and we can split the money, fifty-fifty!"

"What?" Now Alice looked slightly panicked. "I don't feel worthy, really."

"You ought to contact John Grisham." Fanny suggested. "He'd be *panting* for a chance like this."

"Yes, John Grisham," Sara hastened to agree.

"Hey, right!" The man smiled dreamily. "With Grisham attached, it'd go straight to the top of the best-seller list. Tom Cruise could play me in the movie."

"Yes, he'd be perfect," Alice muttered.

"Now, that's settled." Patsy said. "Next question?"

"Miss Stumpff?" A blue-haired woman waved for attention. "I love both your series."

"Thank you."

"But I can't imagine how you find time to write two books a year?"

"Blame a dull life," Fanny replied. "Back home in Montana there's nothing much to do but write. I've got a big house I just rattle around in since my mother died last year. I get home after a day at the library and do some cleaning then fire up my computer. Nights and weekends that's where you'll find me."

A hand was raised down front. "Tell us what's ahead in your delightful Mable Appleby series."

"Well, in the up-coming book, Mable's nephew, Howie Beeker gets accused of killing a cheer-leader."

There were murmurs of alarm down the rows. Apparently all present knew Howie and wished him well."

"But this may be the last of the series," Fanny went on. "My editor has been hounding me to come up with a fresh angle."

"Why mess with success," called a sixtiesh lady in shorts. "Your audience is growing every year."

"I have good back-list action in soft-cover, but I'm afraid some fans are just reading me out of habit. My characters are getting old. Even I'm getting annoyed with Mable Appleby and her snooping. Sometimes I wish she would just stay home and mind her own business." She laughed as if it were a joke though it wasn't really. "But then I'd have no story."

CHAPTER NINE

Most people were still slobbering over lunch as I walked along the Promenade Deck to stake a claim on a deck chair.

I heard a familiar voice and leaned over the railing and looked down on the lower deck where our pre-published friend Gordon Magnuson had waylaid one of the mess boys and just about backed him up against a lifeboat."

".. but the most memorable aspect of this novel is the internal monologue which I know you'll find fascinating.."

The boy squinted up at him and held out his palms. "No spick angliss."

I walked along the row of still-empty deck chairs and selected one that had cushions covered in pink on account of that's my most flattering color. I arranged my book and my tape player with the Sophie Mason seminar on using astrology to time lottery picks.

Fanny wandered along five minutes later, wearing a skirted bathing suit and lugging a heavy book and took the deck chair to the left of mine. Her cushions were midnight blue and suited her well enough. She eyed me reproachfully.

"Margo, what's the point of sitting out here in the Sun if you're going to stay covered up with a hat, kimono and sunglasses?"

"Not to mention a sunblock numbered SPF 32."

Alice joined us then wearing shorts and a halter and carrying a book with her finger saving a place in the middle. As she took the empty chair on my right, I rummaged in my tote bag for my sunblock and held it out to her. "Here you need this."

"None for me, thanks." She waved it away. "I like to get a tan. Nothing damaging, of course, just a light golden."

"Don't kid yourself. It's all damaging." I pulled my caftan down over my wrists. "To answer your question, I hate the sun but I like the view." I nodded toward a blond deck boy, spiffy in his white shorts as he bent over to polish the brass rail."

"That's not a bad reason to sit out here. Too bad he doesn't speak English," Fanny said."He's the captain's Greek nephew-in-law; which is fitting because he looks like a Greek marble statue."

"I disagree," Alice disagreed. "He looks like a *Roman* statue to me. His name is Aleko."

"You remembered?"

Julian ambled into view, impeccable in his white linen suit and matching panama hat.

"May I join you ladies? And Margo?" He moved my feet to one side and sat at the foot of my deck chair.

"Sure, Neg. Say, I thought that suit had got all wrinkled in the bag."

"It did. I ironed it."

"'Irondit?'" Fanny echoed imperfectly."What's 'irondit' mean?"

"Something gay people do," I told her. "You don't want to know. – Julian, we need you to settle an argument. Does that pretty boy over there look like a Greek statue or a Roman one?"

"Neither. Italian Renaissance, no question. He looks like the classic statue of David would have looked if only Michelangelo had got the hands right. – What have you got there, Alice?"

She showed us the cover of her book which was mostly dripping red."I'm reading this unusual new novel about a psychopathic pedophile who strangles his wife and buries her body in a junk yard."

"Unusual?" Julian rejoined. "Sounds like a pretty

standard villain to me."

"But this is the *good* guy."

"The times we live in."

He glanced over at Fanny.

"What are you reading? Your own book?"

"Right." She laughed. "Hanging on every word.– No, this is actually more epic than any story I could invent." Fanny held it up to show the title:"Liz".

I read the cover. "Yet another book about Elizabeth Taylor?"

"Oh yes, and she's *fantastic*," Fanny enthused. "The bitch heroine of the world's greatest long-running soap opera. I myself have read all the Liz biographies and this is the most revealing one yet. And look!" She riffled the pages. "I'm only up to Eddie Fisher!"

Julian vacated my footrest and committed himself to the extent of taking the chair on Fanny's other side. His cushions were burgundy. "Not her again?" He took the book and turned to the photo pages. "Poor Liz Taylor has hardly been able to breathe without an audience since she was five years old. After nearly sixty years of steady coverage in the fanzines and tabloids, nothing more can possibly be said about the woman."

"So you may assume, but more of her history is being brought to light all the time. For example, did you know her father was a practicing homosexual?"

"No," Julian admitted. "But then, why shouldn't he have been? – I wish to goodness *I* were a practicing one. I've been out of practice so long, I feel sorry for myself."

Fanny gave his hand a "There, there" pat. "I hope you meet someone nice right here on board. Maybe around the next corner."

At that point a short, fiftiesh man with an enormous pot belly waddled around the corner, wearing a white thong which barely preserved his modesty.

Julian covered his eyes with his hand until the ill-favored one had passed us and lowered his ungainly corpus into the hot tub. "There ought to be a law about that."

"Yeah, he might scare the whales."

Fanny put on her sunglasses. "When you watch a TV show about a cruise ship, like 'Love Boat', you get the impression that every one aboard is young, beautiful, and all but nude. I have yet to see the real-life counterpart."

"Because," Julian offered. "By the time most people are making enough money to afford a cruise, they're no longer young, and along with the youth went the beauty. And so it would be hoped, the nudity."

Alice sighed. "I had hoped this would be a 'love boat' for Fanny. She's been single too long."

Her friend made a "yuck!" face. "I'm not interested in some ship-board romance."

"It doesn't have to be a tawdry fling, Fanny. Maybe you'll meet a nice guy for the long haul."

"Oh, really? So what man who had anything going for him would be willing to move to a small town in Montana, five hundred miles from nowhere?"

No one among us could think of a soul, and so ended that line of speculation.

"Hey. look!" Fanny stirred. "I just spotted an extra from 'Love Boat'. See that gorgeous young blond in the electric blue bikini? And she's coming this way."

The lovely ingenue was as advertised, fetchingly attired in two strips of cloth, and she sashayed toward us carrying an athletic shoe in each slender, freckled hand.

"So you see," Fanny said. "There are pretty young people who like to cruise."

"I'll bet she's a daughter." I said.

"What?"

"I'll lay five to one odds that girl is not a passenger at all but the *daughter* of a passenger, just along for the ride and bored out of her skull."

"You're covered."

As the bikini model undulated within hailing distance, I

waved at her. "Hi there, kitten."

"Huh? Oh, hi. Mind if I sit a mo?" She perched her trim little behind on my footrest and leaned over to pull her sneakers on.

"Not at all. Are you enjoying the cruise?"

"As if!" The young girl rolled her eyes. "This is a freakin' old age compound. My Grandmother had this big idea we should go somewhere this summer, right? So me, I was like, 'Cool! Let's go to Epcott Center.'. So Grandma was like 'But Tiffany, why travel all the way to Florida when we can catch a cruise ship right here in Louisiana?'. So now I'm like "Jeezums!"

She finished tying her sneakers and arose with the fluid ease of the young and slender. "I think I'll go get my nails done in the salon. − I hope they have cat decals."

"I hope so too," I called after her.

Fanny took a dollar out of her purse, folded it lengthwise and handed it over. "You were right. Not even the daughter of a passenger, the *grand-daughter* of one."

I stuck the dollar in my bra. "So I'm like 'I told you so'."

Julian had stretched out with his hat over his face and spoke now from beneath it. "I've discovered that young people are only good for looking at. Don't ever try to hold a conversation with one of them."

"You know, they all seem so clever on television."

"That's because old people are writing lines for them."

Fanny nodded emphatically. "Were we that dumb at her age?"

"I don't think so," I said. "But we weren't that pretty either."

"Little Tiffany is just like my son's girlfriends." Alice declared. "Have you ever noticed that we don't see ugly high school kids anymore? They have rhinoplasty, orthodontia, dermatology.. And their hair and make-up products are generations superior to the ones we had."

Fanny held up a newspaper. "I saw some good news

in here. Today I'm going to meet a man who will show me a wonderful time. I just read it in the 'Stargazer' column."

"Hogwash."

"There must be something to it, Margo. This writer is a world-renowned astrologer."

"But that's just a sun-sign column," I explained patiently. "It's written for the general public, so no matter how brilliant the astrologer, he's stuck with the premise that there are only twelve kinds of people in the world."

"Then you don't believe it can be accurate?"

I took the paper out of her hand, pulled up my sunglasses, and scanned Aries and Taurus."Sure this will be accurate. – If you were born at dawn on the 22nd of the month." I gave it back to her. "On the equator." I got up, pushed my deck chair back six inches, and sat down again.

"What are you moving around for?" Alice wanted to know.

"To keep up with the shade. Either the ship or the sun has changed angles since we sat down."

"I'll bet you're really following the Greek boy." She looked scandalized. "Are you considering a shipboard romance?"

"Hardly. He's a few decades too young for me. But I can at least admire his pretty blond curls."

"Yes, they're cute. But I like shoulder-length better. Fanny? Do you prefer long hair on a man or short?"

"The question's moot." Fanny stretched her legs out like a cat. "At my age, most of the good ones are bald. – How do you like this set-up? Three glorious sit-down meals a day and two buffets, maid service, pools, constant entertainment.." She flopped over on her belly.

"Not bad, I agreed. "At home, there aren't enough hours in the day for me to be as idle as I'd like to be. But here I have plenty of free time to do nothing. I could live like this forever."

"I, for one, wouldn't dare," Alice warned. "This ship reminds me of 'Pleasure Island' in Pinocchio. Remember how

Pinocchio and his friend Lampwick had nothing to do there all day but play and eat junk food."

"That sounds perfect to me." I allowed.

"It was to them too. – Until they all turned into donkeys."

"Oh, nuts. I'd forgotten that part."

"In the story," Alice went on. "Lampwick turned completely into a donkey then was led away and hitched up to a wagon to spend the rest of his days in ceaseless toil under a whip. I recall that Pinocchio managed to escape with just the ears and tail."

Fanny felt the top of her head. "When I feel something sprouting, I'll switch to carrot juice."

"I'll save this book for tonight. Do you have something else to read?"

I looked in my tote bag. "I've got the latest Playboy." I held up the issue. "It has a spread on Kimberly Conrad Hefner. Gross."

"Gross?" Fanny took the magazine from me, flipped it open and turned it sideways. "I'd bet that adjective has never been applied to her before in her whole entire life."

"Not Kim herself, I meant Hef. I just don't think the guy should be selling naked pictures of his wife."

She cocked her head and her eyes crossed slightly. "He'd be some hypocrite if he believed other everyone *else's* wife should pose naked but not his own."

"Oh, yeah? Well, if he considers published nudity just good clean fun, then how come he never put his *daughter* in the centerfold, flashing her nethers?"

"You kidding?" Julian said under his hat. "Have you ever *seen* his daughter?"

"Okay, so Christie's not exactly Playmate material, I know."

"The best day of her life, the poor thing couldn't have even qualified for that all-dog 'Girls of Kokomo' feature."

"Okay. He's forgiven for leaving Christie out." I put my finger on a full-page head shot. "Kim does look prettier since she got her lips puffed up with collagen. They were too thin before."

"Hef always favored thin-lipped women. Remember Barbie?"

Fanny opened the magazine to a scenic ad for Marlboro cigarettes with its mandatory notice warning Playboy readers that those among them who were pregnant risked fetal damage and low birth weight in the continued use of this product.

"At least the mag doesn't practice age-discrimination. Two months ago, they had Nancy Sinatra. She looked great for a woman in her fifties."

"So you say," Julian droned. "All I saw was a splendid advertisement for some Beverly Hills 'nip and tuck' man. And what did it prove except that she can look good in an airbrushed still picture? She's still an old bag."

"I see it as a strike for the menopausal generation." Fanny declared with some pride. "Every few months, they feature a naked woman who is past forty."

"Yes, and I've detected the pattern there." I held up one finger. "Say, a formerly prominent actress or singer realizes that the public hasn't been paying attention to her for the past ten or twenty or thirty years. She wants to recoup some of her former glory, so what should she do?

"Back to the starting line," Julian said promptly. "She should go to New York, take voice lessons,. ... acting classes... Pay her dues in summer stock or off-off Broadway, wherever they'll have her. If she's got what it takes, she'll gradually work her way back up again."

"Wrong!" I pounded the arm of my deck chair. "That course of action would take too long and be too much work. So our over-age sex symbol sees a short-cut. She goes to a cosmetic surgeon, spends a small fortune on a facelift and body sculpting, then reveals all that fine craftsmanship in a five-page spread in Playboy to show her public she still looks good. That exposure gets her invited on Larry King's show and a few others of lesser note to answer that world-shattering question, "Why did you pose nude for Playboy?"

Fanny took up the narrative. "And she smiles demurely and coos, 'I don't see anything wrong with it'. or 'I'm celebrating my womanhood or 'It's very liberating, really.'"

"Right," I agreed. "Then she goes home and waits for a producer to call with an offer of the come-back role of a lifetime, but none does. Not a one."

"Because if a producer is just looking for beauty," Julian advised. "He has his pick of a thousand juicy, young girls in their twenties who don't need soft-focus and fill lights. Anyone older than that is expected to bring something else to the project. Like talent."

Alice chuckled. "I remember a few years back, one of those former child sit-com stars posed naked 'to show the industry how she had grown up'. Trouble is, once she took her clothes off, it was clear that she had nothing whatever to show. See, the poor skank had been on drugs since she was seventeen, so she was all skin and bones. Not a womanly curve anywhere."

"So how did they photograph her?" Fanny wondered.

"Focused on her vagina, what else? At least she still had one of those. – Hey, look. It's that cute artist, Ward Newcomb."

"Cute *gay* artist, Ward Newcomb," I reminded.

"Nuts." She closed her eyes in a symbolic retreat.

The illustrator was heading our way at a youthful trot. "Mrs. Fortier?" He stopped and sat on the part of the footrest not occupied by my feet. "I've been looking for you."

"Me?"

"Yes. Listen. The art director from Hanover Books is on board. I found out they're starting a new historical romance imprint so I schmoozed him up." He looked excited. "And he may, just *may* commission me to illustrate a new paperback original, 'Umber Passion'."

"A cover illustration? That's marvelous, Ward. Hanover

is a quality house."

"But he wants to see a sample of my work. Naturally, I didn't know he would be here and I didn't bring anything suitable for their line."

"Don't let that hold you back," I encouraged. "Just get out your paint set and dab up something."

"That was my idea." He clasped his hands around his knees. "But first I'll definitely need a model."

"No problem. I see a good candidate right over there." I pointed my bottle of sun-block toward the lissome Tiffany, who had returned poolside to stretch out on her beach towel, face to the *sun*, baking away her youthful complexion. "Did you get a load of that electric blue bikini?" Ward turned toward the exhibit and shrugged. "Yeah, cute. That girl would be fine for a contemporary young adult, but she's too scrawny for the heroine of a period romance. For this I need *buxom*."

He turned back then and looked me up and down, cocking his head.

"I'd like *you* to pose for me, Mrs. Fortier."

"Me? You're kidding."

"Not at all. See, you have the sort of lush over-ripe look that works for the cover of a bodice-ripper."

"I do?"

"You really do." He made a frame of his hands and moved it a quarter turn clockwise, then counter-clockwise and looked through it. "The most picturesque features are the long red hair." He bent toward me, picked up a tendril of my hair and wrapped it around his finger. "And, of course,.. "He held his palms out as though serving two grapefruits. "The full bosom."

"I'm flattered at the idea. But, Ward, isn't there some maximum age for cover models? Under forty-nine, anyway."

"Well, you'll look younger in the painting, naturally." He wielded an imaginary paintbrush. "I'll just make the eyes bigger, the nose smaller, take out the double chin."

"I don't have a.." I stuck out my jaw. "

"And you won't have to spend too much time posing either. I can just take a photograph to work from."

"That sounds like it would be fun." I turned up the brim on my sun hat to present my own idea of chic. "Can I pose with Fabio?"

"I don't think he's aboard." Ward had focused on some point by the railing. "But right this minute, I'm looking at someone who's even more fabulous than Fabio."

The Greek deck boy must have felt Newcomb's eyes on him, because at that moment, he turned and smiled.

"Him? Hey, no!" I nearly levitated out of my seat. "You don't expect me to pose with that young kid?"

"For the sake of art, why not?"

"It's ludicrous is why not! The boy could be my *son!*"

"That won't be evident." Newcomb grinned. "I'll just paint you a little younger and him a little older. Don't worry. In the finished illustration, the two of you will look like you were made for each other."

CHAPTER TEN

I stood in my camisole and slip trying to draw on dramatic-looking eyes. The problem was that I couldn't wear my bifocals while applying eye-liner, or see well enough to draw a fine line without them. Forget trying to manipulate false lashes. I had just wielded the mascara wand with a heavy hand when there was a knock on the cabin door.

"Just a sec." I opened it to the end of the chain.

"I've got the camera, Mrs. Fortier." It was the artist, Ward Newcomb, five minutes early, with a canvas bag slung over his shoulder. "Are you ready for our photo session?"

"Sure, come on in." I took the chain off to admit him. "But I'm not sure what to wear." I paged through the dresses in my Ultravalet. "I don't usually go out in the 18th century."

"That's no problem. I always furnish the costume." He swung the bag down, dug into it and came out with a stiff contraption in nude lace. "If you will just slip this on."

"Huh? What is it? A bustier? A corset?"

"Just an old-fashioned merry-widow with whalebone stays. Simple but effective for enhancing the hourglass shape.

I turned my back, merely for the sake of form, pulled off my camisole and bra and folded the thing around me.

Ward stepped up behind me, pulled the ends together and started hooking, squeezing my innards together.

"Hey," I gasped. "I'm not Scarlet O'Hara with a seventeen inch waist!"

"I wouldn't even fantasize about seventeen inches. I'm

hoping for twenty-four."

"Well, you won't get it."

"Okay, I'll use the outer row of hooks." He still had to pull as tightly as the laws of physics would allow to get the device fastened, then walked around to examine the front. "You know, we could use a little more fullness in the bodice."

"More fullness?" I peered down at my womanly globes which were now bulging out so far that I couldn't see my feet. (And I have big feet.) If these things were hiked up any higher, I'd smother."

"This isn't about breathing, Mrs. Fortier. We're selling voluptuousness, here." He glanced around the cabin. "I know what we need."

Julian had left a fresh pair of tube socks on the dresser and Ward picked them up. "Hold still." He pulled out the top of the merry widow, bunched up one of the socks and stuffed it in the left part of the bra, then did the same with the other sock on the right. If I hadn't been sure he was gay, I would have kicked him in the hangie-downs.

"Now for your costume." He went into his accessories bag again and shook out a white cotton-blend blouse that had a low, sweeping neckline and ruffles instead of sleeves. He held it over my head while I reached up with both arms and flailed into it. "There you go."

I turned to the mirror and pulled it down to my waist.

"This looks like some kind of Gypsy blouse."

"It's the same one all my models wear. I just paint in different colors or designs according to the theme. But the title of this romance suggests its own color scheme. 'Umber Passion'."

"That sounds provocative." I moved the neckline southward. "So what's going to be the plot of 'Umber Passion'?"

"Plot? Oh, I don't know." He fluffed my ruffles. "'Boy meets girl. Boy rapes girl. Girl's father tortures and imprisons boy. Girl forgives, rescues, marries boy.' A to B to C. It doesn't matter."

"Why not?"

"Because this will be for the cover of a paperback original, bodice-ripper. It's always the same plot."

I rummaged in the dresser drawer for my mousse.

"You want lots of hair for the picture, right?"

"Naturally. We want a whole voluminous *waterfall* of hair."

I squirted a puff of the mousse on my palm and began working it into my deceptively brown roots to make them stick up then got out the Aquanet spray.

"First I've got to blow a lot of air into it."

I heard Julian at the cabin door and walked over to open it with my free hand before he had to use his key. He stepped in then frowned and looked me over. Stopping the look twice at my sock-enhanced bosom.

"What are *you* supposed to be?"

"The romantic heroine of 'Umber Passion'."

"Oh?"

"Ward is going to take my picture for a cover illustration."

Ward waved, wiggling his fingers. "We're doing your wife's hair now. It's her main selling point."

"Do tell." Julian moved sideways to get around us and settled on the couch with the ship's activities program. "I always thought Margo's main selling point was the fact that she was for sale to begin with."

I handed Ward the hair spray then bent from the waist, flipped my hair down and swung it around. "Spray it ."

"Okay, but turn the other way toward the porthole." I maneuvered around and shut my eyes while he shook the can and sprayed. "All right. Let it hang down like that until it dries. I shook it around for three minutes then stood upright and flipped it back.

"Magnificent!" Ward applauded. "It looks like a mane!"

"Well, thank you." I twirled my finger around a wave.

"The mane of a horse or a lion?"

Julian muttered behind his program. "Red Guinea Baboon."

"Okay," Ward picked up his totebag. "Bring your hair brush and cosmetics. We'll touch up as we go."

The Greek deckhand was already waiting on the observation deck, for us and his moment of illustrative glory. He must have been told that his customary uniform of white shorts were inappropriate for an historical romance. The kid was wearing dorky-looking khakis that were too long for him and bunched up at the ankles. Certainly borrowed.

"Thank you for helping out, Aleko." Ward shook his hand. "I know this is going to be a great illustration."

"Parakalo," Aleko replied, unintelligibly.

"Now you two stand over there by the rail." Ward pushed Aleko into position while I walked over unaided. "Okay, here's the picture. You're together, madly in love, facing out to the windy sea."

"How do we pull that off, Ward?" I objected. "It's not windy and we've got our *backs* to the sea?"

"Don't be so literal, Mrs. Fortier. I'm looking for a scenic background. – You can practice your passionate gazes while I set up."

It took me two or three minutes to get desensitized to the Greek boy's nerdy outfit and look beyond it to his classic beauty. While Ward screwed his camera to a tripod, I shook my arms out like "Ed Norton" preparing to play his piano and put them around the kid.

Ward bent over to look through the lens then shook his head and straightened up.

"No, that's all wrong, Margo. You don't face him."

"I don't? Geez. Isn't that what lovers do?"

"Not in romance novels, they don't. I mean the whole point is to emphasize the bosom, see? So you have to let go of the boy, turn toward me and bend forward slightly so we can get an eyeful of the cleavage. – That's it. Good. Now pull his arms around your waist and look up at him."

I craned my neck around but could barely see the tip of the kid's nose..

"Ugh. This doesn't feel right."

"It's not supposed to feel right, Mrs. Fortier. It's supposed to *look* right. No, don't hunch your shoulders like that. And arch your back."

"Hanh? How the devil can I bend over forward and arch my back at the same time? I'm not a contortionist, for pity's sake."

"You just bend at the hips." He left the camera again, walked over to us and pushed my back down with his left arm, at the same time putting his right hand under my collarbone and pushing up. "Now hold this pose."

"Ghack! I feel like a rusty slinky!"

CHAPTER ELEVEN

My brief modeling career over, I went back to my stateroom and was relieved to get free of the binding corset. I turned to the full-length mirror and assessed my alabaster nudity. There were big red wells where the whalebone stays had dug into my "waist". I tried to rub them away. My hair was starting to droop and straggle so I groped around for my brush but it wasn't on the dresser.

Then came a knock on the door. I had forgotten to hang out the "Do Not Disturb" sign and cabin attendants are famous for popping in several times a day to tidy up and re-make the beds.

"Hello?" I called. "Who is it?"

"Hello?" The answer was muffled by the door but I heard a male voice, so took Julian's robe off the hook and slipped it on before opening the door.

The arrival was not a steward, but Aleko, the Greek deck boy. He held up my hair brush and grinned.

"Thees, you?"

"Oh, yes." I took it from him turned back to the mirror and ran it through my hair. "I must have left this up on the observation deck. Thank you." He just stepped inside the cabin, still grinning. I tried again. "I mean 'Thank You' in Greek. However you say that. I won't keep you."

"Ooh, Munara. Beeyooteefool!" Then he put his arms around me in the same pose we had assumed for the camera.

I pulled away. "Yeah, that's cute. We looked great together. But you can run along now."

"Munara!" he said again, and put his lips on my neck.

"No!" I waved my hands. "No good!"

"Good?" He seemed confused. "We doo eet, nai?"

"'Nai' is right!" I agreed heartily. "Nai, nai! We can't do it! Nai!"

"Nai, nai!" The boy laughed, threw up his arms and leapt in the air. And I thought I'd never seen anyone so happy to be rejected. Then he shucked his clothes faster than I can take off my hat and stood perfectly still for just a moment with his muscles rippling like a marble sculpture, so I could admire his youthful perfection of form. Before I could pull my jaw back up to object, he had bent over, reached into his discarded shorts and pulled out a wrapped condom. "Thees good, nai?"

And I couldn't help noticing that it was a Magnum, the brand made in the extra-large size. While I was sorting that out, Aleko gently pushed me backward onto my bed, threw up the skirt of my robe and thrust his blond curly head under it.

My resolve faltered.

***

By the time I heard Julian's key card in the door, I was re-dressed up as far as my slip and brushing the tangles out of my hair. Julian stepped in then, stopped with his hand still on the door knob and looked puzzled. "What happened to *you*?"

"To me?" I moved over to the mirror and saw that my face was still flushed. "Well, I'm glad you asked because it was the most dreadful experience! That Greek deck boy was in here."

"Your leading man in 'Umber Passion'?"

"Yes. He just dropped by to bring my hairbrush which I'd left up on deck. Naturally, I thanked him for bringing it and I was very pleasant in a *noblesse oblige* sort of way and then.. and then.."

I was talking too fast, like Marlo Thomas in "That Girl", but I couldn't slow down.

".. And.. then, you know what? He made *advances* toward me. He can't even speak English, for goodness sake, but he made it clear that he wanted to have sex with me right here!"

"Hold on, dear." Julian waved his hands. "I'm trying to sort through this narrative. I mean, are you complaining or bragging?"

"Well, it was terribly insulting, as you can imagine." I pulled on a very modest dirndl dress in pink denim and pointedly buttoned it all the way up to the neck. "I certainly didn't want an animalistic encounter like that. I'm a lady, after all."

My loving husband's eyebrows shot up. "Do tell."

"But then before I knew anything," I continued, nearly sputtering with indignation. "That impudent young man just pushed my legs up over my ears and went right ahead with his plans!"

Julian sauntered over to the couch and made himself comfortable. "Dear me. You should have said something."

"But of course I did. I told him no. That is, 'Nai, nai' I said it, over and over!"

"You said, 'Nai'?"

"Yes. 'Nai, Nai' loud and clear."

Julian picked up the remote and breathed a weary sigh.

"Margo, in Greek, 'nai' means *yes*!"

"Uh oh."

"So, you see, in Aleko's mind, he wasn't being impertinent at all..."

"No wonder there are so many Greeks."

"Just.. well.. helpful. Anyway, the entire sordid episode seems to have come out of a giant misunderstanding."

"Well, that makes me feel better about the whole thing. – That he didn't really mean to be rude." I pulled out my make-up bag and reapplied my lipstick. "Speaking of which, you know what, Julian?" I turned to face him. "It pointed straight up. Right at the ceiling. I'd forgotten that a young man's thing does that."

"I hadn't," he replied glumly. "But then I have a

phenomenal memory." He clicked through the channels, paused briefly at the passengers' talent show on which a fortyish man in a mop wig and "pregnant" housedress lip-synced to "I'm Hurt", passed the cruise director's demonstration of products available in Mazatland and stopped on a commercial from another shipping line.

"See Alaska," quoth the stentorious voice-over. "On our luxurious nine-day cruise."

"It's funny that they'd let a competitor buy ad time."

"Not really. The best market for cruises are the people who take them." He found the channel with the schedule of the day's activities. "There's nothing on the program I want to see. I'm just going to go up and watch the O.J. show."

"Me too."

CHAPTER TWELVE

The ship's Sports Bar featured an enormous 52-inch television with couches and chairs arranged around it. Usually it was tuned to some sports program, but the sport of this hour was the hot game of "Dream Team" vs. the Assistant D.A.'s on the playing field of the Los Angeles courthouse.

As we entered the lounge, all the sports fans were leaning forward in their arm chairs as though watching a photo finish at Churchill Downs, though the action on-screen was just Judge Ito overruling one of Marsha Clark's objections with an admonishing finger. The camera panned over to O.J., looking serene.

Julian and I took armchairs as close as we could get to the TV which was eight or nine rows back.

A few minutes later, a small elfin man crept into the bar and headed for the TV with hand outstretched in dial-twisting mode. "Hey, everybody? Do you mind if I switch over to the weather?"

"Go to Hell!!"

This was boomed by about two dozen voices simultaneously. The elf turned and crept back out the way he had come in.

The TV picture switched from a three-quarter profile of Judge Ito to a sleek black Chrysler. "It's the commercial!" someone called out. "Time for a break."

Nearly everyone in the lounge arose like a wave, split into lines with different focuses of interest and filed out to respectively, the bar, the buffet on deck, the gents', or the ladies'. I held my ground in the spirit of my Granny Armaugh's admonition, "When everyone else runs, you walk."

Julian watched the exodus. "Do you think we could move up closer to the TV?"

Patsy Pickering's bubble hair-do appeared over the back of a wing chair. "I wouldn't dare. They've been fighting over those front seats. Even the *old* people."

So we stayed put. A minute later, Fanny and Alice drifted in, carrying their drinks, and pointed at us. "There they are." They pulled two empty chairs next to ours. "This is the ship's version of 42nd Street and 8th Avenue. If you wait here long enough, everyone on board will come by."

Julian stood up. "I'm not going to wait for the server. Diet for you, Margo? Or Classic."

"Classic. I'm running low on sugar."

"Ladies?" Fanny and Alice held up their drinks to demonstrate that their tanks were full and he made for the bar.

I glanced over to the TV screen where a gaunt "Designing Woman" had just begun rhapsodizing over this delicious "treat" she had recently discovered and what a sumptuous indulgence it was. That caught my attention (as I myself am always looking for new ways to gratify my senses) so I rose from my seat and moved in closer to get the lowdown on this marvelous "treat". Then amidst all her purring and sighing, it finally transpired that the object of this wretched woman's gratification was nothing but a flavored coffee creamer!. I flopped back into my chair. A coffee creamer!

Now I felt an overwhelming pity for the poor hag. I said, "Plainly, she's never put those thin, parched lips around anything really good to eat in her whole *life*. She must never even have gotten *close* to a piece of Vienna pastry from La Marquise."

"I agree," Fanny agreed. "But some fashionable women would rather be a size six than well-fed."

"I would." Patsy Pickering put her finger up to summon

the waiter. "Perrier with lemon, please. – You know what they say at my diet club? 'Nothing tastes as good as thin looks.'"

I waved like erasing the air with a rag. "That's a lie promulgated by someone who never tasted a maple walnut sundae. Besides.." I reached under my neckline and hoisted my bra straps. "I feel more sensuous when I have a little extra on."

"A woman of a certain vintage needs a layer of fat to plump out the wrinkles." Fanny opined. "Or she gets to looking like the Witch of Endor in daylight. As the sophisticated ladies of the continent advise. Save the face and let the thighs go."

Alice smiled. "Rich people, like that actress in the commercial, don't need your youthening layer of fat. They just totter off to the cosmetic surgeon at the first sign of a wrinkle."

At this point, the audience was wafting back in, carrying drinks and snacks to sustain them through the arduous day in court.

A half hour later, the captain walked in then saw that the commercial was on and stood facing us with his arms folded.

"What happened on the trial today?"

"Weren't you watching for yourself?" Fanny asked.

"Sorry. I thought I was supposed to be steering the boat."

"Well, his mother, sister and daughter took the witness stand. All of them completely dressed in yellow."

"Yellow as a team color?" Captain Yeates asked. "What was the theme there?"

"They must have been conveying the spirit of yellow ribbons," I said. "Get it? As if O.J. were the brave and innocent hostage of some evil terrorist group."

The captain nodded. "And what did the mother, sister and daughter have to say about him?"

"Nicest guy you'd ever want to meet."

"Well, that sure convinces *me*." Julian waved his glass. "Send that poor man home."

"I'd send him home all right!" This came from a portly

man in a banlon shirt who had positioned himself close to the TV with liquid provisions around him. "I mean all the *way* home in the gas chamber."

"Gas would be too good for him. I think O.J. should be executed the old fashioned way." I pounded the table in front of me which then shook, jiggling the ice in the glasses. "Hanged by the nuts until he is dead!"

"Neck." Julian murmured.

"What?"

"Neck."

"Did you catch Conan O'Brien?" The banlon shirt had turned to face us. "He said, 'O.J. says he was just hitting golf balls on the patio. And now the Menendez brothers are claiming they were just skeet-shooting in the living room'."

"Conan's great!" whooped a sixtiesh man with a sunburn. "But Charles Grodin is the best talk show host because he gives his honest opinion about the case."

"That's why Wednesday has my favorite TV line-up," called a woman down front. "That's 'O.J. Night' on Charles Grodin."

"Why would you wait for Grodin?" Banlon returned. "On Rivera, *every* night is 'O.J. Night.'"

"Sure," Fanny said. "But then Geraldo gets a lot of grammatically-challenged callers claiming that O.J. is 'innocent until proven guilty.'"

The lounge waiter passed by with a loaded tray.

"They seem not to understand that 'innocent until proven guilty' is a matter of law rather than fact."

"Is that so?" An old woman who heretofore had just been a few wisps of white hair over a chair back joined the discussion. "I go to bed at ten and don't get a chance to watch late-night TV."

"You should set your VCR" I told her. "Geraldo's O.J. hour gets better demographics than he ever did with his dysfunctional family freak shows. He's tapped into the country's new major industry."

"Why not?" Fanny put in. "Anyone with a law degree can ride this story all the way to the Larry King Show. Just get anyone even vaguely connected with the case to retain you."

"How would you go about that?" the old woman asked, bright-eyed.

"Where's the difficulty? You simply look up Al Cowling's girl friend or Kato's hair stylist or Rosa Lopez's dentist and say, 'Give me a buck as a retainer so I can be your lawyer.' Bingo. You're officially part of the case."

"Oh, yes, " the spry one said. "Rosa Lopez had a lawyer who spoke Spanish. I saw her, Maya Hamburger."

"That sounds familiar." I tapped Julian's arm. "Wasn't there a great jurist in history named Hamburger?"

"No there wasn't. You're thinking of Felix Frankfurter."

During the next break in court proceedings, the station had to fill the time with something, so they sent a roving reporter out on the street to interview the common people. Most of those surveyed claimed to be sick of the whole business and declared that they had more important things on their minds and why didn't everybody forget about the O.J. case and get back to their lives.

And how come Johnnie Cochran never wore the same tie twice?

"Bunch of dullards, if you ask me." I said.

"Taking the positive view," Alice observed. "I see the O.J. issue as a great unifier."

"A unifier?"

"Consider that husbands and wives who haven't said more than 'Good morning' to each other in twenty years have at last found common ground for discussion."

"Yes," Fanny said, brightly. "And it's not only fun for the whole family, but it's educational too. This case makes it clear to everyone that beauty and charm are no indication of good character."

Julian stirred his manhattan with the cherry. "I'd thought that had been demonstrated to everyone's enlightenment in

Genesis."

The captain smiled. "Honestly now. You don't think this case is over-exposed?"

"Not really." Alice objected. "What entertainment do we have but O.J.? The Menendez brothers are between trials and there's no media allowed in the Susan Smith court room."

"Where would be the suspense for Susan Smith?" the old woman rejoined. "There's no mystery about the case. She admits that she strapped her poor little baby boys in their car seats and drove her Mazda into the lake."

"The facts aren't in dispute." The waiter said as he picked up more empties. "But Mrs. Smith's attorney is trying for mitigating conditions. He'll claim that she was compelled by circumstance to drown her two kids in that lake."

Patsy Pickering said, "They were such beautiful, white children."

"Absolutely *ruined* the Mazda," Fanny pulled her chair minutely closer to the TV.

"We know the guilty verdict is inevitable. All that's left to decide will be the sentence." The waiter hoisted his tray of glasses. "Capital punishment or room and board for life."

The portly man in Banlon had perched on the arm of his chair to face us. "If I were on that jury, I'd vote that she gets strapped into a car seat and driven into a deep lake."

Julian looked shocked. "And ruin another perfectly good car!?"

"It doesn't have to be a new car," I suggested reasonably. "Just some old junker."

Fanny said, "What puzzles me is that if Susan Smith really didn't want the children anymore, why didn't she simply let their father have custody?"

"That wouldn't have suited her purpose," Julian countered. "If the detestable woman had just given up custody, her friends and relatives, one and all, would have accused her of abandoning her babies and she would have been ostracized forever as a cold, selfish, unnatural mother."

"It would have been better than what's going to happen to her now."

"But remember that in her own conniving, trashy mind, she didn't plan to get caught. She was banking on her 'black car-jacker' story."

All of a sudden, Frank Washington appeared in the doorway behind us.

"Excuse me, folks. But I couldn't help overhearing. Why does a make-believe perpetrator always have to be a *black* man?"

"Easier to describe," I suggested. "Harder to identify."

"Easier to believe the worst of. That's all I'll say."

Julian waved at the chair beside him. "Come join us, Frank. Give us the law enforcement perspective on current events."

"No, thank you. A matter which is merely a light diversion for you people would fall into the category of tedious work for me. I'm taking an hour to myself now, so I'm just going to change into my trunks.." He waved a pair of baggy blue ones. "And spend it wallowing in the hot tub."

I watched him make his lumbering way around armchairs and love seats and open the door to the pool deck.

"Now we know which part of the ship to avert our eyes from during the next hour."

Julian said, "Susan Smith didn't invent a black kidnapper due to racism but to lack of imagination. If only her story had held up, everyone would have felt sorry for the poor grieving mom and she would have become a media darling and been welcome on talk shows everywhere."

"I get it," Alice sat sideways in her chair with her feet dangling over the arm. "Alive those babies were a liability. Dead, they would have been a social entree."

The old woman regarded us over the top of her spectacles. "What about that dreadful ex-boyfriend. I forget his name."

"Findley, the worthless rich kid. Her boss's son."

"Yes. He had sent the horrid woman a 'Dear Jane' letter saying he would have loved her if only she hadn't been encumbered with the children. So, in the hope of making what *she* considered a beneficial marriage," Here a dainty sniff. "She arranged to have herself unencumbered."

The banlon shirt swung his fist. "You mean she murdered her two little kids for that creep? Doesn't anything happen to him?"

"Nothing whatsoever."

"That stinks out loud! – I need a beer." Banlon rose and left us then, marching barward.

The bartender called, "Are you tuning in on that Johnnie Cochran's wardrobe? He must spend two grand on a suit."

"What do you think of Marcia Clark?" I asked.

"I liked her old hairstyle better," the kewpie doll ventured.

The fat man waved his cigar. "If that dame's skirts were any shorter, they'd be collars."

"I meant, what do you think of her as a prosecutor?"

"Pretty timid, for my money," a steward volunteered. "They've got pre-meditated double-murder on the scumbag. I don't understand why they're not asking for the death penalty."

"That's strategy and tactics, hon. The D.A.'s team figured they'd never get a conviction if everybody's favorite negro was in the slightest danger of sucking cyanide gas."

"Hardly anyone does anyway," I reminded them all. "Most condemned murderers are dead of old age by the time all bleeding hearts have bled out and all appeals have been exhausted."

"But capital punishment has become so fashionable in the urban-nightmarish nineties." Julian declared. "These days every town wants its own electric chair."

"Shut up, everyone! Judge Ito's coming back in!"

A hush descended in an instant so that all I could hear was the discreet munching of popcorn.

While the rest of the company hunched forward to catch

Judge Ito's every golden word, I sat back and considered how the climate has changed since we were all young and liberal. I remembered that back in the oblivious seventies, the love generation didn't consider punishment to be a worthy pursuit. That's because criminals were never evil in those days, but just misunderstood victims of a materialistic society. However monstrous, they were supposed to be incarcerated only in the hope of rehabilitating them.

As I recalled TV crime programs of the era, some agonized wretch would be weeping over the raped and mutilated corpse of his four-year old daughter and, as the picture faded into the first commercial, he would sob into the camera, "We must find the poor, sick man who did this and get him some *help*!"

CHAPTER THIRTEEN

I was busy trying on hats when Julian found his way back to the cabin. "I thought I'd run into you in one of the shops in the atrium."

"I was up at the make-it-yourself ice cream bar by the pool. Two scoops of vanilla ladled with hot fudge. That should fix me at least until dinner."

"Well, for my part, I just came from an interview with your young Greek ravisher."

"You talked to Aleko? But I thought he couldn't speak English. Except 'We doo eet' and 'beeyooteefool'."

"That's true. Fortunately though, he has some french. So I was able to explain to the boy that you most definitely did *not* want to have intercourse with him. And that 'Nay' in English means 'No'. He was very apologetic and said it certainly won't happen again."

I looked at my prim self in the mirror and patted my hair.

"Well, I should *hope* not!"

I selected my widest-brimmed hat and put on sunglasses.

"I'm going to take a turn around the deck and then see the movie."

"Why do that here? You could go out to a movie on dry land."

"But on the ship you don't have to pay for it. They even give you a free bag of popcorn."

***

I ran into was Fanny at the elevator.

"Hi, I'm going to the movie. Want to come?"

"Not on your life. It's 'Judge Dredd'."

"Oh, nuts!"

"Say, Margo. Did you notice that old woman up on the Veranda Deck with the thick glasses?"

"Orange dress, fuchsia hat?"

"Right. Well, get this. Fifteen minutes ago, I overheard Magnuson trying to get her to read his stupid manuscript. But she waved her white cane at him and pointed out that she's legally blind and can't see anything smaller than the E on an eye chart."

"Good, she was safe then."

"No, she wasn't. "Cause then Magnuson offered to sit there and *read* the thing to her."

"The whole mess?!"

"You should have seen that old biddy move! I wouldn't dream she was capable of such speed, you know? She just shot out of that deck chair and tottered the hell away from him, tapping her cane a mile a minute." The elevator door slid open.

"Hello, girls!" Sara Luke was in there, smiling and blushing so much that she looked absolutely *pretty*. "Isn't this a magic cruise?"

"Magic?" We stepped in. "Uh. Sure. If you say so."

"I had a wonderful afternoon! I went up to the movie."

"Huh?" Fanny responded. " But it was 'Judge Dredd'!"

"Really? I didn't notice anything about the picture." She clasped her hands to her heart. "I was with the nicest man. His name is Milt Fischman."

Fanny and I smiled at each other and winked with both eyes. Everyone loves romance.

"I don't think I've met Mr. Fischman."

"He's from Brooklyn, Brighton Beach. Doesn't that sound romantic?"

"Uh.."

"And he says he's bought every one of my books," she trilled as she danced off at the Veranda Deck.

"Good for her." I pressed the square light for the Promenade Deck. "Well, instead of the movie, I'll go visit the snakes. Why don't you come?"

"Okay, I'll tag along."

Pete Jarvis was a proud papa and happy to show us his snake motel, walking down the line.

"You see that my larger snakes live in wood cabinets with sliding glass doors. Each has a heating pad but only under half the floor-space so they can choose their own climates." He looked in on a young boa and tapped the glass affectionately. "A snake needs a water bowl, and a hide-box in the corner so he can curl up under a virtual rock when he's feeling unsociable. We need this much space only for the adults. Some of the newborns have enough room in a perforated Tupperware container."

He stepped to the next exhibit which looked like squiggling little bracelets. "Here are some little corn snakes I bred myself. They're not poisonous."

"Oh," I squealed. "They're so cute."

Fanny looked horrified. "Snakes are cute?"

"The babies are."

"It's hard getting the hatchlings to eat." Jarvis unlocked the cover, picked up a pitcher and added water to a little dish. "In the wild, they feed on baby lizards. But I can't readily get hold of those."

"So what do you give them?"

"Newborn mice. Sometimes we have to make it smell like a lizard to get the snake to think of it as food."

"The idea of feeding a higher form of life to a lower creeps me out." Fanny averred. "A mammal to a reptile."

"Me too," I had to agree. "I always wanted a nice snake of my own. But I don't have the heart to feed them live food."

"Some of them can be trained to eat chicken drumsticks," Jarvis said. "And there's an African colubrid, dasypeltis scabra, that eats only bird's eggs."

"Just eggs? Hey, I could get them at the supermarket."

Fanny leaned over the boa's "house". "Say, Pete. Did you ever own an eight-foot Eastern Diamondback Rattler?"

"Nope. I've got a five-foot Western Diamondback at home. But I'd give almost anything to have a snake like the one who killed Schuyler. That must be a beautiful specimen."

CHAPTER FOURTEEN

"Julian? Are you in there?" I knocked in a triplet rhythm.
"Guess not." I was still thinking about my snake friends when
I rummaged in my tote bag and dug out my key card to unlock
the door and so didn't hear the rustling inside the cabin until I
had pushed the door wide open.

Then what did mine horrified eyes behold but the
startled tumbling of two lean male bodies in a swath of
horizontal-striped sheets over which two heads appeared,
Julian's looking flushed and sheepish and the blond, curly one
just looking exuberant.

"Beeyooteefool!"

"Eek!" I skittered through the cabin door and slammed
it shut with my back.

"Julian!"

"Uh.. Yes?"

I flapped my hand. "Well, I certainly hope you have an
explanation for this!"

"Of course, I do!" He groped for the sheet and held it up
to his neck.

"Well?!"

"Well, my explanation is that I.. I thought you were
upstairs at the movie. What happened?"

"It was Judge Dredd."

"Good grief!"

With characteristic prudence, my gently-reared husband
wrapped the sheet around himself like a toga before getting
up. The young Aleko had no such modesty but just tumbled

out of bed in all his well-toned pulchritude. He pulled on his skivvies, his white shorts and his shirt, stepped into his deck shoes, bowed elaborately to us both and made his exit leaving two non-plussed characters on-stage.

I headed for the couch and settled there with my hands folded in my lap.

"Well, Julian?"

"Oh. – Well.." He swallowed hard. "Aleko just stopped by the cabin here to apologize once more for mistakenly having sex with you."

"He did?"

"Yes. He's a very polite person, you know. And I .. uh.. wanted to assure him that he was, indeed, forgiven. So.."

I looked darts at him. "So one assurance led to another."

"Well.. You might say."

"And it had to be on *my* bed?!"

"That was for Aleko." Julian had the good grace to look contrite. "He said it sort of aroused fond memories.

"Ycch!" I picked up a couch cushion and waved it at the bed with both hands, using it as a fan. "I don't want your crummy testosterone all over my sheets."

"Sorry." He cast around for his boxer shorts and finally located them under the dresser. "I'll ring for the steward to change them."

"This is 1995, after all. I should think you would know better than to carry on with a *sailor*."

"We practiced safe sex."

"You shouldn't have been practicing any sex at *all*, you turkey!"

I stood up and busied myself shaking my pillows out of their besmirched cases.

Still clad in his sheet, Julian crawled under the table and scored a sock. "I think I hear the maids outside."

"Well, *you* aren't in any condition to address them, *are* you? I'll go ask for the fresh linens."

I stepped into the corridor and saw two chambermaids in front of their cart, five doors down. They were white and black, and toe to toe.

"That Nicole wasn't nothin' but a stupid tramp anyhow!" charged the black one.

"I'll *say* she was a stupid tramp," the white woman retorted. "She *had* to be to marry one of *your* people!"

The black woman made two fists and held them at waist level. "Well, I'll tell *you* sumpin', honkie bitch...!"

"Excuse me!" I hollered down the corridor, loud enough so it bounced off the walls and made the combatants reel around. "Would one of you bring me some clean bed linens?" I focused on the white one. "Please?"

She shot a malevolent look at her co-worker then, still in fighting mode, marched over to where I was and we walked back to the linen closet together.

"Be cool, sister." I advised. "You don't want to start a race riot around here."

"Those kind make me so mad! They don't care if he killed Nicole and Ron or *not*."

"But justice won't be served by your losing your job."

CHAPTER FIFTEEN

I left the maid to her work and headed for the Lorelei Lounge on the Upper Promenade Deck which was the best room for enjoying the view in lubricated comfort. When I got there, Fanny and Alice had already staked out the couch by the largest unobstructed porthole so I joined them and pulled my shoes off. "Hi, girls. How's the fare?"

"Not so bad, Margo. Try these little cabbage roll thingees."

"I see Sara Luke over there by the door. Why isn't she sitting with you two?"

"I thought you knew. She's a best-selling writer."

"So what?"

Alice handed me the appetizer menu. "In our business, there's an unspoken but well-observed caste system."

"Caste system?"

"Absolutely." She made a sweeping hand motion. "At all our conferences, the front list writers with the six and seven figure advances hang together, have private parties in their suites, or pile into a limousine and ride off to cordon bleu restaurants, while Fanny and I grab a burger with the other subsistence writers."

"Don't you sort of resent that segregation?"

"Not at all. The 'haves' are just uncomfortable with the 'have-nots' and vice-versa."

"After all, what would I say to Sara Luke?" Fanny twirled an onion ring on a toothpick. "'Hey, you make *much* more money than I do. And for writing absolute *dreck*. So why don't you save me all the trouble and frustration and give me some of *yours?*"'

"Me too," Alice agreed. "That's all *I* could think of to tell her."

I picked up the little pasteboard tent on the table. "This says the non-alcoholic drink of the day is a virgin piña colada. If it tastes like a pineapple slurpy, I'll take it."

The waitress stopped by to place another tray of complimentary hors d'oeuvres on the table.

"Excuse me?" Alice asked her. "What are these?"

"Buffalo wings."

"Oh, really? I've read about these in New York Magazine. But I never quite understood what they were."

"They're nothing but fried chicken wings," I informed her kindly. "In New Orleans, that's the part we throw away after serving chicken. Apparently some smart alecs on the east coast found a way to make garbage into a chic appetizer."

Alice shrugged, then glanced at her colleague and said. "Go ahead and ask her."

"No," Fanny returned. "*You* ask."

I looked from one to the other. "Ask what?"

Alice lowered her voice. "If it's not too personal.. We were wondering why a lusty chick like you would have married a homosexual."

"Admittedly, all men have their flaws." Fanny admitted. "But that's rather an unwieldy one, I should think. What brought you two together?"

"Our union was a purely practical matter, girls." I pushed the plate away. "I saw no point in marrying a man I was sexually attracted to since none of my grand passions ever lasted more than two years, anyway."

"How was it practical?" Alice wanted to know. "Does Julian have money?"

"No, but he has something better: social position, old name, old family. You see, 'Mrs. Julian Fortier' gets invited as an honored guest to a lot of events Margie Gowan of Boonton,

New Jersey, could never get into, even as a waitress."

"What about Julian?" Fanny wondered. "Why would he want to be tied down to a traditional marriage?"

"He simply didn't care to spend his life cooking for one in a shotgun apartment in Marigny. He wanted a real home. That is, a house big enough to have a dining room where he could lay out the family silver."

"How very sophisticated an arrangement." Alice raised her glass. "I detected a sort of Gertrude Lawrence-Noel Coward dynamic happening there."

With theatrical timing, "Noel Coward" himself appeared in the doorway of the lounge with the cruiseline's edition of the newspaper under his arm. I waved the little tent to get his attention. He joined us and handed me the paper.

Julian said, "I just spotted Sara Luke by the door, holding hands with a tubby, bald guy."

"I guess that's her Milt Fischman from Brooklyn." Fanny said. "Don't you think they're cute together?"

"You mean because they're both short and fat?"

"Exactly. They could pose for comical salt and pepper shakers."

He put his finger on the paper. "This has an item about the White House press secretary, Dee Dee Myers. You know how she was arrested for drunk-driving?"

"Uh uh," I said. "I didn't even know she was Irish."

Fanny said, "But it was in all the papers."

"I write for a newspaper; I don't have time to read one."

Alice looked reproachful. "Then I guess you don't have time to read mystery novels either, Margo."

"I get my fill of mysteries on television. At least I'm good at figuring out whodunit before Jessica Fletcher does."

"Bradford Dillman," Julian said behind his menu. "It's always Bradford Dillman."

"I love that show!" Alice enthused. "Jessica Fletcher is my exemplar. She only writes three seconds a week and she's already racked up two dozen best-sellers."

Fanny bobbed her head. "Most of them done on a manual typewriter at her kitchen table."

Alice shook her fists in a "Rah Rah" gesture. "She's sent on book tours all over the world, gets lauded and feted by leaders in art and industry, wooed by spies and tycoons, recognized by complete strangers. From her *dust jacket* photo yet." She pulled in the fists. "My own mother wouldn't recognize *me* from *my* dust jacket photo."

"You especially should identify with Jessica," I offered. "According to the back story, the character started out as an English teacher like you."

"What kind of English teacher?" Fanny finally realized that a dried chicken wing isn't worth eating no matter what they call it and dropped it on the plate. "Not like me! Did you ever read that page she pops out of her typewriter during the opening montage?"

"I never paid much attention."

"It starts 'Arnold ran out of the door..'."

Julian shook his head. "Bad usage," and asked the waitress for a carafe of red wine.

"Right" Fanny said. "Now if Jessica Fletcher had really been an English major, she should have known that maybe Arnold could run *out* the door or *through* the door but he couldn't run 'out *of* the door' unless he had been inside the door itself to begin with."

Alice reached for a breaded shrimp. "Maybe Arnold was a termite. — If you don't read mysteries, Margo, why did you come aboard?"

"The air conditioning and those nice snakes."

"I understand the lure of the air conditioning. But what made you so interested in snakes?"

"When I was working on Bourbon Street, back around 1970, I followed Iola the Jungle Girl."

"A real jungle girl?"

"Well, *Gretna's* version of one," I explained. "She used to strip down to a banana leaf." Julian rolled his eyes as he always does when I discuss my early career. "Naturally, she thought she would look more exotic working with a snake. But all she managed to get hold of was this dinky little rat snake, named Robert while she was saving up for a boa. She let me play with him between shows. Robert loved being handled because it warmed him up."

"That sounds cute." Fanny swished the ice around in her drink. "How do you folks feel about being on the same ship with the famous Holden Webb?"

"I'm sort of thrilled, aren't you? It's almost as though we're about to witness a part of history. I was always sorry that I never got to trade stories with Steinbeck or Hemingway." I stirred my daiquiri slurpy. "And we were born too late to bend an elbow with F. Scott Fitzgerald and Thomas Wolfe."

"I ran into Tennessee Williams a few times when he lived on Dumaine Street." Julian was pleased to brag. Then he frowned. "But never when he was sober."

"I've always wanted to meet a great literary figure," Alice said wistfully. "But how often do they come through Iowa? Holden Webb may be my only chance in life for a 'brush with greatness'."

Fanny nodded. "I've been keeping an eye out for the great man but no luck so far."

"I've never even seen a photo of Webb, " Julian said. "How do you know what he looks like?"

"I don't, of course. But I've been checking names on badges."

"Since this man is so famously reclusive," I pointed out. "Don't you think he would demur to wear one."

"Right." Alice said, "I'd bet my next advance that he's hiding away in his cabin and ventures out only in the dead of night. We'll never run into him."

Julian looked shrewd. "But we know he's hiding away in cabin 84, don't we?"

"Really? How do we know that?"

"Patsy let it slip the first afternoon. She said she

knocked on the door of 84, looking for him."

"I've got an idea. One of us should very graciously ask Mr. Webb to join us for a drink." Alice pointed with her swizzle stick. "Meaning you, Julian."

"What? Why me?"

"Because you're a publisher. You have plenty of status."

"I *work* for a publisher," Julian corrected. "I have plenty of *low* status. Besides, my wife is the society lion in the family." He smiled meanly at me. "It is she who issues all the invitations."

"It is? Oh, very well." I leaned over and pulled my shoes on then stretched my legs out to uncreak them before getting up. "What's the number of his cabin again?"

"Eighty-four."

"Eight-four." I levered myself upright. "Wish me luck." And I set out on my mission, making the trip merely to humor the group so they would stop nagging.

While waiting for the elevator, I decided that I wouldn't make a pest of myself but would just give Webb's door a discreet tap. If he wanted to hear me, he would and maybe open it. Or he could ignore me if he chose, in which event I wouldn't have to face him at all but could simply slink away as though I had never been there. My dignity intact.

I took the elevator down to Deck C and made my way along the hall, reading numbers on doors. Before I had quite reached the eighties, I spotted a bearded man striding toward me from the opposite end of the corridor. When he got close enough for me to make out his features without my bifocals, I could see that it was none other than the perennially pre-published Gordon Magnuson. We both stopped in front of Cabin 84.

I put my hand in front of my mouth as though maybe he wouldn't recognize me. "Um.. Hi."

"Yes.. Hi."

He seemed as embarrassed as I was to have bumped heads outside a famous man's door like a couple of groupies.

"I was just going to ask Mr. Webb to come up to the Lorelei Lounge and have a drink with us," I admitted. "But it was Fanny's idea, not mine. Fanny's."

"I'm hoping to talk to him too." The professor hefted his ubiquitous bag of garbage. "I thought he'd want to take a look at my manuscript."

"I'm sure he would," I said with a perfectly straight face.

Magnuson stepped up to the door, put his ear against it and listened with all his might, then turned back to me and whispered. "I think I hear him moving around in there."

"Where else would he be?" I whispered back.

He nodded excitedly then knocked on the door. "Hello, Mr. Webb?!" He called out. "I'm Gordon Magnuson. I teach college English." He knocked again, harder. "I have a manuscript for you to read. Nearly a thousand pages!" Ear to the door again. He frowned and whispered, "Isn't that strange? Now I don't hear anything."

He stood away from the door so I could clap my own ear against it. After a moment, I said, "Neither do I. The guy might well be holding his breath."

I moved back then, figuring there was as good a chance of Judge Crater's walking out that door as the reclusive Mr. Webb and took leave of Magnuson who by then was down on his knees, trying to squint through the keyslot.

When I rejoined the party in the Lorelei Lounge, Fanny looked up eagerly then frowned and looked down again. "I take it that Mr. Webb declined your invitation to join us."

"He probably would have, but I never had a chance to make my pitch. Magnuson's hovering out in the hall waiting to ambush the guy with his stupid manuscript."

"Nuts! Now we'll never get Webb out of that cabin."

Alice took the day's program out of her purse.

"Since he won't be up here to entertain us, do you want to go to the Main Room and watch the funny xylophone player?"

Julian said, "I don't deserve that much fun. Let's see

what movie is playing."

"We can see movies at home," Fanny reminded. "Though of course, we can't see fascinating couples like Margo and Julian at home."

"No, we don't grow those kinds in the mid-west," Alice agreed. "Our main source of diversion is that technological marvel formerly known as the idiot box."

Fanny waved a finger. "The finest invention of the latter twentieth is the VCR so I don't have to choose between Leno and Letterman. I can watch NBC and tape CBS."

I said, "I tape 'The Commish' so I can fast-forward past the sappy family stuff and get to the interesting cop stuff."

"I know what you mean." Alice frowned. "The b-story is usually some warm-hearted domestic tripe like Rachel gets an inconclusive biopsy for breast cancer."

"That's a mandatory plot," Julian averred. "I don't think they're allowed to run any show more than three years without the female lead's getting an inconclusive biopsy for breast cancer."

"That gimmick got old after Edith Bunker," I contended. "I tape 'Chicago Hope' so I can replay Mandy Patinkin. Especially when he sings."

Fanny began erecting a pyramid with swizzle sticks. "I heard that Patinkin's leaving the series."

"He'd better not. Without him, it would just be 'Medical Center' with Jews."

"There are other good actors on the show."

"The difference between Patinkin and other TV actors is like the difference between Elvis and The Belmonts."

Alice bit into a spinach eggroll. "I think The Belmonts are still alive."

"Yeah, but *where*?"

"What happened to E.G. Marshall?" Fanny wondered. "First he was there on the show and he was good and then he was gone."

"He's old."

"He was *always* old. That never stopped him before. – Do you watch 'Touched By An Angel'? Now there's a show that deals with the spiritual element."

"Yes, it's so relevant," Julian said. "From Bosnia we hear about Serbians slaughtering Muslims by the thousands, In Iraq, Saddam is wiping out entire villages with nerve gas, and in Rwanda the Hutus have massacred half a million Tutsis. Right?" He held up his swizzle stick like a magic wand. "So God, with His whimsical order of priorities, sends a lovely Irish angel where she's *really* needed. To some suburb of New Hampshire to help a depressed nine-year-old get into the Little League."

"I don't believe in fantasy anymore." Fanny said. "Lately my set is tuned to CNN around the clock."

"Why not? CNN has replaced the New York Times as the news purveyor of record."

"Myself," I volunteered, "I get all my news standing on line at the supermarket. It takes the tabloids to give you the real scoop."

Julian raised one eyebrow. "You know what kind of material customarily gets scooped?"

"I'm always up for gossip," Fanny admitted. "What did you think of Hugh Grant's being arrested for picking up a street walker?"

"I was dumbfounded to learn that he's heterosexual."

"Of course the poor man is straight," I chided. "Did you get a load of that baggy print shirt he was wearing in the mug shot?"

"Just dreadful," Julian agreed. "No gay man would get arrested looking like that."

"Well, Grant acts sort of pussified," Alice said. "But I guess that's just because he's British."

Fanny reached across her for a shrimp. "The newspapers said they used a mint flavored condom, so no harm done, the way I see it."

"I'd like to hear the poor schlub explain the whole

debacle to his girl friend back in England, that model."

"Elizabeth Hurley."

"Right. If he had his wits together, he would have told her it was all just a gigantic publicity stunt to promote his new film."

"It wouldn't play," Alice objected. "The title of his film is 'Nine Months', not 'Nine Minutes'."

"I saw a picture of the prostitute," Julian said. 'Nine Dollars' would be more germane."

"She probably makes more than I do," Fanny said. "My next royalty check is going right into that fantastic Windows '95. There will be a lot of exciting new stuff bundled with it. An updated Microsoft Word, internet access, I can't wait."

"Everyone will have to wait," Alice announced. "Microsoft won't be shipping the upgrade till August."

"But Office Depot is taking advance orders right now."

"Not from me it isn't," I said. "I just last week figured out how to find a program on my 3.1. It takes nine clicks."

I stopped babbling when the woman I recognized as Duncan Steel's lady friend entered the salon. First she stood in the doorway and glanced around. Then she spotted our motley little party and to my surprise, headed our way. She paused with her hand on the back of an empty chair.

"Hello? Is it all right if I join you people?"

"Look, everybody!" I crowed. "It's the dominatrix! – Sure, sit down."

"Welcome to the conclave." Julian shot me a look and pulled out the chair for her. "I'm Julian and this soul of tact here is my wife, Margo. These ladies are Alice Heckman and Fanny Stumpff."

Fanny looked slightly awe-struck. "Aren't you with Duncan Steel?"

"Yeah." Gratefully, she settled in the chair. "He's taking a nap now so I finally got a few hours to myself. I'm Shane Pederson."

"We haven't seen you around on deck."

"No such luck." She made a face. "Duncan put us in the Royale Suite up on the Veranda Deck. Now he just wants to sit in there and watch video tapes. I was going nuts." She summoned the waiter and ordered a double Scotch and soda.

Alice tapped her lips. "Excuse me for mentioning this. But you wouldn't seem to have much in common with Mr. Steel. How did you happen to meet him?"

Ms. Pederson looked around at us and I guess we impressed her as clued-in because she just shrugged. "He called the Riviera escort service and said he would like some company."

Fanny sat bolt-upright. "Then you're a professional escort?"

"Professional, yeah. That's me."

"Cool!"

"An escort must have the most exciting life," Alice gushed. "You get a date every night, right? So you get a free dinner and paid for your time to boot."

"It's not as glamorous as you might imagine." Shane took out her slim, gold compact, glanced at her reflection in the mirror and frowned, but then snapped the compact closed and returned it to her purse without making any adjustments. "Men invite me out all right, but not to the formal dinners on the upper east side. Oh, no, those are just for the *wives*. They only take me to dimly-lit, second-rate restaurants where they introduce me to other johns who are out with *their* callgirls." She pulled a pack of cigarettes from her purse and knocked out a long, thin one. "Does anybody mind?" Not one of us was a smoker. But neither would any have interrupted the conversation by objecting. She put the cigarette in her mouth and handed her matches to Julian. "Light me." He did and gave back the matches.

Smoke came out with her words. "Of course, if that were all there was to the job, it would be a snap. Anyone could do it."

"What else is entailed?" Fanny asked then giggled at

her boldness.

"Phew. They want all kinds of things. You would be surprised at how minutely detailed these fetishists get about their peculiarities   Some of them give me an elaborate scenario to follow with pages of lines to memorize. The costume I must wear, the appropriate make-up and hair-do to fulfill their fantasies.

The daiquiris were beginning to tell on Fanny. She giggled again and pointed at me.

"If you need a redhead, you can call Margo."

"Oh, no, that wouldn't be necessary." Shane said. "You see, *I'm* the redhead. I'm also the blond, the brunette, and whatever else is called for. I can even be black or Asian, at least on the phone."

Alice held up her glass. "I couldn't even be a *white* sex object on the phone. I wouldn't have any idea what to say."

"You don't have to know anything. If you worked for me, I'd give you a script to read from."

"You write a whole script?"

"It doesn't have to be very imaginative dialogue. 'Kiss my feet, you sniveling slave!' That sort of trash."

Alice looked slightly revolted. "I can't imagine that I would enjoy saying those things."

"Of course you wouldn't enjoy it, Alice. The *trick* enjoys it. He pays. Then *you* enjoy spending the money."

"A job like that would depress me too much," Fanny averred. "The idea of spending one's working day dealing with emotionally twisted men and their aberrant sex drives must be very demoralizing."

"No kidding." Shane inhaled a lungful. "What's more, I'll be forty-five next month and I'm getting tired. Which is why I'm trying like mad to get Duncan to marry me."

"Him? But what would be the sense of that?" I said with no tact whatsoever.

"Sense?"

"I mean, a girl gets married to get *out* of the racket,

right? But if you marry a pervert like Duncan, you'll still be stuck doing the same work."

Julian gave me a chastening look but I didn't feel out of line. We were being candid here, after all. And Shane didn't seem to take offense.

She sighed in a puff of smoke. "That's all too true. But at least this trick would be well-paying and on an exclusive basis so I can drop all the other johns and sell my book."

"Ooh," Alice beamed. "You're writing a book."

I explained. "She means her list of clients, with prices and preferences. She'll sell it to another working girl."

"Margo shouldn't know that," Julian muttered.

Shane blew a smoke ring and watched it float toward the indirect lighting panel. "I realize that ours won't be any fairy tale marriage. But at least I'll be someone."

"'Mrs. Duncan Steel'", I supplied. Not thinking it sounded that great.

"Actually.." She mumbled into her drink. "'Mrs. Sid Muddwort'. That's his real name."

"Are you willing to stare at his ugly old face over your breakfast eggs every morning?"

"That won't be so bad." Shane french inhaled. "I'm very near-sighted. And I don't intend to put my contacts in until I go out of the house. Out will be the best part." She smiled up at some imaginary picture projected on the ceiling. "I'll be able to shop at Bendel's and take in matinees and lunch at the Oak Room."

"With the cream of society?"

"Not exactly." She clicked her tongue and came back down to ground level. "With all the other ex-whores who managed to snag rich husbands. Fortunately, there are a lot of us, so I won't be lonely."

Alice couldn't stifle her curiosity. "How did you decide to pursue that particular.. er.. field of endeavor?"

Shane didn't seem insulted. "No one decides to do that. I mean, you decide to be a fashion model but you're too short.

Or you decide to be a singer, but you don't have the pipes. Or you decide to be an actress, but there's no talent to work with. And while you're hoping.., while you still have hope.." She looked around at the table, meeting our eyes one by one. "See, I was beautiful when I was young."

We all nodded. She was only a little past beautiful now.

"I looked like the original Barbie doll back then but without the plastic. Natural blond, hot figure, You know? Men liked to take me out and give me things. And money. Just to lie there. It was too easy."

"Too easy?" I blurted. "It sounds just right to me."

"Generous men, money and drugs all went together. The problem was that drugs were an inevitable part of the life."

"Drugs?" Now I was ready to drop out.

"Of course, my boyfriends expected me to do lines along with them. First I did it to make them happy." She flicked the cigarette ash. "Then I was doing it to make myself happy. Then I *had* to do it."

"But you must have been making a lot of money."

"For just a few years I did. You realize there's no job security in this business."

"Supply exceeds demand," Julian suggested. "Too many degenerate young women chasing too few horny men in suits."

"You've got it." Shane agreed. She looked rueful for just a second. "Every June, a million cute, blond, cheerleaders graduate from high school and ride Greyhound busses into the cities to be models or singers or actresses, and while they're hoping..

"So a call girl has the shelf-life of a quart of buttermilk. By the time I hit thirty, I had a four-hundred dollar a day habit. But by then the generous men were sharing their coke with a fresh new crop of girls. I could no longer get high-paying dates on my looks alone." She inhaled the cigarette as if it were life-giving oxygen and spoke on the exhale. "So I learned to do extra things."

"Extra?" Fanny bit a knuckle. "Say.. What's the worst thing you ever had to do? In the course of.. your work."

Shane leaned across the table. "Just picture in your mind the most disgusting activity that can possibly occur between two consenting adults."

Fanny closed her eyes then grimaced and, slightly ashamed, opened them again.

"Yes?"

"It's that."

"Eeooo."

"So the work got a lot more specialized and the money came harder, but I still needed it for drugs. I was working around the clock, so what good did all that money do me? It went right up my nose."

Fanny adjusted her bifocals and looked through the lower lenses. "But we can see that you're straight, now."

"Now, yeah. I finally went into rehab eight years ago, and got clean and dry. But when I came out, I was still thirty-seven years old and didn't have a profession. Except this one."

Julian said, "You could always.."

Shane interrupted. "I'm a high school drop-out with no legitimate work history. I could always what?"

He had no answer then and just shook his head.

A steward came to the table, waited politely for a break in the conversation, then addressed Shane. "Excuse me, are you Miss Pederson?"

She inclined her head.

"Mr. Steel sent me to let you know he has finished his nap."

"Thrill me." Dutifully, she picked up her purse and took one last swallow of her drink. "Back to the old salt mines. Well, gang. It's been real."

I watched her walk out of the lounge. Her hips were trim, but she didn't swing them at all. I supposed she didn't act sexy until the credit card had been processed.

"Colorful character, isn't she? Don't you think she would

make a great subject for one of your novels?"

Fanny tapped her chin. "I was thinking it would be fun to use her just as a minor character. I can't very well make a dominatrix the protagonist." She frowned thoughtfully. "Could I?"

"Why not? I see a TV movie here," I wrote in the air. "High-priced callgirl, Victoria Principal, meets her client in his hotel suite and duly hops into the bathroom to put on her Gestapo wardress costume. She goose-steps back out again in her leather boots and Swastika g-string only to find that her client has been shot dead."

Alice wagged her finger. "Not Victoria Principal. Got to be a blond."

"Okay, so Melanie Griffith comes out of the bathroom in her.."

"We couldn't get Griffith," Julian objected. "She only does features."

"Okay, so Judith Light comes out.."

"Too old," Fanny said.

"All right then." I pulled in a deep breath and used it to say, "Kate Vernon comes out of the bathroom in her thigh-high boots and g-string and finds her client spread out across the bed wearing a baby diaper, velvet handcuffs and a bullet hole between the eyes."

Alice held up her glass. "I see a thirty share."

Patsy appeared at the door of the lounge, then hurried over to join us. "Hi, kids!" She took the chair Shane had vacated, rendering it instantly less interesting.

"I got a news magazine down in the gift shop." She held it up.

"Is that O.J. yet again?" Julian took it from her hand. "He's done more covers than Claudia Schiffer."

"Why not?" Fanny returned. "He's a lot more fun to read about than real issues of the day like nuclear testing."

"As to that," Alice wondered. "Why does Chiroc want to test a megaton bomb, anyway? What do those French people need it for?"

"Just flexing their military might," Julian surmised.

"I can't imagine what for," Patsy took an hors d'oeuvre. "Now that the communist bloc is dismantled, our former enemies are no longer a threat to the west. Peace is supposed to prevail so super weapons are out-dated."

"That was the theory worthy of Pollyanna on Valium." Julian said. "But now all the little former U.S.S.R. countries are fighting like weasels."

"Since the Soviet Union is no longer keeping order, the Serbs and the Croats have been slaughtering each other left and right," Fanny said to her drink. "The Russians against the Georgians."

"The 'Witzes' against the 'skis'," Julian remarked. "There seems to be more war than ever, in number and variety if not in scope."

Patsy's voice was muffled in her miniature tamale.

"I don't see how we can get upset about all *those* people. I personally can't even pronounce their names."

I looked up and saw Magnuson stop in the doorway and cast around for a friendly face.

"Here comes the prof." I put my hand up. "Here we are, Gordon!"

As he made his way to our table, Julian reached over and pulled a chair out for him. "How did it go downstairs? Did you manage to catch the great recluse?"

Magnuson held up his manuscript in reply and shook his head.

"The way I see it.." He sank into the chair. "Webb must not have been in his cabin at all."

I pushed over the wine carafe and an extra glass. "But you heard him moving around."

The professor shrugged sadly. "I thought I had, but I must have been mistaken. Maybe I was hearing someone in the cabin next door. After all, if Webb were in there, why wouldn't he have wanted to meet me?"

That train of logic left me with no answer. So I just gaped at him.

"But my visit wasn't entirely unconstructive," Gordon assured us. "Now that we've established that our man isn't always in his cabin, it should be a simple matter to find him."

Fanny raised her head. "Simply how?"

Magnuson drew his fingers across his manuscript in a caress. "We don't know what Webb looks like, but we are aware that he was born in 1932, so he must be sixty-three this year." He smiled cannily. "All I have to do is walk around the deck and check out any white man of that approximate age."

Julian held up a finger. "Consider that *most* of the passengers on a cruise, *any* cruise, are white and of that approximate age."

"Correct." Magnuson looked smug behind his thick glasses. "But most of those men are here with their wives, and we know that Webb came aboard alone."

"That's pretty good," Julian allowed. "You can narrow it down to white men in their sixties who are wandering around by themselves. Interrogate every one of them and make him prove his identity – That's quite an ambitious quest you're undertaking."

"I realize that." Gordon nodded decisively. "But if I have to spend every waking moment of this cruise, it'll be worth it. Because I know that once I find Holden Webb and explain my project to him, he won't be able to resist reading this manuscript."

"We can save Gordon some time at the outset." Julian smiled around the table. "We know there aren't any recent photos of Webb. But there has to be at least one man on the ship who can describe him for us."

"Who is that, pray tell?" Fanny asked.

"The steward who brings his meals to his cabin."

"Hey, right! We'll call him up here."

Gordon frowned. "But what if the employees have signed some sort of confidentiality agreement?"

"We'll explain that we're not asking for anything scandalous," Julian assured. "Just Holden Webb's basic description."

"We'll offer a bribe." I said.

"A tip," Alice corrected.

"Right. So who is assigned to Cabin 84?"

***

Biffie was. The young steward's name tag said "Biffie".

Julian shook hands with him, palming over a twenty. "Hi, Biffie. We're curious about Holden Webb. You've been bringing his meals, right?"

"Yes, sir." The twenty slipped into a jacket pocket, smooth as you please. "Last night, he had the chef's special. Filet mignon, baked potato, summer salad. Flan for dessert."

"Sounds delicious," Julian averred. "But we're more interested in what Mr. Webb looks like."

"'Fraid I can't help you there."

"Wasn't he in his cabin?"

"Sure, he was. But when I knocked on his door, he hollered 'It's open!' so I just brought his tray in and set a place at his table in front of the couch."

"So you saw him?"

"Yes, but not vory woll, as thc passenger had his back to me."

"What was he wearing?'

"Nothing."

"You mean..?"

"Not a stitch. No sir."

After that conversation-stopper, Biffie was excused to go back about his appointed rounds. Julian hmmed. "That doesn't tell us much."

Gordon had listened intently to the interview, pen in hand to take notes. Now he just unclicked the pen and put it away unused. "Thanks for trying, at any rate."

"You're right in that." Fanny sighed. "If Webb's only distinguishing characteristic is a bent toward nudism, there's no way of identifying him once he has his clothes on."

"That may be why the man is such a recluse." Alice speculated. "If he's like that all the time, it explains why there were never any photos."

Our waitress was standing at the end of the bar, adding up the bill. I looked around the table and didn't see a sucker to take it, so guessed I was the sucker. Julian caught my eye and nodded, then made a little writing motion behind his head so that only the waitress and I saw it and twirled his finger to designate the whole table.

CHAPTER SIXTEEN

For one of the conference's highlight events, "An Evening With Lord Reggie", the stage was set like the old "David Frost Show" with nothing but two padded swivel chairs. Patsy Pickering was alone onstage, occupying the left chair. When her little watch said six o'clock, she swiveled to face front and called us to order. "Thank you all for joining us. You're in for a special treat. This evening, we are honored to have Lord Reggie Micklewhite of Caldster as one of our expert lecturers. He is going to tell us about some cases of real-life theft and how they were solved." She tugged at her too-short-for-her-age skirt and continued. "Lord Reggie had a very interesting history. He began his career working outside the law, as a thief in London. But in 1980 he turned away from his life of crime, committing it, that is." She laughed lightly. "And now Lord Reggie lends his considerable talents to preventing it. During the past fifteen years, our guest speaker has been working his way up the corporate ladder and has just been named the vice-president in charge of security for the Steinmetz chain of jewelry stores."

As the 'special treat' came down the aisle to take the right chair there was applause, rocking applause, from the audience. (Reformed criminals get much more glory than people who have never done a dishonest thing in their lives.)

After the noise subsided, Patsy assumed the posture of a talk show host.

"Now, Lord Reggie.."

"No, no." He waved a modest hand. "It's just Rege."

"Very well then. What made you decide to cross the line from career outlaw to good guy?"

He chuckled. "I wuz gettin' on forty and didn't 'ave the 'eart to spend another ten years standin' on me 'ead in the nick. I knew one bloke as was in Brixton Prison for murder since a boy of sixteen. 'E were fifty years old and never bought a suit 'o clothes or drove a car or loved a woman." He sighed and took a sip of his Evian water. "Ain't no way fer a man."

"So you embraced a life of honesty." Patsy chirped. "How does a career criminal manage that?"

"The prison chaplain got to like me. Once I was hout, he found me a job workin' in the security section fer a chain o' jewelers."

Patsy nodded. "Oh, I get it. There's an old saying,'It takes one to catch one.'"

"It were nothing fancy. I started out just wearin' a uniform an' carryin' a flashlight. But after time I was able to make meself useful in what you yanks call 'inventory control' action." He smiled slyly. "That amounted to just spottin' all me own old tricks." The audience laughed along with him.

"That worked well enough for some ten years. I'm a bit out o' date since most illegal doings are carried off by computer nowadays. But there's still the odd Gypsy woman who flounces into a shop dressed up like the Duchess of Kent, and carrying her beloved smiley-faced babe."

Patsy looked puzzled. "A babe?"

"To cache the swag, luv. Soon as the clerk can be distracted, she throws a gem or two down the little blighter's throat. You know, I got to put the arm on 'em then call for a warrant to search the baby's poo. Been losin' me 'eart fer the job, I kin tell you."

CHAPTER SEVENTEEN

The seating in the ship's auditorium was more comfortable than that of a theater on land. There were well-stuffed arm chairs and matching sofas and love seats with low tables in front of them. One of which was occupied by Harvey Gould and his new love of his life, Letty Buell. Liveried waiters were weaving in and out with drink orders. Our party commandeered three couches in the front row of the balcony.

Fanny said, "Naturally, it would be an awfully short show if Vinnie Moretti just sang his own songs. So he's covering the hits of great Brian Epstein discoveries."

"John and Paul?"

"Freddy McCreedy and Peter Noone. – Look at the program." She held it up. "I just found out their third number is going to be that Freddy and the Dreamers classic, 'I'm Telling You Now'. See? So we're all going to get up and do the 'Freddy'."

"*All* of us."

"All except Julian," said Julian. "Julian doesn't know the Freddy."

"It's very easy." Fanny popped up and stood in the space between the couches.. "You stand on your left leg like this and flap out your right arm and right leg twice." She demonstrated. "Then you switch to your right leg and flap out your left arm and leg." And she did just that. "See? Anyone can do it."

"Anyone can," Julian allowed. "But no one should."

Moretti strutted out on-stage costumed a la Carnaby Street, in a frock coat of burgundy velvet with a matching cap, under the bill of which poked a fringe of dark bangs. His hair was still black. Or again black.

From our table and in that flattering pink light he could have passed for the younger Vinnie as he plucked the microphone off the stand and waved to us all.

"Welcome back to the year 1967. I have three hits on the charts. You are my fans. And we're all young." There was some rueful laughter at that little fantasy. "Jimi Hendrix is alive. Janis Joplin is alive and the Beatles are still together."

As he played and sang, the strobe light blinked on and off to the eerie effect of making his movements look jerky and disconnected like an old-time movie.

And we middle-aged groovers in the balcony felt as though we were back at one of those parties where cats and chicks sit on pillows on the floor, drink Bali Hai out of a wineskin, and play "Greensleeves" on their alto recorders.

***

After the show, Fanny grabbed my arm. "I want his autograph!"

"Me too!" I whooped.

"What on earth will you do with Moretti's autograph?" Julian objected.

"We don't care about the autograph per se," I informed him. "We just want to meet Vinnie."

Four minutes later, our little group of groupies was giggling and "Ooh-ing" around the singer who, with the panache of his profession, smiled and talked to each of us as though he really cared where we were from and what we did.

Up close, I saw that his face looked like a cracked and oozed version of the one I remembered from the album covers.

"I'm from New Jersey," I said proudly.

"Me too," he admitted. "Mountain Lakes in my case."

"Mountain Lakes? I was at your concert in Central Park, New York City, July of '67."

"You were?   Uh, sorry I don't remember seeing you there."

"As one of ten thousand, I wouldn't expect so. But I can still picture every number in your act. Hey, what happened to the snake you used to perform with? That boa?"

"Christine? I miss her. – My second wife got the snake as part of her settlement." He smiled and his teeth were lovely. They must have been capped. "My first wife got the kids. – I miss the snake more."

"This is a marvelous treat." Fanny swung her hair. "I was surprised to see you performing here on the ship."

"Not like *I* am," he laughed. "I hate boats. I get so nauseated that I have to knock back Sea Calm like Tic-Tacs. It does a worse number on my head than weed and everything is a blur."

"Then what was your motivation for coming aboard?"

"I sincerely need the money."

"Money?" I echoed, "But I remember you were playing *stadiums* back in the sixties."

"My band and I were really hot for one summer. But then the leaves fell." He blew a long breath upward at his forelock. "Stadiums became big auditoriums, which after time booamo smallor auditoriums, thcn onto showrooms, high school assemblies and 'intimate little bistros'. This here is the best gig I could get."

"But you must have made millions when you were still at the top."

"The promoters made millions. I made almost a million. Made it, blew it, drank it, smoked it. Drugs for me and all my friends. You'd be surprised how many friends I had back then. Until I went bankrupt in '78. I was forced to sign over my royalty rights just to pay my debts. Then it was to start all over as a vocalist for hire. There isn't an oldies gig anywhere I haven't played."

CHAPTER EIGHTEEN

I'm always timid about approaching very beautiful women, but Stefani Wyeth was sitting all by her lonesome in the Lorelei Lounge, so I figured my company would be as welcome as any and approached her table.

"Hi, Ms. Wyeth. I really enjoyed your class this morning."

"Hi." She checked my badge and proffered a slender hand. "Margo. Call me Stefani and have a seat."

She pointed to her bottle of red wine. "Like some? I'll ask for another glass."

"Not my poison." I called the waiter and ordered a glass with Coke in it.

Stefani said, "I'm sitting here waiting for Schmelvis to come on. Isn't he a kick?"

"Unique in the world." Then I saw Frank Washington at the door of the lounge. As he paused and looked around, I decided to make him owe me a favor and waved.

"Hey, Frank! Over here." He looked pleased at the sight of me, then stupefied at the sight of my companion. I watched him rearrange his features into "What the hell. Why not?" and casually ankle over to meet us.

"Stefani," I said, "This is Lieutenant Frank Washington, the homicide detective in charge of the Schuyler investigation."

"Are you really?" She held out the hand again. Frank took it delicately pumped it a modest twice and relinquished it as he took the chair across from us.

"I'm afraid so."

"I was personally affected when Ridley died." Stefani leaned back, graceful as a cat, and crossed her long legs. "I had a history with the man."

"I know," Frank said. He couldn't take his eyes from her, but, gentleman that he is, kept them focused above her neck. "I read about the 'Behind Bars' writers program."

"That was fifteen years ago, when I was young and still brimming with ideals. We went into the prison as part of our graduate school practicum." She smiled wryly. "My mission was to teach "inmate number 29763," Ridley Schuyler, to exorcise his demons by committing his thoughts and feelings to paper."

"You were more than successful."

"I don't take all the credit. My pupil was what you would call highly motivated. It seemed Ridley didn't have very much status inside the prison."

"For the excellent reason that he was a punk," Frank put in.

"Well, he was a small man and something of a physical coward. I understood that he had no money or influence so he made whatever bargains he had to."

"On his knees for cigarettes, probably."

Stefani squeezed her eyes shut to banish that picture.

"For whatever reason, he wasn't very popular among the other inmates and he was grateful to have any visitor at all and willing enough to talk."

I was incredulous. "And in that setting, he talked the whole book, *Deep Lock*?"

"It wasn't quite so simple. He told me about all his experiences from his childhood vandalism, through adolescent delinquency, all the way into his life as a career criminal. I recorded nearly two hundred hours of narrative over the next three months. Then I put them in some logical order, edited, paraphrased, polished, revised..."

I leaned in. "Essentially reduced the whole thing to thoughts, words, even syllables, then reconstructed the mess into a cohesive unit."

"Yes."

"It sounds as though you actually wrote *Deep Lock* yourself."

She gazed down at her manicure for a moment.

"If truth be known, I *did*."

Frank looked perplexed. "But according to the notices, the book was supposed to be entirely in Schuyler's own words."

She laughed a close-mouthed laugh. "Like any good ghost, I wrote my subject's story the way he himself would have written it if he had known how to write."

"But.." Frank adjusted his chair to sit minutely closer."The voice in the book was explicitly masculine. There were the expressions and thought-processes of a rough-hewn career criminal. How did you manage to convey that?"

Stefani blinked her golden eyes in slow-motion.

"You'd be surprised how easy it is to assume the speech patterns of a man. If you love him." She made a church and steeple out of her hands and studied them. "As I did."

"You and Schuyler?!" I exclaimed with more volume than tact.

She nodded ruefully. "The twenty-one year old me and Schuyler. It didn't seem so ludicrous at the time."

Frank absorbed that revelation for an uncomfortable moment then said, "How come your name wasn't on the cover of the book, as 'written with' or 'as told to'?"

She turned the golden eyes out the porthole to the dark sea and repeated a story she had certainly told before. If only to herself.

"Ridley convinced me that we wouldn't be able to sell the book with *my* by-line. A graduate assistant who can write doesn't ring anybody's bells. But when the publishers thought they had a career criminal who was also a brilliant wordsmith, they saw a great marketing device. They offered a hundred-thousand-dollar advance then moved *Deep Lock* to the head of their Fall list, threw most of their advertising budget into putting Ridley's personal history before the public and made him into a household name."

I tried not to sound mad. "So Schuyler became rich and famous. What were *you* supposed to get out of it?"

"Fifty percent. Supposed to. He promised to share the money with me." She clasped her hands. "Well, he had promised to love me too."

"You didn't get any of it?"

She sighed mightily, but was so thin that it hardly moved her blouse. "He kept putting me off, saying that he had bills, expenses, gambling debts to pay... At first I believed him. Then almost all the advance money was gone within a few months and still he persuaded me to be patient with him. He said the advance was chickenfeed compared with all that was coming."

"Coming?" I echoed. "Did he mean the payments for film rights? Foreign editions?"

"More than that. We had planned to continue writing books as a team. His colorful experiences and my literary talent. It would be like printing money, he said."

"But that's not what happened," Frank averred.

"No, that's not what happened because then Ridley was sent on his first national book tour. And he got the V.I.P. treatment all the way." She counted the elements on long fingers. "The Four Seasons Hotels, the limousines, the fawning interviewers. So he became a celebrity overnight and naturally found himself surrounded by girls."

"Star-boppers abound," I was cynical enough to suggest.

"And the very sort he had always fantasized about in his jail cell. Young, blond, beautiful, pliant.. Some were even rich. He quickly realized that he didn't need a black sweetheart. Especially one who had known him during the bad time. Having me around just reminded him of the powerlessness, the bars, the locks, the guards. Where he had been."

"Where he still belonged," Frank said grimly.

"He somehow lost sight of my part in his success." Stefani lifted the wine bottle to pour another glass but then just held it as though she had forgotten how. "Because I had done such a good job of rendering his voice, Ridley managed to convince himself that those really were his own words in the book and that I had just written them down, like a stenographer taking dictation."

"What a scumbag!" I erupted. "If he'd done that to me, I'd have.." Then I clapped my mouth shut.

Frank looked up. "Killed him?"

"Maybe. If I could have gotten away with it."

Stefani moved her classic head from side to side. "I know I couldn't have. I'm not that lucky."

Frank took the wine bottle from her hand and poured it for her. "So it was Schuyler's story, but your writing. That explains why Deep Lock was so good."

"But then the ungrateful slime ended his partnership with you," I added."Which explains why his other books were trash."

Frank shook his head. "Did he actually try to write those himself?"

"He couldn't possibly have," Stefani said firmly. "Ridley never even wrote a long letter. He must have used another ghost writer."

"Hello?" Patsy Pickering was waving from the door. "Miss Wyeth? The ship's officers have asked to meet you."

"My public." Stefani rose with an apologetic smile and followed Patsy out of the lounge.

"Well, Frank.." I kicked my shoes off and tucked my feet under me. "I understand why she wrote for Schuyler. However misguidedly, the girl was in love with him. But who else would be willing and able to write books in his name?"

"Probably some barely-competent hack who couldn't crack six figures under his own name."

Ten minutes later, Letty Buell came in looking conspicuously unattached.

I waved her over and asked, "So? How went your romantic tête a tête?"

"Romantic?"

"With Harvey Gould."

Letty shook her head vigorously and her earrings bobbled.

"Would you believe that Harvey asked to come to my cabin with me. And he meant just that *minute*."

Frank and I exchanged a "Here we go again" look.

She fluttered her hands. "He said he had lost the key to his own cabin and would like to rest in mine."

"Hoo hah!" I rejoined. "The old 'I lost my key' trick."

"Well, I couldn't help being skeptical either. So I just called over the nearest steward who said he could have a duplicate key made in only a few minutes."

Letty stuck out her lower lip. "Then Harvey acted very annoyed. I tried to explain that we would have plenty of time to be alone together." She settled into her chair, making it creak. "For goodness sake, we were just getting to know each other. Before we did anything so intimate, I wanted to meet his family after all. And I was sure he would want to meet mine!" Her voice quivered. "I was still trying to explain my feelings when he just turned around and walked away!"

I leaned over and patted her shoulder. "That's the way it is when you're attractive, Letty. All kinds of men come on to you. Some will be nice and some will be.. like Harvey Gould."

"*Most* will be like Gould." Frank interposed. "But stick to your high standards and you'll strain those out. – I just talked to the creep again."

"Did he give you any new information on Schuyler?"

"He promised some. Gould said he had an appointment to talk to his partner in New York at ten o'clock. Maybe there would be some more relevant details."

"He's going to his cabin to make a phone call? It must

be important at eight bucks a minute."

"Not important to me unless it involves something pertaining to the case."

"Ten o'clock?" I held my watch close to the candle. "It's a quarter to. By the way, what cabin is Gould in?"

"Ninety-three," Letty said. "My goodness. Are *you* interested?"

"Not that way."

Frank narrowed his eyes. "What are you up to, Margo?"

"Nothing. I just have to go to the ladies room. Carry on!"

CHAPTER NINETEEN

On alighting from the elevator, I saw Lord Reggie step in from the deck outside. "Just the guy I want to see! Lord Reggie, could I ask you something?"

"Mrs. Fortier? Yes, mum."

I took his arm and walked him all the way down the hall to Stateroom Ninety-three.

"You see," I whispered, "Harvey Gould is making a call in there, probably to his partner in New York and probably about Ridley Schuyler's murder. I'd like to know what he's saying."

He whispered back. "So you're going to stand out 'ere in the flippin' 'allway with your ear stuck against the door."

"I don't have to. See, right over there next to Gould's cabin is the linen closet. And the maids are mostly off-duty."

"So you can crouch insoyd the bloomin' linen closet with your ear stuck to the wall. And now one will nowtice."

"That's my plan, but.." I turned the knob and pulled. "You see the closet is locked."

"So hit seems."

"So I was thinking, say, you must know your way around all kinds of locks. Do you think you could..?"

"Oh, no ma'am." He took a step backwards. "Oi couldn't open that door. That'ould be 'ighly illegal."

"Geez. It's only a linen closet. It's nobody's private property, after all."

"If hit was meant fer ye to go inside, there wouldn't be no lock on't."

"Please, Lord Reggie. I don't want to take anything. I just want to use the wall for a few minutes."

"Oi can't help ye." He looked up and down the empty hall. "However if ye sort o' take yerself on a walk 'round the corner, when ye come back, the door might o' fallen open by hitself. Niver can tell, can ye?"

"Why.. uh. No. Anything can happen on a boat."

I took a walk out on deck to the refreshment bar, bought myself a Coke, drank it down quickly and carried the glass back to where I had left his Lordship. By the time I returned to the storage room, Reggie had departed and there was a matchbook with the ship's logo on it stuck between the door and the jam to hold it open.

I reached in and turned on the light switch, then closed the door as far as the match book, and tiptoed in. The wall adjoining Gould's cabin was all shelves, crammed with linens. On the floor under the bottom shelf were stacked rolls of toilet paper and boxes of tissue. I got down on my knees and moved enough of them aside so that I could wiggle in, then held the glass to the wall to amplify the sound and put my ear against it. I could hear Gould clearly. He must have been on the phone. "Hey, putz! What the fuck..!!"   Then he lowered his voice for at least a paragraph. I waited for him to speak loudly again and give me some exposition.

My ear was getting sore, pressing against the glass. (Someday I'll go to a medical supply house and buy a stethoscope. Every snoop should have one.)

A few minutes later, I heard the door open and close.

Now there was no movement inside the cabin next door. Then there was a ringing sound. Someone must have been trying to call Gould. But the phone just rang twice more, then gave up. After several more minutes huddled against the closet wall, I gave up too. Gould must have gone out for the evening and by now was probably up in the Sports Bar, telling the septuagenarian mixologist that she was the most beautiful woman on the ship. I wiggled out from under the shelf and replaced all the paper products, then grasped the steel brace overhead for use as a crutch. I pulled my slightly arthritic limbs to a standing configuration, made my way around mops, brooms and bottles of cleaning fluids and reached for the doorknob.

I turned it and pulled but the thing stayed stuck just as though it were locked. I turned it the other way and pulled again and it still didn't budge. Then the adrenalin pumped inside me and I started pounding.

"Hey, someone open up! Someone?!"

I stepped back and drew a deep breath for some stronger shouting, then out of the corner of my eye, I caught a movement of ringed colors and swung around to see a snake uncoiling atop a stack of bath towels. "Oh Hi, Pedro! What the devil are you do..?"

But when I focused on the order of colored rings I realized that what came slithering toward me now was not my friend Pedro the Mexican milk snake. In this case, red met yellow.

Kill a fellow.

CHAPTER TWENTY

After I had followed the second hand on my watch for nearly an hour. I was still sitting with my back to the door. Every few minutes, the coral snake would rear up and flick his long forked tongue side to side to take my measure. I had turned to face him, tucked my head down, folded into myself and sunk slowly to the floor. Then the snake satisfied himself that I was neither predator nor prey and curled up, inches from my bare legs and made himself comfortable.

I had heard several sets of footsteps way down at the other end of the corridor and the creaking of wheels, as the room stewards went about their appointed rounds. But I didn't dare upset the snake by calling out to them. At last I heard footsteps come toward me and pass the cart. Some man called a friendly word to the maid and he stopped outside the door to my closet. The doorknob turned.

I didn't move but strove to make my voice a whisper, all breath. I've heard that snakes are deaf but I didn't want to set up any vibrations for this one to feel and maybe not like.

"Get Jarvis," I rasped. "His coral snake is in here with me."

"Uh oh", the man whispered back. "Listen. Sit perfectly *still*. I'll go for help." Now I realized that it had been the pre-published Gordon Magnuson speaking as the footsteps pivoted and sprinted back down the hallway from whence they had come. Seventy-five "Chimpanzees" later, I heard more footsteps coming toward me then it was Jarvis's voice outside the door.

"Hello in the closet."

"It's Margo in the closet," I stage-whispered.

"Margo Fortier? That's good. Because I know you can keep cool around a snake. Do you have your back to the door?"

"Yes," I breathed. The snake must have sensed something because in that moment he raised his beautiful but deadly head.

"Okay, Margo. I've got the steward here to unlock the door. Now, with a minimum of motion, I want you to shift slowly to your right so I can open it."

I heard the key click in the lock and moved sideways on geologic time as the snake scoped me out with his tongue.

Then the door opened just a crack and a steel pole with a crook on the end poked through. Once I had scrunched against the wall to make room for him, Jarvis himself stepped in after it, and, holding the stick in both hands, planted his feet. This roused the snake to the point of uncoiling and undulating from side to side, flicking its tongue around curiously. Jarvis swayed to match the rhythm of the snake. Then moving slowly and smoothly he slid the pole under the snake's belly and lifted it in the air. He reeled the pole in and picked the fugitive up by the back of the neck.

"Come back to papa, you bad boy. How did you take it into your head to wander off like that. I was so worried about you." He called behind him. "You've got his house?"

"Yes, sir, right here." The steward tip-toed up behind him, holding a terrarium out with both hands and put it down as softly as though it were a bomb.

Jarvis chided gently. "Now, back into your house, Eugene."

I got to my feet. "Eugene?"

"I named him after my lawyer. – Poor little snake. You must have been scared out there all by yourself." He fastened the lid on the terrarium.

"As if Eugene had a lot to fear from *me*."

"Margo?" Magnuson came up and patted my shoulder. "I'm absolutely scared and *repelled* by snakes. I can't imagine how you managed to sit alone in a room with one for a solid hour without panicking."

I shook my head. "Without *seeming* to panic which worked just as well."

"It's lucky I happened to come to this closet for an extra pillow." He slipped around me and took a pillow off the top shelf.

"To rest your manuscript?"

By now, a group had gathered at the other end of the corridor. When their consensus was satisfied that the snake had been securely confined, they moved forward en masse a foot at a time. Fanny and Alice were at the head of the assemblage.

"Margo," Fanny asked. "How did you discourage that creature from biting you?"

"By making it unprofitable." Now that I was free to stretch out my arms and legs, I did a sort of unattractive dance as I explained. "Consider that a poisonous snake's venom is his currency. He spends it only for self-defense and for food." I described my own outline in a circle. "Obviously I'm too big to swallow whole, so I wasn't food. And I put all my concentration into assuring him that I was no threat either."

Alice clasped her hands at arms' length. "How can you be so brave! I would have screamed my head off."

"If you had, you would have frightened him and got yourself bitten."

The steward turned to face me, looking concerned.

"I'm terribly sorry this happened, Mrs. Fortier. But what were you doing in that linen closet, anyway?"

"Why.. I just wanted an extra sheet.. blanket. The door was open, so I stepped in and, what do you know, it slammed shut behind me."

"If your stateroom is too cold, Ma'am, you can adjust the

temperature with the climate control switch."

"Oh, no. I *like* it cold. I just wanted the blanket to..uh.. to play *tent*."

"Play tent?"

"Yeah. See, I like to pretend I'm an Indian and .."

Fanny caught my eye then and, somewhat agitatedly, tapped her lips with her finger. I put a metaphorical sock in it and just smiled a "You know how it is."

The steward didn't actually care. He simply stepped into the closet and fetched me a blanket. With horizontal stripes. I hugged it as though that were just exactly what I had craved all along.

Captain Yeates came down the corridor at a fast trot.

"Was anybody hurt down here?"

"No, we were extremely lucky."

Jarvis put a drape over the glass case, making nighty-night for Eugene.

"I travel with a supply of anti-venin of course. But if Mrs. Fortier had been bitten in an artery by a snake this size and we hadn't found her in this length of time..."

I held my palm out in a "Stop" sign. "Let's leave that to our imaginations."

The captain kept his voice low but his face had become pink. "Jarvis, you assured me that all those poisonous snakes were securely locked up. And now one of them seemed to have himself the run of the ship. That thing could have killed Mrs. Fortier!"

"Don't remind me."

"I didn't see Eugene when I was putting them to bed. But I just assumed that he was in his hide box." Jarvis got down on his knees to examine the lid of his terrarium. "Captain, I'm not a man to make excuses, but this was secured. Look right here. The lock was pried open. This is all too scary. – He might have been hurt."

The captain joined him on the floor and studied the lock.

"You know it couldn't have been an accident. That lock

looks awfully strong. And the snake wasn't particularly muscular."

"Right."

"But who would do that? Liberating a coral snake would be a surreal way of committing suicide."

"Not for an experienced snake handler."

"Do we have any on board aside from you?"

"Here's proof that there's at least one. To make good and sure nothing else happens," Jarvis patted the top of the terrarium. "I'm going to take Eugene back to my room and milk him."

"Good luck trying to get milk from a snake." someone muttered.

"I didn't mean real milk. I'm going to feed him and take his venom. If this boy bites anyone during the rest of the trip," He grinned. "It will just be for fun."

"That's cute."

CHAPTER TWENTY-ONE

Our little group adjourned to the Lorelei Lounge and met up with Frank to mull the turn of events.

"Here's a mystery for you, Lieutenant." Fanny stirred her daiquiri. "'The case of the vanishing and reappearing snake.'"

"There's nothing supernatural about it," Frank said. "Theoretically, Jarvis could have left the lock unsecured then noticed that his snake was missing and broken the lock after the escape to make it look as if someone else were involved."

"But I don't think so." Alice said. "People who handle poisonous snakes must learn to be pretty careful or they would keep losing family members."

"You seem knowledgeable, on the subject." Julian remarked.

"We see lots of snakes in Montana. Side-winders wriggle out of their caves in the heat of the day and sun themselves on the blacktop.

"Lieutenant Washington?" It was Pete Jarvis who hailed us as he came through the door, waving. "Listen. I've got some news." He came to our table and stood still a moment before saying, "I milked Eugene."

"Eugene?"

"My coral snake."

"Oh.. uh.. Good."

"Not entirely good." He looked uneasy. "You see, I hadn't milked him since the last time he ate, so he should have had a full sac but this time hardly any venom came out."

Frank pushed his chair back. "You mean he was full this morning, and now he's hitting on empty. So what happened?"

"So.. Well.. He must have bitten something while he was running around loose."

I piped up. "We can hope it was only a rat."

"It'd have to be several rats of some size to take all that poison." The herpetologist clapped a hand over his face. "Also, it couldn't have been food he bit into, because when I got him back, he still hadn't eaten anything."

"How do you know?" Frank asked.

Jarvis peered over the hand. "A snake has to swallow his prey whole, you know; he can't chew. So you can always tell when he's just eaten because there's a big bulge around the middle of his body."

"As with Margo," Julian offered.

CHAPTER TWENTY-TWO

The next morning, Julian woke me when he came into the cabin at the ungodly hour of 10 A.M..

"Margo, I hate to admit it, but I think you're right about your unaccountably aryan-looking Abram Weissman."

"Wha..?" I turned over on my back. "Why?"

"I was just having my orange smoothie out by the pool and he was sitting three chairs away, fiddling with his laptop."

"Huh?" The mean old sun was blazing through the porthole, even penetrating the curtains. I pulled the pillow over my eyes. "So, what happened?"

"This very old man, wearing a yarmulke, tottered up to him and said, 'Mr. Weissman? We have nine men and we need a minyan.'"

"Really?" I got up on one elbow. "So what did he say?"

"He acted really insulted and said, '*I'm* not a minion!'"

"Hoo! I love it."

"Then they just stared at each other. I mean neither had an idea in the world what the other was talking about.

I levered myself fully upright. "So then what happened?"

"There was this chubby kid splashing around in the pool. He looked about ten years old but he must have been thirteen because he popped right up and yelled, '*I'll* come.' Well, that was it. The old man and the boy went off together to have their prayer service. Weissman just sort of looked disgusted and went back to his computer."

We went to have lunch in the dining room which takes longer than the buffet out on the pool deck, but the food is better and I enjoy being served. At lunch time, the seats aren't assigned, so we headed for a table big enough to hold the whole gang.

By the time I had sat down and discreetly pulled my shoes off, Gordon Magnuson had already selected a chair but when the waiter brought him the menu he ordered only a green salad. I ordered the braised swordfish.

The good professor didn't pay much attention to his salad when it was in front of him, but just sat there, not even reaching for a fork.

"What's wrong, Gordon? You don't like seafood?"

"I love it." Magnuson patted his midsection. "Trouble is, I've been putting away too much of this great cruise cuisine; I'm trying to go easy."

So, I wondered, if the child of God wasn't hungry, why was he even sitting at the table with us? I had just opened my big mouth to ask that very question when I spotted the brown paper wrapping of the cruddy manuscript on his lap. Obviously, he was there in the dining room to network. I closed the big mouth over a forkful of sauteed artichoke hearts.

Apparently Letty Buell was still trying to catch Magnuson's attention. She stopped by the table and simpered. "That's a nice shirt, Gordon."

"It should be. It cost thirty-five dollars."

CHAPTER TWENTY-THREE

Only minutes after Fanny, Alice, Julian and I had taken our usual deck chairs, the artist, Ward Newcomb, arrived toting a portfolio and springing on his feet. "Margo, he bought it! Hanover is going to use our illustration for the cover of *Umber Passion*."

"Coming to a supermarket near you," Julian mumbled.

"What's more, he's signing me for a new series." Ward opened the portfolio. "And here it is. That job-clinching illustration!" He held out the painting, swelling with pride. "Beautiful, isn't it?"

I hope I managed to conceal my anger and disappointment when I said, "*Too* beautiful!"

"Fantastic," Julian exclaimed, meaning it literally, I'm sure.

Ward graciously accepted what he took to be praise. "I've got to run down to the bar a few minutes. I'll leave it here for you to admire a while longer." He propped it on the table in front of us and scampered off.

Only after he was well out of sight, did I say, "That doesn't look like me!"

Fanny stepped back for optimum viewing distance. "Well,.. maybe twenty-five years ago."

"Never! I was never that candy-box pretty in my *life*. Nuts! Ward was just using me as a stand-in for Arlene Dahl or Rhonda Fleming or somebody. I thought he liked *my* face."

"Give him a break, dear," Julian said. "Maybe he didn't

have enough paint to do the whole nose."

The kewpie doll came around the corner and stopped to admire the portrait. "That's beautiful. Paulette Goddard?"

"No, actually..." Julian began.

"Susan Hayward," I interrupted. "How are you doing, Letty? Getting around and meeting people?"

"Not really." She sighed. "I wish that Professor Magnuson would pay more attention to me. I think we would have a lot in common." Letty patted her own "pre-published" manuscript and I had to agree with her.

"Magnuson doesn't have time to socialize now. He's combing the ship from stem to stern looking for Holden Webb."

"Hmmf! He's missing a good opportunity if you ask *me*." And she flounced away.

"Oh, Julian?" Fanny twirled her straw in her glass.

"Yes?"

"I have a question."

"Go ahead."

"Hypothetically speaking, say if someone saw your wife in a passionate embrace with a teen-aged Greek deck boy. Would you want to know about it?"

"Not really."

"Never mind then."

Then I espied a decrepit-looking gnome crouched on the farthermost deck chair, sort of babbling out at the sea. I was preoccupied with feeling sorry for the old coot when Magnuson came into view, stopped and knelt on the deck beside him, cuddling his manuscript. I waited while he talked at the gnome for a few minutes. Then when he arose with a defeated shrug and spotted me, I waved him over.

"Hi, Gordon." Julian said, "I take it that old man wasn't our Holden Webb."

Magnuson shook his head. "Jules Weinstein, Dubuque, hardware."

"What makes you so sure?" I asked. "Did you check his I.D.?"

"No, but he told me how to get my windows to stop rattling. – Weinstein would have read my manuscript, though."

"'Would have'?"

"He was really interested, but he left his good glasses back in Dubuque." Magnuson looked past me, over my shoulder. "Hey there's someone else the right age. Catch you later." And off he scrambled.

"Dubuque." I said. "I think that's where I left *my* good glasses."

"You left mine there too," Julian said from behind his copy of the ship's program.

"What's on the calendar today? Any good lectures scheduled?"

"No, at least nothing with snakes. But they give dancing lessons on board."

"I'm not interested unless I can be an Ito."

(The chorus line of the hour is Jay Leno's 'Dancing Itos'. Appropriately bearded and black-robed, they look like the His ineffable Honor above the waist and Can Can dancers below.)

"The real party seems to be going on over there by the buffet, around Mrs. Sather."

"Who?"

He pointed with his program. Mrs. Sather, properly labeled, was a petite elderly woman with wispy white hair. Fanny had risen to direct her to a deck chair close to ours then practically got down on one knee to hand her a drink while Alice hovered around obsequiously waiting to light her cigarette.

I watched as Fanny solicitously wrapped a napkin around the highball glass, maybe to insure that the frail creature wouldn't get chilblains. "Can I get you some shrimp, Mrs. Sather?"

The ancient soul's hands fluttered. "I guess I could eat a small portion."

Fanny bustled toward the buffet and I grabbed her on the way.

"Why are you kissing up the that old lady? Is she an editor?"

"More important than that," Fanny whispered. "She's a *librarian*."

Alice was arranging the flatware on a tray according to a diagram in Emily Post's forties-era etiquette book. "I've already got an editor. I can never get enough librarians."

"I didn't imagine they were such big deals."

"You kidding? They're practically the only people who buy mid-list fiction like ours in hardcover. And consider that one small-town librarian can bring me a hundred new readers a year. – If she likes me. So it's mine to make her like me."

Mrs. Sather thanked the volunteer waitresses and chatted while daintily picking at her shrimp."This will be my fortieth year with the Parsipany library system."

"You must enjoy it," I averred, without adding "I can't imagine why."

"I guess I live my work. I'm an incorrigible bookworm."

Mrs. Sather gestured with her Pall Mall cigarette. "When I learned which writers were coming to lecture here, I made it a project to read their books and I discovered something very interesting."

Her revelation was interrupted when Duncan Steel bore down on us, lurching, limping on his four-pronged cane. "Hey! Did any of you see my girl friend?"

"You mean Shane?" Fanny said, "I think she went up to the health spa."

"Hah?"

"Up on the Observation Deck." He needed directions. Certainly he had never been near any such place himself.

"Why don't you hang out here awhile," I offered generously. "We're all hoping to get a glimpse of Holden Webb."

"What for?," Duncan Steel snapped. "He's a has-been."

"He's a classic," Fanny contradicted firmly. "I know he hasn't written anything since the fifties aside from the occasional review. But I enjoy those."

Steel pursed his lips which made him look even worse than usual. "What does Webb know about good writing? He stinks!"

"He..?"

"Stinks!"

With that, he moved forward on his cane and made his way down the deck with somewhat less speed than requisite for the proper emphasis.

Alice watched his progress. "Why does that poor wretched man have it in for Webb, I wonder."

"Maybe Webb wrote a criticism one of Steel's novels."

"Impossible," Fanny declared. "An author of his stature would never even stoop to *read* Steel's perverted spewings, never mind waste time writing a review of it."

"That's what I was about to tell you," Mrs Sather said quietly. "I read books by all the authors attending this conference and I discovered that the thrillers of Ridley Schuyler's Dick Duel series were very similar in style to those of Duncan Steel."

Julian leaned forward. "How similar?"

Mrs. Sather inclined her head. "So much so that I would bet my house they were written by the same person."

Julian clapped his knees. "So Steel was Schuyler's ghost writer? That anonymous hack?"

"For fifty percent of the take," Fanny said, "Why not?"

"But none of the glory."

Alice snorted delicately. "Did you see any 'glory' to be realized from those 'Dick Duel' books? If they were mine, I'd put *Fanny's* name on them."

"Oh, no you wouldn't," Fanny objected. "Not for fifty percent of a *million*."

CHAPTER TWENTY-FOUR

Shane Pederson came along in her exercise costume of spandex shorts and a tank top. She sat at the foot of my deck chair and lit a Virginia Slim while looking over "Umber Passion".

"What a great painting of Debra Paget!"

"Yes. Uh.. Your boyfriend was here looking for you. He didn't know you were upstairs exercising."

"I did it early today so I wouldn't run into that sleeze ball Harvey Gould."

"You know him?"

She did a french inhale and spoke on the exhale. "I met him about ten years ago, at the kind of party I get invited to. You know. This wholesaler in office supplies was throwing a bash for his new customers and ordered a dozen assorted hostesses to provide companionship. We were just supposed to light their cigarettes, laugh at their jokes, wriggle and coo. You know the bit."

I just looked wide-eyed as though I had no idea.

So, fine, I did what I was paid to do. Professionally. Then at the end of the evening, Gould invited me to meet him for cocktails the next day. So okay, I assumed he was asking for a date, right?"

"A paid date?"

She gave me a pitying look. There's no other kind, hon. So I made with the spandex, the make-up, the four-inch heels and met him in Marly's Lounge on the dot of six, ready for work."

"Great!" I said, then covered my mouth.

"Not great. First off, he went into this song and dance about how beautiful I was. Like I didn't know it, right? Beauty is my stock in trade. It costs me a fortune to look like this." She frowned hard and momentarily looked unbeautiful.

"Then, he started in on how excited he was, just to be near me. I didn't need to hear all that trash. I wanted to move ahead to the money issue.

"Then he comes on with, 'I've been told that I'm a very giving person.'" She did a creditable imitation of Gould's New York accent with hard final g's. "So I said, 'Great, let's buzz on over the Harry Winston and pick me up a few baubles.' So he comes back with 'I'm not into jewelry exactly.'"

After listening this far, I was getting ahead of her.

"Let me guess. He didn't bring any money."

"You must know the creep. Enough for the drinks and that was it. He actually thought he could *seduce* me. Do you believe that? Then he explained that he couldn't spend much money because his wife had him on an *allowance*."

"A man on an allowance," I made Eartha Kitt growling noises. "That'd make *me* hot."

"It would anyone, so then he said he would be very generous with his *time*."

I gasped. "His *time?*"

"So just to play this farce out to the final curtain, I said. 'Neat. You can come to my apartment and clean out my cabinets, do some painting, wallpaper my hallway.'

"So he just shifted around like 'Heh heh, that's not what I was thinking of.'"

"So I said, 'Well, if you're really offering to give me your time, that's how I would like you to spend it.'

And he comes back with, 'Heh Heh. To be perfectly honest with you..' Then he gives me this nasty leer that's supposed to be 'sexy'. and says, 'I had something more romantic in mind.'"

"So I told him, 'It sounds like you don't want to give me your time, but just want to rip off mine.' and picked up my purse and charged the hell out of there. So you see, counting prep time, I wasted a frigging hour and a half on the creep. I mean, I could have been home cleaning my oven."

"Huh?" I looked up. "Why would you clean an *oven*?"

"Pardon?"

"I mean it doesn't actually touch the food. So why would you go to all the trouble of.."

"Margo." Julian interrupted without moving his lips. "Don't embarrass us all."

Fanny spoke with ice in her mouth. "Did you ever notice that the less a man has to offer a woman, the more likely he is to be out looking for one?"

"No kidding," Shane said. "So yesterday, I working out up in the spa, doing my curls, and along comes Harvey Gould. He must have seen me through the window. He barreled in and sat his fat ass on the rowing machine across from me and started rattling on and on, all about *himself*. About how smart he is and how successful he's going to be when *In Deeper* hits the bookstores." She snorted. "Well, he wasn't paying for my company and I sure didn't feel like giving it away free, so I told him to bug off. Then he got nasty."

"Nasty, how?"

He said he'd tell Duncan all about my past if I wasn't nice to him. For nothing!"

She looked as though she wanted to spit.

Alice said, "So he threatened to tell your fiancé that you were a working girl?"

"Naturally, I laughed in his face and said that would be a shock, all right. How did he think I met Duncan in the first place?"

Fanny giggled. "So you're essentially blackmail-proof."

"Not really. I can tell you guys that was a bluff. For myself, I don't care. God!" She mashed out her cigarette. "But

Duncan would be mortified if it became public knowledge. Not that I *am* one but that he *needs* one. It worked though."

"Gould bought the bluff?"

"Must have. He hasn't bothered me since."

Julian nodded. "If he revealed your profession, Gould would have to tell the world, including his scary wife, how he found out about you. — I'd like your professional opinion." He showed her the gift-shop copy of Newsweek. "What do you think of Paula Jones?"

"I think she gives us bimbos a bad name."

Fanny smiled slyly. "You don't believe Clinton showed her his thing?"

"Oh, sure I believe Clinton showed her his thing. But it's not such a big deal."

Julian smiled. "*'De minimus non curat lex.'*"

"What?"

"That will be Clinton's defense in court."

"He hasn't got anything to worry about, anyhow." Fanny said. "Powerful people are immune to prosecution. Look at William Kennedy Smith."

"The poster boy for date-rape?"

"Yes, he could endorse Rufies. The point is that Smith had sexually assaulted at least three young women before one finally pressed charges, but the other victims weren't allowed to testify."

Shane smirked. "The word in Palm Beach is that everyone knows the Kennedys are pigs and no decent girl would go anywhere with any one of them."

"I'm fairly decent," I protested, "But if John-John invited me for a walk along the beach behind his house, I'd go."

"So would I," said Alice

"So would I," said Fanny.

"So would I," said Julian.

CHAPTER TWENTY-FIVE

We stood on the aft end of the Promenade Deck where the wind was a little milder and we could watch the ship's wake billow out behind us.

"Isn't this romantic," I said. "Drinking in the river?"

"Drinking it in?" Julian rejoined.

"Basking in the night, with the soft glow of the lights on the shore, the band playing behind us? – It's glorious. If only I were here with someone besides you."

"Look down there." He pointed into the murky water. "There must be a party going on forward. Someone seems to be throwing confetti in the river."

"Those pieces of paper look too big to be confetti."

"Then they're littering."

"You can only litter on land. When you do it on water, you're polluting."

Julian leaned over the railing and shook his head. "The poor old Mississippi is so polluted already, I'm surprised that anything sinks."

Frank Washington was ten feet over, smoking the end of his daily cigar. "What are you two doing outdoors in the humidity?"

"This voyage stirs up the genetic memory in both of us," Julian explained. "The first Fortier to reach the new world had sailed here as a French officer in seventeen twenty-five. He was a warrior and a pioneer. Margo's people, by contrast." He flicked a hand. "Were mere Irish peasants who crossed the Atlantic as refugees from the famine. In steerage class."

Frank frowned darkly. "It beat 'tween decks."

In that second, some white entity streaked around the corner, headed our way. I lifted my sunglasses and saw the white streak resolve into a young room steward running for all he was worth. He didn't see us coming in time to veer and careened into Frank who dodged lithely enough so that the guy only grazed his shoulder then reached out and grabbed his arm to keep the steward from continuing his trajectory all the way over the rail and into the muddy water.

"Hold on, fella! What's the matter?"

The steward's face had turned as white as his jacket.

"You're the policeman, right?"

"NOPD Homicide. Yes."

"I think – I'm *sure* that man in there is *dead*!"

"What man?"

"The gray-haired man in Cabin Ninety-three. It's Mr. Gould!"

"Show me where." Frank followed the steward with one hand on his shoulder. Morbid curiosity dictated that I shamble along behind.

"Mr. Gould got a phone call from New York but there was no answer in his cabin. He'd left the 'Do Not Disturb' sign on his door, so the maid didn't go in. The partner said to go wake him up!" The steward's voice rose in pitch as he babbled. "She tried ringing his cabin, but there was no response so she sent me. When he didn't answer the knock, I let myself in." He pointed to the door that was still ajar and stood out of the way while Frank looked in then looked out again.

"You're right. He certainly appears dead."

"I'll go run for the doc," the steward volunteered. "He's down in the infirmary on A Deck."

"Just to declare him, yes. And someone has to get the captain," Frank said.

"That should be me." I raised my hand.

"In his office," The steward called behind him. "Upper Promenade Deck, Aft."

I didn't attempt to make speed comparable to the young man's but set what was for me an uncharacteristically brisk pace through the corridor, took the elevator to the promenade deck then turned around a few times to get my bearings. Which way was fore and which aft? I studied the diagram of the ship bolted up between the elevators in which I myself was represented by a little red dot. The square part was the aft. My right hand flailed to point the way. Okay. After a minimum amount of wandering and back-tracking, I finally located the man, as promised, in his office, in front of his computer, clicking away on lists of figures."

I poked my head in. "Captain?!"

He looked startled at my sudden appearance but not panicked.

"Yes, Mrs. Fortier? What is it?"

"Emergency in Cabin Ninety-three."

He exited the program, rose, and reached for his cap. "What kind of emergency?"

"You're going to hate this."

***

By the time I showed the captain back to the fatal cabin, a small group had gathered outside it. Fanny and Alice were there leaning against the wall and giggling like sorority sisters at the prom.

Alice grinned. "Looks like Harvey Gould has run his last base."

"Gould the publisher? How?" Someone said behind me. Maybe it was Magnuson but I didn't turn to look. "He was too young to die spontaneously."

"He couldn't die young enough to suit me."

That was definitely Fanny.

Captain Yeates pushed aside the rubber-neckers and stepped into the cabin. Then, shaking his head at the futility of it all, knelt beside the body and felt for a pulse in the throat. In that moment the steward appeared with the ship's doctor in tow. The captain waved him in.

"It's too late for your good offices; that's for sure. But you have to come in and make it official."

He changed places with the doctor who picked his stethoscope up, then dropped it and leaned low over the deceased.

"These two marks.. Something I've never seen in my life, much less on a ship. But I think I know what it is."

"I saw it just the other day," Frank said. "Get that herpetologist up here."

"The herpetologist?"

"I'd bet my badge this man died of a poisonous snake bite."

I was about to take a gander at the scene but the captain put his arm across the door protectively.

"Mrs. Fortier, you'd better not go in there."

"Why not? I work for the newspaper."

"I'm aware of that but you're a *society* columnist. High teas. Debutante balls.."

"Hey, I cover crime scenes all the time."

"This one's nothing for a sensitive lady to witness."

"Don't worry, Captain." Frank waved at me to come ahead. "Mrs. Fortier isn't the least bit sensitive and she can't even *define* lady."

I hoisted my nose up in the air. "Why, thank you, Frank."

While Captain Yeates was cudgeling his brain for a reply, I smiled sweetly and brushed past him, taking a single step in. Then I stood with my back to the wall and my arms folded in an "I know all the rules and won't touch anything" stance.

Harvey Gould still lay where he had fallen, on his side, curled up. (Necessarily as there wouldn't have been room between the couch and the dresser for any other configuration.) And staring hard at nothing.

I considered that now, perhaps for the first time in Gould's existence, something was sticking out more than his teeth. Too bad for him it was his tongue.

Frank was trying hard to convey that he didn't mind interrupting his cruise to go back to work. He had already found a legal pad somewhere and drawn a diagram of the cabin.

Jarvis was located and delivered within minutes. He stood, nodding glumly. "I'm sorry to say it looks like death due to the bite of a poisonous snake, applied to the left side of his neck. See the brown spot here? There are two puncture marks where the fangs hit him."

"It was the same scene as before." Frank observed. "Except the bite marks are closer together. Smaller snake."

"But there's no snake in here now," the doctor noted. "Does anyone have an idea where it came from or where it went afterward?"

"Regrettably, yes." The captain took in a deep breath. "Now we can guess what that coral snake was doing between the time he was stolen from his terrarium and when he showed up in the closet with Mrs. Fortier."

"Then someone deliberately freed that snake." I said. "Could it have been Gould himself? Could he have been a snake fancier?"

"Maybe," Frank replied. "But then after the snake bit him fatally, are we to suppose he carried it to the linen closet, locked it in, then returned to his cabin and lay on the floor to die? – All right, Captain Yeates. I'm not familiar with Maritime Law. What procedures are supposed to be enacted for homicide on the high seas?"

The captain put his hands to his temples. "It's a matter beyond my purview. Nothing like this has ever happened on any vessel under my command. All I can do is ask for your help."

"I'll work on it, but this is going to take some time. We'll start with the people who had contact with the deceased, those actually attending the conference, and then go on to interview everybody in the vicinity and work outward."

"Lieutenant?" Fanny fairly bounced with excitement. "Are you going to force us all to stay here on the boat until you find the murderer?"

He showed his teeth in a fake smile. "Wouldn't that be nice for us all? No."

"No?" A faint hope dashed.

"All I can do is take everyone's name and address, verify identities, and let you all scatter to the four corners of the earth."

"Then you would have to solve a case with no access to the suspects?" I asked. "What that means is that if you don't solve this crime before we dock, you never will."

"That's pretty much what it means." He glanced around at the eager company. "Do any of you know of someone who wished ill to Mr. Gould? Even so far as wanting to see him dead?"

I noted that, with the efficiency of his calling, he had already started a list with a heading, underlined, but no names on it.

"Excuse me? There's one enemy I'm sure of." Fanny stood up on her toes, looked over his shoulder and pointed to the pad. "That's S-t-u-m-p-f-f. Stumpff, Fanny." She pointed to her chest. "Me. I would have *loved* to kill him."

"Put me down too, lieutenant." Alice stepped up behind her. "My name is Heckman. H-e-c-k-m-a-n, Alice. I'm thrilled that he's dead."

"And you might as well add me to the list," Patsy Pickering stepped out of the crowd. "I certainly didn't think much of him."

Frank looked at me quizzically and I shook my head, "Hey, I didn't know him well enough yet to really hate him."

Julian flicked a smile. "You're lucky it didn't happen at the end of the trip. I gather the whole ship would have come under suspicion."

Of the next dozen crime conferees interviewed, Professor Gordon Magnuson was the only one who showed real grief.

"This is a tragedy beyond comprehension." He was twisting his handkerchief. I was waiting for him to wring out a waterfall the way they do in cartoons. "Harvey Gould was a wonderful person."

Frank tapped his pen. "You were a friend of his?"

"I'm sorry to say that I knew him only for a fleeting moment. But from our all-too-brief discussion, I could intuit that this man was dedicated to fine literature. The real tragedy is that he never had a chance to see my manuscript." He was still hugging the referred-to treasure tightly. "Mr. Gould invited me to Fed-Ex The Second Awakening to his office in New York. And he even advised me to mark it 'Requested Material'!"

Gordon made a fist around the handkerchief as he contemplated the magical promise of a literary career, now lying cold and dead in Cabin Ninety-three.

"Would you like me to call the nurse for you, professor?"

"No, no. I'll be all right."

Our next interview prospect, the bookseller, Mary Maggie Mason, was stacking her wares and checking inventory sheets.

"A few questions, Ms. Mason?"

"Go ahead," she invited, but didn't stop working.

"How well did you know the deceased?"

"Better than I wanted to," she admitted without looking up. "For years I've been running into him at conferences: Seattle, Toronto, Milwaukee... The first time we met, he tried to get me to go out for cocktails. Said I was the most beautiful woman at the conference. Yada, yada, yada." She flapped a charge slip. "I told him all I was selling was books, and I wasn't giving *anything* away. Gould finally gave up the struggle and launched his gross self at some other target. But even now, every time I see him, he forgets that he hit on me before and tries his line again."

Frank bent over an enormous tome titled *Authors' Pseudonyms* then opened it in the middle and flipped through the pages while speaking. "Say, Margo, did you know Ed McBain's real name is Evan Hunter whose real name is Salvatore Lombino? – You understand Ms. Mason, that we're making a thorough search of the ship and we'll have to look through all of your books."

"You think I might have hidden something in that edition of *Authors' Pseudonyms*? Like a murder weapon?"

"No, Ma'am. We've already got the murder weapon. It's a snake."

"A snake?" Her blue eyes got wider. "But that's absurd! I'd use a serrated knife!" She turned her head from one to the other of us as though observing a tennis match. "Ask all my friends. *They'll* tell you."

I hadn't seen Fanny behind us until she stepped forward now. "She's right, Frank. I have known Mary over fifteen years and I can personally attest that she would definitely use a serrated knife."

"I guess that's all we need from you, Ms. Mason. Thank you." We headed for the elevator.

***

Duncan Steel's suite on the Veranda deck was luxurious on a small scale with real paintings on the walls and Louis Quinze furniture that looked authentic. (At least to me).

"Mr. Steel," Frank said, "We have to speak with everyone who knew Harvey Gould. Did you talk to him during the conference?"

"Gould!" Steel's eyes bugged dangerously. "I wouldn't give him the satisfaction! I came to this stupid boat for only one reason. I wanted to face Ridley Schuyler in person." His gnarled fist whitened around the head of his cane. "Face him down. Man to man!"

"You knew Schuyler?" Frank asked quietly.

"More than knew him. I *was* him!"

"You *were* him?"

"In a manner of speaking, anyway." He tapped his cavern chest. "I was Ridley Schuyler's ghost writer."

"Then it was you who wrote the books published under his name?"

"All except the first one." He flicked away at "the first one" with arthritic fingers as though Schuyler's single fine work hadn't counted for much.

"So those 'Dick Duel' books with all the mayhem and sadism, those were *your* doing?"

"The sensational thrillers, yes." He squared his narrow shoulders with pride. "I was enlisted as a worker for hire and received a flat rate of a hundred thousand per book. No royalties. My contract with Schuyler stipulated that I never disclose our business relationship. But now that he's dead, there's nothing to prevent my saying that I was the creator of those novels."

"Except good taste," Julian muttered behind his hand.

"But you did not, I presume, write the book about to come out, *In Deeper.*"

(Which we knew for a fact because Fanny had sworn that Schuyler's last book was actually *good*.)

"You're very perceptive, Mrs. Fortier." Steel waggled his head. "That's true. You see, it was my talent that kept Schuyler in the game all those years. And now that he was about to break through with a big-time gimmick, a new tell-all autobiography, he wanted to shut me out! I could have killed him with my bare hands!" Those bare hands shook.

***

Back in the elevator, Frank re-capped aloud.

"Duncan Steel was turning out six to eight paperback originals a year, mostly genre books: 'Swords and Sorcery', westerns, even romance. He could barely meet his alimony payments writing under his own name, so he was happy to team up with Ridley for a hundred thousand a pop. Ridley got his name and picture on the books and went on tour to promote them while Steel stayed home in Rego Park and did the actual writing."

"The arrangement must have suited Steel's bill exactly. It gave him a chance to vent his darker side. The stuff so depraved that he was ashamed to write under his own name, he could credit to Ridley."

"Now we have a motive for Steel. He hated Gould for leaving him out of the new book deal. And he was supposedly alone in his cabin at the time of the murder."

"You really believe Steel had the strength?"

"Not really. But Miss Pederson certainly does."

"You think she'd commit murder for him? Theirs isn't exactly a love match, you know."

"What if he paid her to do it? She already made her living doing unacceptable things for money. – So Schuyler and Gould were in business together and they're both dead of snake bites. Coincidence?"

CHAPTER TWENTY-SIX

The next interview was conducted in the Lorelei Lounge and must have been more pleasant for Frank.

"Ms. Wyeth, I'm forced to interview everyone who had contact with Harvey Gould."

"Really, Lieutenant? Then by all means interview me." Stefani was curled up on the couch against the rear wall, graceful as a cat.

"Thank you," he said, pulling out chairs for both of us. "Do you mind if Mrs. Fortier sits in?"

"Margo? No."

"I hate to tell you, Ms. Wyeth." Frank certainly did. "But we think Gould's murder may be connected to Schuyler's. And regarding that, your name would be on anyone's suspect list."

"Dear me. The old 'woman scorned' motive?"

"It's cliché but common."

"Gee, Frank," I horned in. "If Stefani were angry enough to off her ex-lover, would she have managed to hold her temper for some fifteen years?"

"Maybe. As the Italians say 'Vengeance is a dish best eaten cold.'"

"But I'm not Italian, Lieutenant," Stefani reminded. "I'm Swazi. And I don't like *anything* cold. – Anyhow, I can ease your mind. I'm the last person who would want Ridley dead now."

"You had become friends again?" Frank found that contingency distasteful.

"Never friends. But we were *partners* again."

"Partners? What for?"

"The publisher swore me to secrecy, but under a legal interrogation I would have to divulge it."

"That's just what this is," Frank assured her.

"Very well then." She paused for dramatic effect. "It was I who wrote the new book for Ridley."

"You?"

"Yes. It was all Harvey Gould's brainstorm. He noticed that *Deep Lock* was a well-crafted piece of literature and that all of the subsequent novels were garbage. So he took Ridley to one of those bars around the Flatiron building, got him very drunk and shook my name out of him."

"I see," Frank said. "Then he put the winning combination together again."

"And again, I was to remain anonymous. But this time I was being paid for it." She crossed her long legs and reminded me of a hosiery commercial. "Two hundred thousand against half the royalties."

"That sounds pretty good."

"And, don't worry. I didn't even turn on my word processor until the check had cleared." The corners of her lips turned up. "I'm not your suspect, lieutenant. You see, I was the only person on the ship who had reason to be grateful to Harvey Gould. It was his idea to put me back together with Ridley. To my enormous profit."

CHAPTER TWENTY-SEVEN

"I don't know why you're interested in me, Lieutenant. I'm not one of those crime conference people."

"No, Mr. Moretti, but we would like to talk to you anyhow."

We had caught up with the singer by the coffee station in the cafeteria. His dyed black hair looked indigo in the bright light.

Frank took a cup of coffee to foster the attitude of "just chats". I swigged a Coke.

"I heard that you were from Mountain Lakes, New Jersey," Frank went on. "Did you happen to know Frederick Ihde?"

"Sure," Vinnie said easily. "I dated his daughter Louise, one summer. Why?"

"Because he was a victim of theft seven years ago. And the late Ridley Schuyler was a suspect."

"I know. Rotten thing to happen to Fred."

"Did you happen to know Harvey Gould?"

"Gould? Sure. That hand-job offered $50,000 for my 'tell-all' autobiography if I would say I slept with Patti Smith." Vinnie dumped two packets of sweetener into his coffee. "I said, I never slept with Patti Smith. He said she was probably so high back in the mid-seventies that she wouldn't remember whether we did it or not. But the only girls I got were the groupies who lined up outside the stage door."

Frank nodded. "So you rejected his bid."

"Then he offered a *hundred* thousand if I would say I

slept with any one of the Monkees. Well, they're all *guys*, so no thanks."   ***

We were stepping out of the cafeteria when we were ambushed by Professor Magnuson, stepping up to Frank.

"Lieutenant?"

From my angle, I could see that he was holding his dreadful manuscript behind his back. But I had no opportunity to pull my old friend out of tedium's way.

Gordon smiled benignly. "I have something that I know will interest you as an officer of the law."

Frank raised both eyebrows. "Oh, really? Do you have something to add to your statement?"

"Not exactly." And then in a lightening move he must have practiced, the good professor thrust his treasure into Frank's startled hands.

"This?" Frank hefted the bale of waste paper. "Why would it interest me? Are there policemen in this story?"

"Well, not in a mundane sense," Magnuson averred. "But the protagonist's internal monologue deals with authority issues in the profound abstract."

"I'm sure it does, Gordon. And I'm dying to read it, but.." Frank tried to hand the mess back. "Right now, though, I'm sort of caught up in this murder thing. Some people think it's important that I.."

"Oh, at your leisure!" Magnuson backed away out of reach and waved his hands. "Just look it over when you have nothing else to do." Then he turned heel and fairly sprinted down the corridor leaving Frank to stare down at his new burden in pure irritation.

"You're in for a treat." I patted his shoulder. "The greatest suspense is in the title but the solution is revealed on page 849."

"Good grief! – Well, I'm certainly not going to carry this piece of garbage around with me for the rest of the day." He held it at arms' length, turning his face away and beckoned to a steward. "Excuse me. Would you put this in my cabin?"

"Right away, sir. On the desk?"

"Sure." Frank smiled affably as the young man went off on his errand then muttered. "On the other side of the porthole would be even better. – I phoned ashore." He put a hand to his brow. "At eight dollars a minute. And I got some news from Duffy on the bank which may be relevant. The theft of Fred Ihde's Fabergé egg was reported on July 11th, 1988."

"And today's July the 10th, so – Holy cow!" I snapped my fingers for emphasis on the second try.

"Yes. That makes it seven years tomorrow. We weren't even considering that it's a significant number. Now, assuming Ridley Schuyler actually did commit the burglary.."

I finished the sentence. "The statute of limitations would be up this week. If he so chose, the thief could produce his swag with no fear of being indicted for grand larceny."

Frank finger-combed his mustache. "It's true that he couldn't be prosecuted, but he couldn't exactly keep the stolen property either. At the very least, he'd be liable for a huge civil suit."

"Okay, now." I held my hands over my eyes in a swami position. "I'm putting myself in the mindset of a fame-hungry ex-crook."

"Like Ridley P. Schuyler."

"Sure. My guess is that he stole the egg, but intended to return it to the owner, preferably in front of a bank of TV cameras. The whole caper could have been staged just for publicity to show what a 'master criminal' the guy could have been if he had stayed on the wrong side of the law. I see it as his ticket to ride on the talk show circuit."

Frank nodded. "If that great revelation was supposed to promote his book, he must have shared the secret with his publisher."

"The late Harvey Gould."

"Which made him an accessory after the fact. That deepens the connection. Now we have two conspirators in a theft, both dead of snake bites."

CHAPTER TWENTY-EIGHT

Frank had news for the conclave up in the Lorelei Lounge. "Margo's theory held water, as it happens. We finally got a call through to Gould's partner in New York, Dunn Meechum. And, while equivocating and disclaiming and excusing the hell out of himself, Meechum managed to admit that they were planning an enormous promotional campaign around the stolen and restored egg. As of last month, they had already reserved ad space in twenty major markets. The actual copy, of course, had been kept under wraps."

Julian ordered another round of drinks for the table, only Captain Yates demurred. "So that was the plan last month. But Meechum and Gould must have cancelled the big campaign after Schuyler was killed in his hotel room."

"Wrong. Why cancel? Schuyler's murder made it a bigger story. They were still going ahead with all the promotion as recently as yesterday. Meechum admitted they'd arranged for the New Orleans photographer, Logan Bishop, to meet the boat the evening we docked. He was commissioned to take publicity pictures."

"Then the campaign was proceeding as scheduled?" Fanny shook her head. "I can't envision Katie Couric conducting an interview with a cold and stiff author."

"Gould himself had planned to meet Ms. Couric and fill all the other promotional dates."

"Ah ha! I can just see him weeping copiously about the shocking murder of his posthumous best friend."

I said, "But considering that since the whole campaign was based on the stolen egg, then Meechum and Gould must have been able to produce it themselves."

"You're right. It appears that sometime before he was murdered. Schuyler passed it along to Gould who must have brought it on board with him."

"So if we assume that Gould had it, how come he doesn't have it now?"

"He doesn't have anything now," Fanny smiled.

Frank said, "But the second officer went through every inch of the dead man's cabin to pack his bags and he couldn't have missed anything bigger than the head of a match."

Julian nodded. "So it's fair to hypothesize that whoever iced Harvey Gould then helped himself to the egg."

"Or herself," Frank added.

"You don't think Gould's murderer could be a 'her'?"

"Why not? An attractive woman could more easily have got herself invited to his cabin."

"Or an unattractive woman," Patsy Pickering interposed. "Anything in a skirt."

"And we know Gould had a way with the ladies that made them want to kill him. But consider that this couldn't have been a spontaneous act. The murderer had to be someone who knew how to handle poisonous snakes." Frank looked around the table. "Not a common skill or one quickly acquired."

"So what's next?" It was Fanny who asked that.

Frank turned to Captain Yeates. "Now that Gould's cabin has been cleaned out, what's left for us to do is make a search of the rest of the ship."

"*Every* cabin?"

"It has to be done. I mean we have to examine every piece of luggage of every passenger and crew member, all the common areas and every nook and cranny of every stateroom."

I tapped Frank's hand.

"And every person?"

"Person?" He screwed up his face. "Margo, no one could *swallow* a Fabergé egg."

"What if not exactly swallowed but..?"

He looked horrified. "Impossible! You realize that, including the stand, the thing is over eight inches in length and *pointed*, for pity's sake?"

The waiter reappeared with our drinks and Julian handed me my Coke. "If someone on this boat were concealing the swag in that manner, he wouldn't be able to walk into dinner."

"That's true." I took a long gulp and stood up to get ready for the sugar rush. "But I seem to remember that not everybody on board *has* walked into dinner."

"What?"

"Consider that at least one passenger has taken every meal in his room."

"I presume you're alluding to the invisible Mr. Holden Webb."

Alice nodded. "A sworn enemy."

"That's a far-fetched connection," Frank said. "Oh, wait! Let me present your motive. Webb was so offended by the poor quality of Schuyler's ouevre that he talked his way into the victim's hotel room, grabbed the nearest snake and killed him."

"No," Alice said. "But I'm not referring to Schuyler's murder. Webb had an excellent reason to kill Harvey Gould. There was an issue of long-standing."

Frank sat back and held his palms behind his ears in an all-listening mode.

Back in the late fifties," Alice began. "Webb's older sister, Harriet, donated a bundle of his letters to her university library. They were only allowed to be read on the premises, not reproduced in any way. But ten years ago, a young PhD candidate named Sikes was rooting around in the archives of that library and he happened on the letters. The enterprising scholar used them as a basis for his dissertation and made an A. Then he put them together in a book and Meechum and

Gould's company, 'Goldmark Incorporated', published them without permission."

"How could they?" Julian objected. "Published or not, Webb held the copyright to his own letters."

"They contrived to get around that technicality by paraphrasing the letters. Of course they didn't paraphrase them far enough. In substance, what they came out with was still Webb's creative property. His gang of attorneys took them to court and won, but won what?"

Frank said, "If the judgement was high enough, maybe the whole publishing company."

"But the publishing company was nothing but a box of letterhead stationary. 'Goldmark Incorporated' had no capital, operated out of rented desk space, leased all their equipment, owned no printing facilities and contracted out all their work. After the judgement, they dissolved Goldmark and re-formed as Meechum and Gould."

"So Webb was left with nothing but a pile of legal bills to bless himself with." Julian said. " A good reason to hate Gould."

"I'll admit we have a puzzle there. Holden Webb, who hasn't been seen in public for thirty years, who, in fact, would be welcome almost anywhere in the literate world, agrees to make an appearance at a third-rate writers' conference. – No offense, Patsy."

"What? No." She flapped her hand. "Third-rate."

"Webb arranges to board a boat with at least two people he despises and before he debarks, both of those people are dead."

Frank was writing on his pad. "Let's explore some other mysteries. I can't understand why a recluse like Holden Webb would sign onto the cruise at the last minute. Or why he agreed to come at all, considering that he despised the guest of honor."

Fanny laughed. "Maybe he wanted to mend fences."

"From what we know of him, Webb is a notorious

curmudgeon. He doesn't particularly enjoy associating with people he *approves* of, so it's not likely that he would go out of his way to cultivate Schuyler."

Frank underlined something on the pad. "But there's a more plausible explanation. What if he were aware that Schuyler would never actually make the cruise?"

"You're saying he had a premonition?"

"Hardly that, Margo." Frank issued me a look of tactful condescension. "A person can know in advance that another person isn't going to be in a certain place without calling on any paranormal abilities." He put down his pen. "For example, what if the person himself intends to prevent that other person from going to that place. – Let's interview Mr. Webb."

A steward whose name-tag said "Julio" was unable to help us.

"I'm sorry, sir, but Holden Webb is nowhere to be found."

"You looked in his cabin?"

"I did, sir, and it's completely empty. Not only is the man gone, but there isn't a single personal item left in there. I mean, not a thread of clothing or anything else. He seems to have packed up his suitcases and skipped. Even the waste basket is empty."

"I don't care about the waste basket. I'd like to know where the man himself has gone."

"Well, he must be on the ship somewhere. We haven't docked since Gould's murder."

An hour later, the captain was shaking his head.

"On your orders, Lieutenant, we've shaken down every passenger and every crew member. We've even swept the *rest* rooms. It's as though Holden Webb jumped over the side, and took his bags with him."

Frank pressed his lips together. "It's more like he was never on board at all. I'm going to contact his residence, in Scardia, Maine."

***

By the time Frank met us again in the Lorelei Lounge, we had thoroughly rehashed all the details of the day's trial coverage, so we were ready for any diversion he might furnish.

"I've been on the phone with Tulane and Broad and you're going to love this one." Frank dropped his notebook on the table in front of us and looked peeved. "We finally found Holden Webb?"

"Found him?" Alice whooped. "That's great! How?"

"With a long-distance phone call. We contacted the Scardia police station which sent a patrolman up to Webb's house to knock on his door."

I sat upright. "My stars! He must have got himself back to Maine awfully fast."

"He didn't have to get back there, Margo, because he never left."

"That's impossible."

"According to one Patrolman Hiram Beatty, Webb is recovering from an appendectomy and has been in bed for a week."

I personally wasn't convinced. "Maybe he just told the *cop* he was and had been."

Frank picked up his pad and read from it. "A Doctor Thomas Oldfield also told him. The general practitioner who originally diagnosed Webb made two housecalls to follow up on the surgery, Sunday and Tuesday. That was during the same period our man was supposedly in Cabin 84."

"So Webb never came aboard at all?" I said.

"Comes the dawn? Not only that; he never booked the cruise. It turns out Holden Webb had never even heard of the Riverside Crime Writers' Conference."

Fanny let her mouth fall open. "Then he couldn't have e-mailed Patsy asking for an invite?"

"Or anyone else about anything else. Webb claims he never in his life owned a personal computer and doesn't know how to use one."

"Then who e-mailed the conference using his name?"

I snapped my fingers in a hip manner. "Did Patsy save the message? It's easy enough to trace the return address."

"She did and we can't. It transpires that the imposter had corresponded through some re-mailing service in California that stripped the original address."

Julian sat back and folded his arms.

"That development brings us, hell-bent, to this question. Who was sitting naked in Cabin 84 when our friend Biffie brought the dinner trays?"

Ten minutes later, Cruise-Director Richter was at the table, looking ready to chew his clip board.

Frank spoke with no accusation in his tone. "You did check Webb in, didn't you?"

"Well, yes." Richter stuttered. "I.. I don't actually remember the man; I *must* have, though. No one can get the key to his stateroom without handing me his boarding pass. And at the end of the evening I had Webb's pass. Here it is." He put it on the table in front of us. "But then I noticed that I hadn't put a check next to his name on the passenger list. I had an extra key left too. I figured it was an oversight."

Frank cogitated a minute before saying, "Could someone have checked in as himself with one boarding pass, then dropped another boarding pass, Webb's, into your box? You were looking ahead to make sure no unauthorized people got on. But you weren't looking behind you."

Richter's face was red to the roots of his hair. "It's possible. But he still wouldn't have Webb's key."

"So we'll hypothesize that someone who was on the boat as a passenger or crewman posed as Holden Webb in Cabin eighty-four." I ventured. "But at the same time, he had to be appearing elsewhere as himself. There couldn't be *two* never-seen mystery men on-board."

"There weren't, according to the cabin stewards," Frank admitted. "Now let me think about that. Did anyone actually see this man?"

"So far as we know," Fanny volunteered, "Only Biffie the

steward."

"Then, by all means," Frank rubbed his hands together. "Let's have a chat with Biffie the steward."

Four minutes later, the young man joined us at a fast trot, bright-eyed and all eagerness to take part in the news of the day.

"You wanted me, lieutenant?"

"Yes. Sit down a moment, Biffie. I think you can help us."

"I hope so, sir. What can I do?"

"You're the only one we know who can describe Holden Webb. You brought him all his meals?"

"Yes, sir." The young steward took a chair but remained perched on the end of it. "He ordered three a day: a continental breakfast, a light lunch at one and a full-course dinner at six."

"When you brought them to him, was he inside the cabin?"

"Every time. I knocked on the door and he yelled 'It's open!' So I carried in his tray, set it on the table and laid out his silver. Mr. Webb was just sitting at the desk, hunkered down over a book. Naked as a muffin."

"Naked? He was like that every time you brought him a meal?"

"Yep. Must be a nudist or something.

"Oh." Frank looked nonplussed. Then recovered with, "What can you tell us about.."

"Nothing!" Biffie covered his eyes. "He had his back to me and I didn't exactly want to stare, you know? I don't look at guys. I like girls, see? So I just looked down at my shoes, arranged the plates on the table, and beat it out of there."

"Okay, then. Was he tall or short?"

"Neither. In between." The steward waved his hands. "I didn't really notice what he was. He was bent over his desk."

"Fat or thin?"

Biffie held his palms out. "How can I describe him? He

was non-descript."

Julian shook his head. "So far, it could be any white man on this ship, from the captain himself on down to 'Schmelvis'."

"Now, Biffie," Frank persisted. "Did he say anything to you besides, 'It's open'?"

"Well, that was funny."

Frank lowered his voice almost to a whisper. "Please tell me what was funny."

"Well, 'course, it's my job to be friendly. It's part of the cruise line service, you know? So I would always say, "I got you set up here, Mr. Webb. Enjoy your meal. And then he would say ..'Mmf ..mmf.' something like that."

"Would you recognize his voice if you heard it again?"

"You kidding? 'It's open' from the other side of the door then 'Mmf.. Mmf'."

"What about later when you went back to pick up the tray?"

"It was always left on the floor outside the door. So I didn't have to go inside again."

Frank tapped his pen.

"What did Webb eat?"

"How should I know?"

"By extrapolation. What did he leave on his tray?"

The steward seemed to study his eyebrows for a moment. "Nothing but the utensils."

Frank heaved a sigh. "So we're looking for a naked man with a healthy appetite. Is there anything else you remember about him?"

"All I can tell you is, there was nothing about his body that I would envy."

"Then we can rule out Aleko the deck boy," I said helpfully.

Frank let Biffie go back to work and ordered a light beer.

"I already interviewed the maid assigned to that section. She went into the cabin every day to clean, but Webb was out during those times. She said all she had to do was make the bed. And he seemed to have gone the whole voyage without taking a shower, or even washing his hands."

"How does she know that?" Fanny asked.

"The soap was never used."

I piped up. "Maybe he's like me. *I* don't use soap."

Julian said, "We all *know* that, Margo."

"Because it dries up the natural oils. I use cleansing cream, and I brought my own aboard."

Frank was given his beer and he took a sip. "We've got: middle-aged, not remarkably tall, short, fat or thin. Our subject either stinks to high heaven or he's obsessed with keeping a baby-soft complexion."

"We've never seen anyone like that."

"Do we know exactly what we're looking for? Maybe we have seen him but didn't know what we were seeing."

"Any ideas, Margo?"

"First, I would look at a guy who is not what he appears to be."

Julian said, "We already know one man like that." He glanced over to the bar where Gordon was warning Abram Weissman that the suspense about his title might be excruciating until he got to page eight-hundred and forty-nine.

I said, "You can't be referring to our friend Gordon Magnuson. He's everything he appears to be and less. His life is an open dull book."

"No, I didn't mean the good professor. I was thinking about our manifestly gentile Mr. Weissman."

"You're right. That story of his never did hold borscht."

***

Weissman came over to our table when summoned, but looked puzzled. "Lieutenant? What is this about?"

Frank pointed to a chair, looking as tired as I've ever seen him. When the witness took it, he said, "About the fact that you're not really Abram Weissman, junior or senior."

"But.. Well.."

Frank spoke in a police report monotone. "I've put a call through to Abram Weissman of Avenue O in Brooklyn. He has two sons, Morris and Leonard. No 'Junior'."

"Of course not," I put in. "That wouldn't be kosher."

"As of this afternoon, the father and both sons were doing their quarterly taxes in the family furniture store. That's all I could get; but it was enough."

"Well, concerning that.." Blue eyes shifted uneasily. "Heh heh. It's certainly not a police matter."

"No?"

"I mean, I wasn't doing anything illegal. I'm not using that name to defraud anybody."

"What for, then?"

"For personal reasons."

"In the light of a murder's occurring right here on board," Frank leaned forward till he was inches from Weissman's face. "There isn't much left that's personal."

"All right, Lieutenant. I'll come clean. I'm Ed Hansen, from Denville, New Jersey." Our suspect produced a folder with a picture I.D. and held it out.

Frank took it from him, adjusted his glasses and read carefully, moving his lips. "According to this, you're a private investigator with your own agency."

"Of fifteen years' standing. You see, I'm on this ship in pursuit of an investigation."

Frank handed back the folder. "Which leads inevitably to the next question. Upon whose behalf are you pursuing it?"

"I can't tell you that. Confidentiality is part of the service."

"Maybe it's part of the service, Mr. Hansen. But unless you're working through an attorney, it's *not* part of the law."

"All right, man, before you get out the rubber hoses. I don't think he would mind if I revealed it. I was hired by Frederick Ihde to track down his stolen Fabergé egg."

"But why did he spend his own money to hire you? I heard the property was insured."

"Yeah. Insured for about one-fifth of its current value

and Ihde's reputation wasn't insured at all. That's mainly what he wanted back. And I believed Ridley Schuyler was responsible."

"That's what your investigation was all about? You booked yourself on board to follow Schuyler?"

Hansen hefted the I.D. folder in his hand, feeling its weight, then shoved it back in his pocket. "I suspected him from the beginning. By now, it had been nearly seven years since the theft and the statute of limitations was running out. And the word was that Schuyler's new book would feature a newsworthy revelation, so I put two and two together and figured this trip would be significant. I paid old Mr. Weissman to let me take his place."

"Why didn't you cancel after Schuyler was killed?"

"I had a thought that he might have passed it to his new publisher, Harvey Gould. I was going to search his cabin at some point."

"And did you have that opportunity?"

"No."

"Then you never found the egg. It must be very frustrating."

"Sir Galahad went after his Holy Grail. – Look here." Hansen opened his note book and fanned four eight-by-ten color photos on the table. "These are copies of the pictures supplied to the insurance company. Four views, back, front, top and bottom."

"Holy smoke!" Frank breathed.

"You see the outside of the egg was gold mesh encrusted with diamond, ruby and sapphire flowers with emerald leaves wrought by Fabergé's most talented workmaster Mikhail Perkhin."

"Who is that in the picture?"

"The portrait set in the top was of the Czarina herself painted by the famous miniaturist, Constantin Krijitski."

"And these are just pictures of the egg itself. It was set on a gold stand with the double-headed golden eagle. Pavé with sapphires."

I nudged Julian. "What does pavé mean?"

"Paved."

"Than why don't they just say paved?"

Hansen continued. "As with all the commissioned Easter eggs there was a 'surprise' inside and this one was a miniature replica of the Imperial cradle. It was mechanical and when you wound it with a little key, the cradle would rock."

I held one of the photos toward the light. "How much would something like that run?"

"It's priceless!"

"But not free."

"Certainly not. It originally cost the Czar 10,000 rubles. Ihde bought it at an auction at Sothby's in 1962 for two hundred and fifty thousand which was reasonable at the time. But if a piece of that quality came under the gavel today, it would run close to five million."

"At the least."

"Say, Lieutenant!" It was Biffie the steward hurrying through the lounge, waving at us. "When the morning maid cleaned cabin 84, she saw that it was empty, so she thought the passenger had moved to another cabin. But there was one thing he left, propped up on his pillow. So she turned it into purser's office. – This little gizmo." He pulled something out of his jacket pocket and twirled it carelessly around one finger.

Hansen leapt to catch it. "That's it!"

"What?"

"The *stand* Fabergé made for the egg. See, gold filigree with double eagles! Kee-Rist, you might have dropped this thing and bent it!"

Frank took it from his hand. "This is very valuable, isn't it? Why would anyone have left it behind?"

Hansen said, "The quickest conclusion is that the occupant of that cabin took the egg and then discarded the stand to allow for easier concealment."

CHAPTER TWENTY-NINE

At lunch in the dining room, the captain stood up on the landing of the staircase with a cordless microphone to his lips.

"Ladies and gentlemen, I am sorry to be interrupting your meal. But this is the only time of day when we can get such a large group of you together."

A big guy in a funny tourist shirt who looked as though he made a lot of money at whatever it was he did on dry land waved as if to summon a waiter.

"We heard there was a fatality on board! What's the story, Captain?"

"Most of you have already been informed of the tragedy that occurred yesterday. The deceased was the distinguished publisher, Harvey Gould."

The passengers looked around at one another and shrugged. None of them seemed to know or much care who the distinguished Mr. Gould was.

"First of all, let me assure you all that the voyage will proceed as scheduled. No part of the program will be changed."

"Was it an accident?" an old woman trilled with more volume than her thin body appeared capable of emitting.

"I don't think so, ma'am. I'm sorry to say that we have to suspect murder at this point."

"Murder by what means, Captain?"

"Murder by – Well, it appeared to be by snake."

This intelligence caused more of a stir then the identity of the late-lamented.

Our one advantage is that we happen to have a New Orleans homicide policeman on board, Lieutenant Frank Washington. Every action is being taken to sort out this matter and now Lieutenant Washington has a few words to say to you all."

He handed over the microphone, then stepped back and assumed the "at ease" position.

"Ladies and gentlemen," Frank announced. "I'm here to ask for your help. For the loan of your eyes and ears. We need information about the passenger who stayed in cabin 84, who identified himself as Holden Webb. We know now that the man was an imposter, but if anyone got a glimpse of him, say entering or leaving his cabin, we're asking you to come speak to me about it. And your confidence will be kept. So far, all we know is that our subject was white and somewhere in his middle years. If anyone can be more definitive than that, we will be most grateful."

"Lieutenant?" Magnuson raised his hand. "I have something important to say."

"Yes?" Frank cocked his ear. "What is it, Gordon?"

"When you get to the third paragraph on page 563, you'll notice an unconventional use of the subjunctive mood. I want to know whether you think it's an effective device or just distracting."

"You.. What?"

"In *The Second Awakening*. I don't want to resort to stylistic forms that merely call attention to themselves."

"Magnuson, I'm in the middle of a *murder* investigation!"

"Very well then. Later when you have more time."

The good professor resumed his seat then and kept his peace.

The captain took the microphone again. "Thank you, Lieutenant. Will that be all?"

Frank tilted his head toward the mike. "I can only add that we will be using the Pirate's Nook on Deck C as a command post."

"Thank you, then," the captain said, nodding. "I'm sure we will do all we can to help the lieutenant resolve this.."

A young steward stepped into the room behind them and waved his arm.

"Hey everybody, court's back in session!"

In that instant, the whole population of the dining room rose as one and there came the roar of a stampede. I jumped up and scrambled out of the way so as not to be knocked down and trampled flat by the crowd careening toward the television in the sports lounge to consume their eight-times daily O.J. fix.

"Hey, you people!" I called after them. "We've got a murder of our own right here on the ship. A human being who actually walked among us lies dead! Isn't that important.. too?" My voice trailed off on the "ooo" part as I glanced around and realized that the only person left in the dining room was Julian, smiling at me and shaking his head. "It was no contest, dear. We don't have any good-looking celebrities in ours."

I sat down at the nearest table and addressed an abandoned piece of strawberry short cake.

"Does anyone really pay attention to every minute of the trial? The testimony itself is so slow and boring with all those pop-up objections, that I just wait for the 'comfort break' so Roger Cossack and Greta Van Susteren can tell me what's actually going on."

CHAPTER THIRTY

Julian and I were so blasé that the Sports Bar was almost full by the time we ambled in. We were lucky that there were still unclaimed chairs in the back row near Fanny and Alice.

"I was roped in by the Bronco chase." someone down front was admitting.

"It was downright stupid," a heavy man retorted. "Chasing a car down the highway at forty miles an hour."

"But it developed into a real drama when he threatened suicide!"

"You think so?" I joined in. "It just reminded me of that scene in 'Blazing Saddles'. The part where Cleavon Little put a gun to his *own* head and took *himself* hostage."

A woman raised her hand. "Did anyone consider that maybe Jason did it and O.J. was covering up for his son?"

"Why would Jason do it?"

"Because O.J. paid him."

"So of course O.J. would be blameless in that case," Julian drawled. "Anyhow, Jason worked as a chef in a restaurant and he was on-duty till eleven at night."

Someone over at the bar raised a glass. "Does anyone know where Al Cowling was?"

"A. C. was at a kid's birthday party all evening." The bartender flapped his rag contemptuously. "Everyone saw him there but *you*."

Before the commercial was over, Frank Washington wandered in as though he didn't know quite where he was. I waved and pointed to the empty chair next to me.

"How is your 'command post' going?"

Frank just looked weary. "Nothing."

"No one has come forward with a description of Cabin 84?"

"We asked everyone in the neighboring staterooms. But they didn't remember seeing him."

"No wonder. I couldn't tell you who is in the cabin next to mine either."

"Frank," Alice said, "You must have mixed feelings about the trial. Are you on the black side or the white side?"

"I'm on the *blue* side. I'm a cop, remember?"

A rumbling sound came from one of the front couches. "I wouldn't put it past the cops to frame someone!"

"Oh?" Frank looked mildly interested. "Has any policeman ever tried to frame *you*?"

"No, but they're a pain in the ass about my expired brake tag."

"So, get a new brake tag."

"I been *busy*."

"Speaking for this one cop," Frank smiled dangerously. "I barely have time to do the paperwork on *guilty* people. So, I'm going to go out of my way to get an innocent man indicted? Would I get paid extra for this?"

Captain Yeates came in then, too distracted even to ask for an update of the trial. "Lieutenant? We've searched the whole ship for your Fabergé egg. Nothing."

"But no one could have left this vessel since we pulled anchor. Therefore the item didn't leave on two feet."

Fanny clapped her hands. "Maybe the murderer put the egg in a big jar and threw it overboard!"

"To a friendly turtle?"

"No, but suppose he had a friendly human waiting alongside in a motor boat."

Frank tapped his pen. "That's a worthy scenario."

"No, it isn't," the captain interjected. "You think we pilot this vessel without looking? Someone on the bridge would have seen a motor boat, friendly or unfriendly, hovering in the middle of the blasted gulf."

Now we saw Gordon Magnuson come through the door of the Sports Bar and approach us at a trot. "Lieutenant? I think I can help find that Fabergé Egg."

"Really?" Frank smiled as widely as the rising sun. "I wish you would."

"I just got a brainstorm. Suppose the egg isn't on the ship or entirely off it either."

"Say, what?!"

"Yes, indeed. I was just thinking about where Ray Milland hid his liquor."

"In the vacuum cleaner bag?" Fanny recalled.

"In the light fixture." Alice said.

"No, no. I meant in the first scene of 'The Lost Weekend'." Gordon spread his hands. "The camera pans across the New York city skyline, and stops under Ray Milland's window. There it is, his whiskey bottle, hanging outside by a rope."

"So you think the egg is..?"

"Exactly! What if it's been dangling from a rope all this time, trailing through the water behind us."

Shane Pederson entered the room sprinting and came to a halt at our row. "Say, girls?! – Excuse me, Lieutenant."

"Don't mind me. I've got calls to make." Then Frank rose from his chair and Shane slipped into it.

"Have I got news!" She was breathless with it. "Duncan said Harvey's murder reminded him of how short life is. He's ready to *marry* me!"

"Great!" Alice whooped. "You're getting your wish!"

"That is.." Shane clutched her heart. "If he doesn't change his mind by the time we get back to New York."

"Don't give him a chance," I advised. "Get him to do it

right here on the ship."

"Is that possible?"

"I see it in the movies all the time," Alice said helpfully. "Old movies."

Shane clasped her hands together in a praying configuration. "Come up to the suite with me. We'll call the captain."

***

"That's right, Captain Yeates. We're ready to get married."

Steel executed his most joyful smile which looked as though someone had split his face with a hatchet. "It's time I made an honest woman of my girl here." He put his arm around his bride-to-be to the extent that his arthritis would permit. "And I think we're old enough to do it without our parents permission. Huh huh."

He finished the sentence with a coughing fit.

"We would like to do it right away." Shane said. "Can you marry us, Captain?"

"Sorry, Miss Pederson." He shook his head. "I can't. You see, the master of a vessel doesn't really have the authority to officiate at weddings. That's a myth. All I can do is record an on-board marriage by entering it into the ship's log. But you would have to find a qualified judge or clergyman to solemnize it."

Shane stomped her alligator-shod foot. "Damn! What are the chances there's a judge or a minister on this bucket?"

"I'm afraid there's no 'Reverend' or 'Rabbi' listed on the passenger manifest," the captain advised. And if we have a judge, he's being modest about it."

Julian and I exchanged a look. "Where is he? Do you know?"

"Down in the card room. I saw him on the way up. – Excuse us, please." And we headed for the elevator.

Father Kevin Dawes was sitting by himself at a card table for four, opening new decks and shuffling them.

"Hi, Julian. Margo.." He waved a deck. "You play cards?"

"Not right now." Julian took the chair next to his. "Kevin, we would like you to break your incognito for an hour or so and perform a wedding ceremony."

"A wedding?"

"Two of the passengers are very anxious to get married."

The priest did a two-handed riffle. "They can wait till we get to port tomorrow, can't they? And hunt up a justice of the peace there."

"I think time is of the essence for this particular ceremony."

"Why? Is the bride pregnant?"

"No. Rather the groom is facing the other end of the life-table."

"He's dying?"

Julian shrugged. "Actually looks as though he already has."

Five minutes later, we were back up in the suite making introductions. Father Kevin Dawes, this is Shane Pederson and her fiance, Sid Muddwort, also known as Duncan Steel."

Shane rushed forward. "You're a priest?" Dawes nodded and she clapped her hands. "Then you can marry us?"

"Is at least one of you Catholic?"

The groom looked angry. "Shit! Presbyterian."

"I am," the bride trilled.

"Ms. Pederson? *You* are?"

"Sure. I was raised to be a good little Catholic girl. Sex is a sin. Even *thinking* about sex is a sin. How did you think I got where I am today?"

There was no argument for that so I just looked down at my shoes which were Easy Spirit. Rather graceful pumps in a beige leather with a two and a half inch heel.

The priest looked around distractedly. "We don't have

much time for a pre-Cana conference."

"What's that?"

"Okay, we'll do this fast. Sit down."

Shane took a chair and Steel had to be helped into an adjoining one.

Dawes remained standing, folded his hands in front of him and addressed the blissful couple. "Shane and Duncan.." He looked from one to other. "As you embark on your new life together, you are taking on the Lord's most supreme challenge."

Shane smiled politely and a snore escaped from Duncan. She nudged him somewhat roughly and he put his head up. "What?"

"The sacrament of marriage is a gift bestowed on two young.. uh.. two people in love. And in exchange for this gift, you undertake a vital responsibility. You are not making this union merely to populate the earth, but to populate *heaven* as well."

I stepped over and said into his ear. "He's fading. You'd better sum it up quickly."

"Okay, uh.." Then he blurted, "Don't use birth control."

The bride-to-be laughed though her nose. "I can promise that won't be a temptation."

There was a knock on the door and Patsy came in chirping excitedly. "This is going to be such fun! Professor Magnuson has agreed to be the best man. The captain will give the bride away. I'm the maid of honor. The rest of you get to be bridesmaids.

Fanny sighed. "Always a bridesmaid."

"Come on." I took Shane's elbow. "Let's get you into your bedroom and dressed properly."

She looked down. "What's wrong with this outfit?"

"You can't wear black leather with chains to your wedding."

"You're right. This is better for the honeymoon."

***

When we re-convened for the wedding an hour later, there was a basket of fresh flowers in the center of the table. I peeked at the card: "Best Wishes to the Bride And Groom from the crew of the Santa Luisa."

I heard a tap on the door and opened it to Fanny, wearing her polyester party dress and holding up a bunch of white flowers. "Here's the bridal bouquet! The florist just bunched together some orchids, a few streamers, and a doily."

"Why it's *beautiful*!" Shane fairly squealed. And her eyes shone and she blushed lightly, for all the world like a real bride.

Gordon Magnuson appeared exactly on time, looking spiffy in a blue suit and tie to assume his duties as best man.

Patsy arrived, perky in peach taffeta and positioned herself as maid-of-honor behind the bride. Captain Yeates was the last member of the wedding to arrive, impeccable as always in his uniform. He offered his arm to Shane and escorted her the few steps to Father Dawes who stood waiting in front of the porthole.

Dawes hadn't brought his priest outfit along on the trip. He looked clerical enough, though, in black pants and a black sweater over a white button-down shirt.

He didn't have a book in his hands. But of course he had performed the ceremony often enough to wing it by now.

"Ladies and gentlemen, we are gathered together in the sight of our lord, Jesus Christ, to see these two people united in holy matrimony. Shane and Duncan, you are about to embark on a journey together that entails a great mutual responsibility.

"In the words of St. Paul, 'Wives be subject to your husband, for the husband is the head of his wife, even as Christ is the head of the church.'"

I whispered to Julian, "The analogy *stinks*."

Julian whispered back, "Shh."

"Do you promise to love, honor and obey.."

"I do," Steel interrupted.

"This is the vow for the *bride*," Dawes corrected softly.

"Oh, yeah. – Sorry."

"Habit," I mumbled to Julian.

"For better or for worse, in sickness and in health.."

Steel looked as though he were about to sink to the floor. I realized that Gordon was discreetly holding him up by the back of his collar.

"For richer or for poorer, as long as you both shall live?"

"Yeah!" Shane said quickly.

"And do you, Duncan take Shane to be your lawfully wedded wife, to love, honor and protect, in sickness and in health, for richer, for poorer, as long as you both shall live?"

The groom appeared to be dozing now. So Gordon grabbed the back of his belt and moved him up and down till he awoke and realized where he was and what he was supposed to be doing.

"Yeah, sure. I'm here to marry her. Go ahead."

"With the power vested in me by Holy Mother Church and the current jurisdiction, I pronounce you man and wife."

Instead of the traditional recession, the bride and the best man just helped the groom to the nearest couch, where he collapsed with an "ah" sound.

In that tender moment, I heard the sweet strains of "Hawaiian Wedding Song" then a familiar baritone singing, "De moment hob ich lang ehrvarted.." I whirled around. Sure enough, there he was in the corner crooning to the accompaniment of a battery tape player.

"You hired *Schmelvis* to sing for the reception?"

"Damn right!" Steel pounded his cane on the rug. "I go first class!"

Shane linked her arm in his, sighed happily and listened to her wedding song.

"..Hient shmaicheled de blueh himmel fon Havaii auf unser chupeh.."

CHAPTER THIRTY-ONE

The stalwart lieutenant caught up to me at the rail on the observation deck, looking as though he had been forty hours without sleep.

"I spend more time on the phone than Judy the Time-Life operator. I've been checking up on Mr. Hansen. He was telling the truth about how he got into the case. Ihde did hire him."

I turned into the breeze so my hair would blow away from my face. "He's clean then."

"Not exactly." Frank looked smug. "It transpires that Ihde had run out of money, given up the chase, and cancelled the account three years ago. So Hansen was chasing Schuyler on his own time."

"Three years of work for nothing?"

"Admittedly, that was a big gamble of his time and resources so he must have figured the pay-off would be worth it."

"Worth what? The insurance company's reward couldn't have been more than ten percent of the policy which works out to a mere seventy-five thousand."

"That's true." Frank leered. "But just think what the thief would have paid him *not* to claim that reward."

"You're saying he intended to blackmail Schuyler?"

"I'm not saying it for the record, mind you, because I can't prove this. But he was no longer on Ihde's payroll, so it was the only way he could have made a profit. Hansen had to catch his thief with the loot in hand before the seven years were up, or Schuyler would be out of danger of prosecution and he'd have nothing to be blackmailed about."

"He could have been the nudist in cabin eighty-four."

Professor Magnuson walked toward us, with his hand on the rail, looking into the water, so he didn't notice us until he was a foot away. "Oh, Lieutenant! Did you happen to read.."

"I'm sorry, no." Frank wasn't good at sounding regretful. "I haven't had the opportunity."

"Well, I'd really be interested in your thoughts. And tonight's your last chance," Magnuson warned. "We dock at Cancun tomorrow." He continued his walk along the rail.

Letty Buell hove into view, holding her delicately-adorned binder. "There he goes again. You know, Gordon hasn't spoken a word to me all day."

"Don't mind him. He's been running around the deck looking over all the railings for an egg dangling from a rope."

"Well, that's important, I suppose." Her little mouth formed a pout. "I guess I'll go to the ice cream bar. Since I came aboard, I've been eating what I shouldn't and not eating what I should."

"Not eating *when* I should," I said, watching her bustle off. "And eating when I shouldn't. Do we all do that?"

"I don't know," Frank said. "My concern is that this ship will put in at Cancun tomorrow and that Fabergé egg is liable to walk down the gangplank in somebody's bellypack, never to be seen again."

"Isn't it more likely that it wasn't on the ship at all? Maybe only the stand was brought aboard as a diversion."

CHAPTER THIRTY-TWO

As we docked at Cancun, the tourists were already crowding the exit ramp, buzzing about the restaurants and shops and the beaches.

Frank Washington was looking unusually festive in a new guayabera from the gift shop. He waved his arms, unencumbered by a stupid manuscript, which he had just dumped back on its perpetrator.

"I'm going to check out the police station. – On a guided tour, of course."

Lord Reggie was standing at the rail. "Oim gown t' boy one o' them big 'ats."

Jarvis bounced on his feet. "They have a fantastic selection of snakes in Mexico. I hope to get a nice girl friend for Pedro."

Letty Buell was hanging on Magnuson's arm. The one that wasn't holding his manuscript. "I sure will miss you, Gordon. I guess you're looking forward to the Paco Taibo seminar."

"I certainly am. Taibo is the foremost crime writer in the Spanish language."

I turned around. "Paco Taibo?"

Patsy tapped Gordon's shoulder. "I hope you enjoyed the conference."

"I still haven't found my publisher, but at least this adventure will be grist for the creative mill."

I pointed to the manuscript which he, as ever, had folded in his arms. "Say Gordon, I'm in the mood to read that now."

"Right now, Margo?"

"Sure."

He laughed uneasily and took a step backwards. "I'm flattered but we hardly have time.."

"I just wanted to take a peek."

"Great!" He looked around at the debarking passengers, as if hoping for an interruption. "But I've been working on this copy and it's all out of order. What I can do is send you a fresh one from home."

"I honestly can't wait that long."

"Professor?" Julian stepped between us. "The little woman has an outlandish theory about your work in progress." He held his hands out and smiled. "Shall we humor her?"

Magnuson only relaxed his grip slightly, but Julian took that for acquiescence and wrested the manuscript from his hands. He gave the prof a "Women! Can't live without 'em." smirk and pulled the covers of the manuscript apart so it opened halfway through, and held them on his hands.

An oval-shaped hole had been cut into the pages and nestled therein was a gold mesh egg, decorated with flowers fashioned of precious stones.

Frank stepped forward. "That's it! Just like the picture. The Ihde Fabergé Egg!"

The captain whistled low. "Well, I'll be a monkey's uncle. I had the whole ship searched top to bottom, stem to stern, and never found it. The blasted thing was tucked in there all the time..!"

"Gor!, I niver copped anythin' that posh." Lord Reggie affected a slight bow. "You 'ave me professional admiration, mate."

Frank said, "Don't be so admiring, Lord Micklewhite. The professor killed two people to make this particular score."

"Killed?"

"Ridley Schuyler and Harvey Gould. Yes."

Magnuson sighed and threw his hands up. "There was only one thing I regret. I hated to let go of Jake."

"Jake?"

"The rattlesnake."

"Oh, that was yours?"

"Actually, it belonged to my uncle Ned. He found the diamondback rattler on the road when it was just a baby and kept it in a cage in his house in Richmond, secretly of course."

Jarvis nodded. "Because keeping poisonous snakes is illegal most places."

My uncle didn't remove Jake's venom sac, because he lived near the water and he was having trouble with rats. So whenever it was time to feed Jake, he'd just take him down to the basement and turn him loose."

Julian nodded approval. "Cheaper than arsenic poisoning and more ecologically sound."

"Yes. When my uncle became ill, I had to learn how to handle the rattler so I could take care of it for him."

"Again secretly."

"Of course. Then just before he died, Uncle Ned asked me to find Jake a good home. I couldn't keep him at my house. I take a lot of trips and he would be lonely. So I was bringing him down here to hand over to Jarvis for his reptile farm."

"Then that was the big surprise you promised him."

"Right. I customized a valise to transport Jake comfortably."

"So you had it planned all along. To murder Schuyler and steal the egg."

"No, it wasn't like that at all. When I went up to his suite, the snake just happened to be in my bag. You must understand that I never would have harmed Schuyler. He had been my literary idol."

"And you just met him in his hotel room to tell him so?"

"Exactly! That's when I proposed that I write his authorized biography. After all, I had been his greatest admirer since 'Deep Lock' and had done all the research on his life and works. I'd been loyal to him all through the bad times. Certainly, I deserved the chance. He just laughed."

"He refused you?"

"For no reason but pure meanness. After all the years I spent studying Schuyler, I was surely the best candidate for the job."

"But I can imagine that he didn't see any profit there for himself," Julian said.

"Then I told him that I knew all about him, including the fact that he had stolen the Fabergé egg."

"Blackmail in mind?" Frank suggested.

"Oh, not at all! I just wanted to demonstrate what a good researcher I was." Magnuson looked thoughtful. "But I guess he did mistake it for blackmail because all of a sudden, he became very angry. Murderously so, and he came at me. He wasn't very big and I guess I could have taken him, but you see.." He patted his chest. "I was wearing this shirt which was brand new."

"And cost thirty-five dollars," I recalled.

"Yes. You understand, then. There's no question that he would have torn it. That's when I backed up and unzipped my valise. It didn't occur to me that Jake would be a viable weapon until I was actually threatened. I showed Schuyler the snake just to scare him away from me."

"And you're saying it didn't work?" Frank's eyebrows shot up. "That he wasn't scared of a big em-effin' *rattlesnake*?"

"I didn't have a chance to find out, because Jake was very irritable after being confined so long, and was in a striking mood. He just sprang forward and bit. As luck will have it, he hit an artery at the first strike so there was no point in calling 911. It was only going to be a few minutes."

"A very bad few minutes," Frank suggested.

"Yes. But what about *me*? I had to stand there and watch him die. I felt that all my research had been for nothing. The least Schuyler could do now was let me have the egg. For all my trouble, I mean."

"But he was dead."

"So he wouldn't miss it. Unfortunately, it wasn't anywhere in the room. I searched every inch." Magnuson shrugged sadly. "Then I realized he must have passed it to Harvey Gould, his only connection in New Orleans."

"So after the snake killed Schuyler, you just left it there in the suite."

"Considering what happened, I couldn't very well show up on the ship waving a rattlesnake. I covered by telling Jarvis my manuscript was the surprise." He smiled and the light glinted off his glasses. "We're old friends, but I knew he didn't like me enough to try to read it."

"So you had to continue your search on board the ship."

"I decided to create a phantom passenger to divert suspicion. Holden Webb was ideal, because he's the most famous man nobody knows."

"And you framed him by leaving the stand for the egg in his cabin, eighty-four."

Frank unhooked his hand cuffs from his belt. "Professor Magnuson, I'm afraid you don't get to see Mexico. And you'll have to ride to our next U.S. port in the brig. I'll call for a unit to meet us."

"I won't make any trouble, Lieutenant. I'm not a violent person."

"You couldn't prove it by Mr. Gould."

"But I never meant to harm the man."

"You have the right to remain silent.."

"I just wanted to look for the egg."

"If you give up this right, any thing you say.."

"And that sealed his doom," I said.

"Not at all, Margo. I was going to go after the egg in a subtle manner. So when I introduced myself to Gould, I explained that I was an author then sat next to him and put my manuscript on his lap. That distracted him so that he didn't notice my taking the key out of his jacket pocket."

"So Gould wasn't lying when he told Letty he had lost his key."

"I meant only to sneak into his cabin, locate the egg and carry it away with no harm done."

"I get it. Sort of like Raffles!" the kewpie doll cooed.

"Exactly. And who could blame me? I was only thieving from thieves."–"Later I saw Gould kissing Miss Buell here and then overheard him telling the steward to send wine up to her cabin, I assumed he would be out of his own all night."

I said, "You made a serious overestimation of his charm."

"Almost to the extent that he did himself," Fanny mumbled.

Frank was still reciting. "..may be taken down and used against you in a court of law."

"I felt that I needed some kind of protection. I'm not exactly a fighter." Magnuson looked apologetic. "And I didn't have a gun so I got hold of another snake."

"That was one weapon that could never be traced to you," Frank said. "You have the right to an attorney. If you can not afford one, one will be appointed for you."

"The coral snake, Eugene, was the smallest of the poisonous ones on display, so I pried open the lock on Jarvis's terrarium, put him in an empty ice bucket, and carried him along with me." Sheepishly, he turned to Jarvis. "I'm really sorry Pete."

"S'all right, Gordon. Eugene's okay. No harm done."

"I used Gould's key to let myself into his cabin and had just found the egg in his shoe box in the closet when he walked in on me."

I said, "When I heard him shouting at you, I assumed he was yelling at his partner on the phone."

"He was loud, wasn't he?.. Awful." Magnuson made a gesture to cover his ears, but with his hands cuffed, could cover only one. He chose the right. "So what happened then was *his* fault. I shook up the ice bucket to agitate the snake and aimed it right at Gould's throat. It was frightened enough to strike hard and fatally."

Letty Buell put her hand on the binder. "Then this wasn't a manuscript at all."

"I'm afraid not. There was a load of freshman term papers in the trunk of my car. I just gathered a bale of them and stuck them in a binder. I only had to type the cover page."

"And there never was a 'Second Awakening'."

"There never was." Magnuson patted the binder. "It would have been a great novel though."

"Now you'll have plenty of time to write it," Frank assured him. "I'd guess twenty-five to life. – Do you understand these rights as I've explained them to you?"

"Yes, certainly, lieutenant. – Don't worry; It hit Gould's carotid artery and worked very quickly. He couldn't have suffered much."

"Hmmpf." Fanny looked down at her shoes. "That's not good news to *me*."

"I knew Eugene couldn't have had a fatal amount of venom anymore, since he'd given Harvey Gould a double dose. But by then, Jarvis might have realized that the snake was missing, so I couldn't risk carrying him downstairs to put him back in his terrarium. When I saw the door to the linen closet ajar, I locked him in there."

Indignantly, I got up on my toes. "And me in with him."

"I'm sorry about that, Margo. I thought no one would be using that closet for the rest of the evening. I was going to come back later, on the pretext of looking for a pillow then happen to discover the snake and sound the alarm to Jarvis. But then I discovered you in there too."

"Come on, Gordon." Frank took his elbow.

The kewpie doll was circling around the group, sideways.

"Gordon? We can still write!"

CHAPTER THIRTY-THREE

For our last gathering in the Lorelei Lounge, the group had grown so that we needed two tables pulled together.

Fanny stood up to address us all. "I propose a toast and present this non-alcoholic ersatz daiquiri to Margo! The heroine of the hour."

"Oh, you shouldn't have!" I reached for it with both hands.

"Yes, indeed," Fanny continued. "It was you who solved the case. Now tell us all. How did you come to suspect Magnuson? I mean he looked so harmless with his silly manuscript."

"He had me fooled too. But he claimed he was getting off in Mexico to see Paco Taibo."

Alice leaned forward. "Paco is in Spain all month."

"So you had told me. Then I recalled something Gordon said after I got locked in the closet with the coral snake. Remember? He was amazed that I could have stood it for a whole hour."

"Who wouldn't be?"

"But at that point, no one could have known exactly how long we'd been in there, except me, the snake, and whoever had locked us in there together."

"Hey, I should have caught that."

"And I realized that he ate when he wasn't supposed to and he didn't eat when he *was* supposed to."

"What do you mean?"

"Magnuson claimed that snakes frightened and repulsed him."

"Right. I remember that."

"But I recalled that the first time I saw him he was in Jarvis's herpetorium, looking down at one of the snakes and eating a sandwich."

Julian nodded. "What's wrong with a sandwich?"

"Nothing with the sandwich itself. But can you eat within sight of something that disgusts you?"

"No I can't." He gave me a sneaky look. "Maybe that's why I'm so thin."

"So he was eating when he shouldn't have been, unless he wasn't really repelled by snakes." I made a dramatic pause. "But when the braised swordfish was served in the dining room, he didn't have any of it. Why would anyone turn down fresh seafood?"

"Yes, why?"

"Because he had to establish a presence in Holden Webb's cabin. And he did that by eating the full meals that Biffie was delivering."

Fanny said, "But what about the lifeboat drill? Both Gordon and his alter-ego were accounted for."

"Too easy," Julian told her. "Both of his cabins were at the same lifeboat station and all they called out was the numbers. So he stood on the edge of the crowd and answered for the first number, then walked around to the other side and answered to the second. Nobody noticed."

Frank pursed his lips and closed his notebook in a loud, clapping motion. "Magnuson sure made a clown out of *me*. All the while we were searching the ship, stem to stern, for that egg, it was on the desk in my own cabin, hidden in that ridiculous manuscript."

"There was no safer place." Fanny's eyes were wide. "I guess no one thought of opening "The Second Awakening"."

"That was the whole idea," Julian surmised. "Magnuson brought his fake manuscript on board intending it for a hiding place. Then he groveled around the ship begging everyone in sight to read it just to make sure that no one would want to touch the silly thing."

I took up the narrative. "After he killed Gould, and found the egg in his room, he cut out the center part of the pages to make the right size hole." I turned to Julian. "That must have been the 'confetti' we saw in the water the other night."

"He was perfectly aware that no one would read that asinine bundle of trash even at *gunpoint*."

"Now it's clear that Magnuson was using reverse psychology." Frank looked peeved. "The way he described his stupid story, I'd have been as eager to open a box of wasps."

"He's pretty smart for a college professor."

"Those guys'll fool you."

"But how did he get a key to cabin 84. He never came aboard as Webb."

Frank said, "He admitted to me that he simply went up the front desk and claimed he had misplaced his key. He showed them the Webb boarding pass with the stateroom number and they issued him a duplicate. They didn't notice the name."

CHAPTER THIRTY-FOUR

When we docked at the Julia Street Wharf in New Orleans, Julian and I were in no hurry to get back to the steam bath that is our home. We decided to hang out by the gangway and bid farewell to all of our new best friends whom we never expected to see again.

Ward Newcomb was among the first to arrive at the gangplank with Aleko in tow. "Greetings, friends and lovers! I'd like to introduce you all to my new model."

Julian looked at me sideways. "We've actually had the pleasure."

"Bee-yoo-tee-fool!" the boy agreed.

"I'm going to use him for all the covers of a new sci-fi series, 'Lance Apollo'." Ward patted his find on the head then paused a moment to untangle a blond curl. "You watch. This kid will be bigger than Fabio."

"He is already," I affirmed.

A minute later, Alice arrived arm in arm with the white-haired Mrs. Sather.

The librarian was smiling. "We're going to do some sight-seeing in New Orleans before flying our separate ways. Until next year."

"Next year?" I repeated.

Alice grinned and bounced on her feet. "Guess who is going to be the guest of honor at next year's American Library Association Conference! You see? It pays to know people!"

"Wonderful! Your sales will go to the sky!"

"Well, it sure won't hurt."

Fanny came through the corridor with Lord Reggie one step behind her, wheeling her suitcase and carrying his own.

"Guess what, Margo." She stopped in front of us. "I'm starting a new series about a suave British jewel thief."

"That sounds original."

Julian shot me a dubious look.

"Well, of course it's not original," Fanny chided. My character will be an updated version of Raffles and Simon Templar. But the theme is about due to come around again, don't you think."

"No doubt at all," I was able to agree. "And Lord Reggie there probably has enough stories to fill twenty books."

"No kidding. I've already e-mailed my editor in New York and she's very excited about the project. She wants Reggie and me to go on a promotional tour together. – After we're married, of course."

"You're going to get married?! Oh, best wishes, Lady Micklewhite."

Fanny blushed at the title, but looked flattered.

"Hey, I'm no romantic fool. I realize that he's not exactly the Duke of Marlborough." She held his hand fondly. "But home in Montana even a scrub Scottish laird would be impressive at the church suppers."

Julian clapped Reggie's shoulder. "Congratulations, old man! I know you'll be happy!"

"Fanny says as she 'as one o' them ridin' lawnmowers. An' oim to plant me own rose garden in the back."

The newlyweds, Mr. and Mrs. Duncan Steel, needed a steward to carry their bags because the bride was pretty much occupied with carrying the groom, his arm around her shoulders.

"Hi, Margo, Julian.." Shane waved with her free hand. "We're going to spend the last part of our trip in the suite where Ridley Schuyler died."

"Sounds romantic," I said.

Father Dawes was the only passenger who walked

down the gang plank solo. There was a jaunty spring in his step and he swung his duffle bag. "Julian and Margo! Thank you for everything." He hugged us both at once.

"We've enjoyed our cruise so much," I volunteered. "We're sorry it's all over."

"Not I. This was enough vacation to last a long time." He rubbed his hands together. "It will be good to get back to the parish."

"You're returning to your church then."

"Absolutely. I've come to the realization that as a priest, I can make a real difference, inside the system." He lowered his voice. "De-frocked and disgraced, I wouldn't be any good to anyone."

I looked around to check for eavesdroppers and whispered. "What about the celibacy part?"

"I think I can hack it," he whispered back. "With God's grace and a full schedule. I have a whole new operation to set up."

"Like maybe a chapter of Dignity?" Julian asked.

Father Dawes winked and held his hand out in a peace sign. "Come to Mass sometime. It won't hurt you."

The next passenger we saw was Sara Luke bustling through the corridor hand-in-hand with her bald, tubby new swain, as a steward walked behind her pushing a pile of purple suitcases on a dolly.

"Hi,.." She giggled. "Milt and I are coming back to the ship next month. On our honeymoon."

"Well, best wishes to you, Sara." Julian said. "And congratulations to you, Milt. I know you'll be happy together."

Milt grinned and tick-tocked his head sideways.

"That's neat!" I said. "But if you're coming back so soon, Milt will have to take more time off his job."

Sara's jaw dropped, giving her an extra chin, her fourth or fifth. "Goodness, why would he have to take time off when he works right on board!"

And I watched them depart, still holding hands in the

spirit of young lovers cavorting through a meadow.

"He works on the ship?"

Julian smiled. "I thought you knew that Milt is one of the entertainers here."

"How could I? I never saw him perform."

"Not without his wig and white jumpsuit."

"She's marrying *Schmelvis?!*"